BUSKER

A BROADWAY TROUBADOUR

BY

GREGORY A. KOMPES

Fabulist Flash Publishing
Selbyville, DE

ISBN: Print Edition: 979-8-950241-01-7
ISBN: Digital Edition: 979-8-950241-00-0

Editor: Leslie E. Hoffman
Cover & Interior Design: Gregory A. Kompes
Cover Photo: Jefferson Santos

Fabulist Flash Publishing
PO Box 122
Selbyville, DE 19975

For more books by Gregory A. Kompes, please visit www.Kompes.com.

DEDICATED TO:

All the musicians
I've had the pleasure of
making music with

BUSKER
A BROADWAY TROUBADOUR

BY

GREGORY A. KOMPES

ONE

Around Charlie, three women dressed for work or the theater, with comfy coats and woolen hats, listened to him singing Jim Croce's "Time in a Bottle." Charlie's voice mimicked Croce's. That lilt that matched the meter of the song. In the eyes of one of the women, tears glossed. In the eyes of another, an obvious memory of some youthful time. He had them. When you had them, you made money. Not a few quarters, but bills. Cash money.

Down the subway corridor, two transit cops. They didn't seem interested in Charlie, but he'd already been harassed twice that week. He knew the law. He could perform alone on his acoustic Seagull guitar anywhere in the city without the need of a license or permit. However, in the big stations, Times Square, Port Authority, 34th Street, the cops got a bit pushy.

Charlie played for those women, channeling Croce. All the while, in his brain, "Hey, Ya," by OutKast circled. He'd heard it the night before for the first time, while drinking his third or fourth beer. Yesterday had been a good day. Lots of cash had been dropped into his case. He'd made his daily nut times two. Thinking about that now, he thirsted for a beer. His nightly reward for a day well played. Normally, he'd buy a cold six-pack and take it back to his rented room. But on nights following days like yesterday, especially when that day was a Tuesday, like yesterday, he splurged on two-for-one beers at one of the gay bars in The Village. Sometimes, he'd go home with a handsome guy. Most nights, it was only him and the Seagull riding the subway uptown.

He strummed now, changed keys, fingerpicked the bridge. The women continued to sway.

"Hey, Ya!" looped in his head. While he played "Time in a Bottle," he continued to try to work out the chord pattern for the OutKast tune. It would be a good addition to his dance sequence. Charlie liked fun music and the boys in the gay bar all danced when that song had come on the jukebox, or did they have a DJ?

He'd been playing guitar almost as long as he could remember, more than twenty years, okay, twenty-five years was closer. Charlie often played one song, while others wandered around in his brain. Often, new music showed up while he played. If he played for a passerby, he could stop the song he was playing and work out the new one. But those women might not offer tip money if he abruptly stopped. The goal: money in the case.

As much as he liked the songs he played, even the requested ones that weren't his favorites, his brain reached for new and interesting music: Great poetry. Brilliant chord changes. Lyrical lines. Fascinating harmonies. When he was twenty-seven, he met another busker on a hilly street in San Francisco—a city where the locals and tourists take pride in supporting the street musicians—when he discovered that most other musicians played and thought about one song at a time. Most musicians, he'd been told, if they thought about a different song, a different set of chord changes, they couldn't play the one they played. He'd been told by a guy with laughing hazel eyes that he, Charlie, was a freak. He'd said it kindly. Then, he'd kissed him passionately. After spending the night together, and thinking about two songs at once while the passionate man slept next to him, Charlie dressed and picked up his ever-present Seagull guitar, and jumped the next bus south to San Diego. The San Fran money was good, but Charlie wanted to be warm.

Entering the last chorus of the Croce, Charlie worked out the final chord changes for the Outkast song. He longed now to hear it again, to discover if he'd put the puzzle together correctly. But first, he had to finish this tune. Hopefully, the women would tip him well and the transit cops would ignore him.

Deep down, his blood raced a little. He maintained a perfect pace for "Time in a Bottle," yet he longed to play "Hey, Ya!" for strangers. He longed to earn enough money to warrant a six-pack. He longed for...

On a strong, slow, downward strum, Charlie played the final chord. While it rang, he plucked those two little last notes, the haunting outcome of the memory in the song. While they rang, Charlie heard Outkast sing, "My baby don't mess around..." in his head. The song had a lot of lyrics. He'd have to find them somewhere to get them right. Music, he remembered. Melody and harmony. Words, the poetry of music, required more effort.

Finishing the song, that last strum, the women applauded kindly. A moment later, one dropped a dollar. Another, the one with the tears, flashed a twenty, smiled through her damp eyes, and dropped the big bill into his guitar case. The transit cops drew closer. A different lyric, "alright, alright, alright, alright," rattled in his head.

That twenty translated to two slices and a six-pack of beer.

The women headed off into the station. The cops now focused his way. Charlie slipped his Seagull into the case, snapped the clasps, swung the case over his back, and headed out the exit he'd been standing near.

Times Square. Cold. People everywhere. Twilight. Almost time for shows. Folks on the way to the theaters were too rushed and ignored him. He usually took a break then. Had dinner. Had a beer or two. Somewhere warm. One of the small bars a few blocks below Times Square. A few blocks west. A few blocks east even, that were cheaper than the tourist places near the theaters. He repositioned his Seagull onto his back, the strap across his chest, the body of the instrument against him. Comfortable. Safe. His life and livelihood strapped there cradled him.

South. Down Broadway. Into an old industrial block that hadn't yet been usurped by the modernization of Times Square. Not that Charlie minded the changes. Making the theater district into a theme park brought more people at all hours of the day. More people equaled more money.

There, in the middle of the block, Milo's, an old, old bar with battered wooden floors, ancient curled black and white photographs on the wall of eras gone by, and a working steam table. One of the few left in the city. Good, cheap, hot food. Although, he'd missed two-for-one happy hour by ten minutes so would have to pay full price for his beer.

"Hey, Charlie," called Milo from behind the bar.

"Hey, Milo."

Milo's Pub, narrow and long and steamy and warm, smelled of cabbage and slow-cooked meat. In metal bins on the steam table, the carrots dull, the green beans grey in a bath of salt water. There was a draft beer sitting on the bar by the time Charlie made it to the end spot.

"Play me 'Moon River' and this beer is on the house," said Milo.

"Feeling nostalgic?" Charlie quickly swung off his guitar and took it from the case.

"I am." Milo pulled a draft for another patron.

After a quick moment of thought, Charlie adjusted the tuning—his E-string needed to be replaced—found the right first chord, and played a soft, easy version of the song from *Breakfast at Tiffany's*. By the end of the song, Milo and another man at the bar were crooning the song, "My Huckleberry Friend…"

"Your dinner's on me," said the guy at the bar, a regular whose name Charlie didn't know.

"Really?" Charlie gathered the bills and change from the guitar case, tucked the money into his pockets without counting it.

"Yep. I bet him you wouldn't know that old song and Milo said you knew everything. I should have listened," said the regular.

It all sounded like bunk. Those guys knew him. "Moon River" was a standard. Everyone knew it. Milo loved that song. Charlie had played it for him at least a dozen times over the past year. That might have been the first free-beer song he'd played for him. Charlie zipped the guitar into its case and headed right to the steam table for a big helping of cabbage and corned beef. He'd fart all night, but didn't care. Hearty warm food, all he could eat, would keep him through until tomorrow. It didn't matter how he'd come by it. And that meant he was ahead financially for the day. After a long swig of beer, he devoured the heap of hot food.

"Get enough?" the regular asked.

For a long moment, Charlie didn't know if the question was criticism or concern. "Yeah," he pushed the empty plate away with a quiet belch.

"Another?" asked Milo, holding up a glass near the taps.

"Yes." He headed into the john, a smelly little room. He locked the door. It always seemed clean, yet smelled to high heaven, the urinal he pissed in full of ice. After washing his hands, he pulled out the bills from his pocket, straightened them so all the faces were turned in the same direction, sorted the bills into similar groupings, and counted. Thirty-seven dollars. Not a bad hour thanks to the lady's generous twenty. He squirreled money into several different pockets. He'd been robbed enough to know that you don't keep it all together. Although, he never went so far as to tuck money into his socks or shoes.

Back at the bar, he dropped five crumpled dollars down for his beer and drank half of it off in a single swallow. Cold beer in a cold mug. So cold there were hints of ice crystals on the rim.

Nothing better.

Around him, except for the regular and Milo, everyone in the place had their heads down in their phones. No one watched the world anymore.

"Where you gonna play tonight?" asked Milo, wiping down some bar real estate. He kept the place clean—or tried.

"Near the theaters about ten. Then, probably The Village tonight," said Charlie.

"It's getting cold. You don't look dressed to be outside all night." Milo stopped wiping and looked right at Charlie. His black, black eyelids created a droopy frame around tired yellowed eyes. The whites had been deteriorating all summer.

"I meant to stop by the thrift shop today to look for a sweater. Maybe a scarf. I just didn't make it down there." That wasn't true. He hadn't thought of that, but he didn't want Milo to think he didn't know how to take care of himself.

"Bed bugs. Anything you get from those shops'll be full of bugs," said the regular who'd insinuated himself into the conversation. He did buy dinner.

"Hold on," said Milo. He headed to the far end of the bar, near the front windows, and returned with a beat-up cardboard box that had seen much better days.

"What the hell's that?" asked the regular.

"Lost-n-Found. People leave shit here all the time. Let's see..." he rummaged elbow deep into the box. "No sweaters." He pulled out a foam Statue of Liberty crown. A T-shirt. A pair of oversized 2020 New Year's eyeglasses.

"Why do you keep that shit. It's trash?" asked the regular.

Milo waved him off. "Looky here." Like a magician performing a trick, he pulled and pulled and pulled a long, blue, wool scarf from the box. "Want it?"

"Does it smell?" asked the regular.

Charlie finished his beer. He liked the color of the scarf. It would highlight his eyes. He had dark hair and warm brown skin tones, but deep blue eyes. In some light, they sparkled like diamonds. In sunlight, especially on a blue-skied day, the blue radiated. On those days, especially if he played in Central Park, he'd make big tips because people were mystically drawn to him. He'd dated a guy once who said: "If the music ever fails, with those amazing eyes, you could become a tarot card reader, tell fortunes." He liked when Charlie sucked his cock while looking up into his eyes. A big turn on for the guy. That was down in Key West. A few winters ago.

"It doesn't," said Milo before he pulled the edge of the scarf up to his nose. "Well, maybe a little like cabbage."

"Everything here smells like cabbage," said Charlie.

The guys laughed.

"It's yours if you want it. It'll air out or you could Febreze it or something," said Milo. He carried the scarf in a ball toward

Charlie. "Better yet," he pulled his head back, "you can have it for a song."

"Always a catch with you," said the regular.

He never wanted to be in debt, so happy to pay with the best currency he had: Music. "What do you want to hear?"

Milo, after a look outside into the darkness, smiled broadly. The gap in his front teeth prominent. "Autumn Leaves."

"So nostalgic," said Charlie. He appreciated the easy song choice. Another classic.

"I miss my Mable," said Milo. "We'd a been married fifty years in a few weeks."

The regular whistled appreciatively.

"That was her favorite song. She'd always play it when she shifted our closet from summer to winter," said Milo. "No one does that anymore."

After tuning that damn E-string, Charlie played and sang the sweetest version of "Autumn Leaves" he could. He couldn't even imagine fifty years with the same person. Especially now that he was thirty-seven. Charlie figured he'd die some cold night clutching his guitar on a street corner hoping for one more dollar to be dropped in his case. Not a bad way for a busker to go.

Before he'd finished, Milo set the lost-and-found scarf near Charlie on the bar. Then, filled another mug with beer and set it next to the scarf as he wiped tears from his eyes. "On the house."

When Charlie finished, the few patrons applauded. One said, "His next beer is on me."

"Just give the kid the money," said Milo.

And to Charlie's surprise, the guy who'd spoken up, came over, smile on his face, and handed him a five-dollar bill.

With the money shoved into his shirt pocket, Charlie picked up the scarf, gave it a sniff. It didn't smell nearly as bad as he'd suspected. It smelled better than he did.

Charlie once more cased up his guitar, strapped it to his back, and drank off the second free beer of the evening. Free beer. Free food. A comfy, warm scarf. More than forty dollars in his pocket, plus a handful of change he hadn't yet counted.

He wrapped the long blue scarf around his neck several

times. Probably a woman's scarf, but it was warm, soft wool. The real deal. Not some fashion piece of crap, but a well-made scarf with tight stitches or whatever they were called.

He found Milo watching him and said, "Thanks for this."

TWO

In Times Square, near the TKTS booth, as the theater goers exited the shows, standing near the high-rise rows of seats, Charlie played "Havin' a Heatwave." The people all around him dug their hands deep into their pockets, trying to fend off the frigid air, sadly not reaching for tips.

The scarf from Milo's Lost-n-Found box helped deter the cold. Charlie wrapped it around his neck one more time as two girls applauded with gloved hands, creating a muffled sound Charlie enjoyed. It had been an hour since anyone had dropped any money in his guitar case.

He tuned his E-string. It needed to be replaced.

"Summertime" might be a good next song for the theme of his set, but he wanted something upbeat to help him stay warm. He was still at least seventeen dollars short for his daily goal. Seventeen dollars, at least, to get him to a hundred. That was his daily nut. That kept a roof over his head and food in his belly. That got him twenty dollars in the savings account, his other goal. Travel funds. He should have already headed south by now, or west. But he was short a few hundred dollars to make the trip and transition comfortably. He never minded living on the edge, but lately…

So, instead of "Summertime," but sticking with his summer hit theme on this cold, cold night, he launched into "Under the Boardwalk." Still on the edge of a ballad, but people loved it and it seemed like the right choice for his location with the bleachers. He liked the song, too. It sat in that warm, gooey spot in his range. Plus, people generally tipped for it.

He'd learned over his lifetime of busking that there were lots of songs people liked, but not all songs generated tips. Sometimes, he played those tipless tunes because he liked them or they were requested. Generally, he stuck to the tried and true that earned him his daily bread.

Maybe it was because of the weather, maybe some other reason, there weren't any cops out on the street. That took some of the pressure off, although Charlie had only ever been harassed when playing in the subway. He was thankful when they went around.

An older couple stopped to listen, they didn't sit on the cold benches, but swayed to the music, his arm around her, a Playbill in her coat pocket. Charlie could imagine this woman in a long, fur coat. No one wore real fur anymore, but it seemed like it would be a good choice for a night like tonight.

The older couple dropped a bill in the instrument case. From his angle, Charlie thought it might be a five. He nodded his thanks. "Any requests?" he asked.

The woman's eyes brightened. "My favorite—"

"He's a young guy, he won't know our song," said the man.

"Try me," said Charlie. He had a terrific repertoire and knew just about everything up to the last few years.

"Well, at our wedding we danced our first dance together to 'Passing Strangers.'"

"Billy Eckstine and Sarah Vaughan," said Charlie, and he tuned the damn E-string and launched into the slow, romantic song. Considering the lyrics, thought it a strange choice for a first dance, but to each their own.

The couple danced, spinning slowly, surely imagining a different time, yet unselfconscious in this moment, passionate, soft, in step in a way only a long-married couple could be together.

Charlie played and sang and thought about Milo and his late wife. He wanted this. Someone to love and be loved by. Someone to dance to dreamy songs with after a lifetime together.

A half dozen people gathered and listened and watched. When the song ended, they applauded. Money, bills mostly, dropped into the instrument case.

The older man, his arm still around his wife, held out

a twenty to Charlie. "Thank you, young man. That was wonderful."

Charlie took the bill and shoved it in his pocket. "You're very welcome." He immediately played, "Isn't this a Lovely Day," another song Sarah and Billy sang together. That garnered more applause from the older couple who immediately swayed together to the song. Not quite summer irony, but he'd now made his nut and that meant he could stop whenever he chose. Yet, he'd play for these people all night, even out in the cold, if they continued to enjoy, and pay for what he offered.

THREE

Charlie's tiny room in the little old hotel was freezing cold when he arrived. He stashed his guitar in the corner, turned on the little lamp next to the creaky bed, and placed a hand on the icy radiator: the flaked, once-white paint rough against his hand, the cast iron frigid.

There weren't many choices. No one would be at the front desk at this hour. The super never answered the phone, day or night. But...the hallway had been warm...Charlie opened the door and stepped into the hall. At the end, the radiator there knocked and banged. He approached it, reached out to touch it, but couldn't get close because of its heat. He warmed his hands, turned, warmed his cold ass. He considered sleeping there in the hall, but that was nothing more than an invitation to being mugged or murdered.

He'd never met his neighbors. Charlie's hours were rather unconventional. The hallway, most nights, remained silent. He dropped down to the floor, moved his body as close to the radiator as he could without touching it, and breathed in the dusty heat while his body warmed. Charlie kept his coat on, and scarf, but after an awkward finagle, he shoved off his boots so his stockinged feet would warm up. He examined the hole in his sock.

It was only November.

At this rate, he didn't know that he'd make it through the

holidays in New York. He had almost enough money saved that he could get down South or somewhere warm out West.

He'd wintered in Florida several times. Spent one of those in Key West. In other years, he'd wintered in New Orleans and Tucson and San Diego and Vegas, although desert winters were nearly as cold as the north.

The trouble: housing. He'd found this terrible hotel. An old, men's only SRO, short for "sleeping room only," although they didn't call these places that anymore, they certainly and thankfully still existed. He had his room and a tiny stove and a miniature fridge, that never really kept anything cold. He shared a bathroom, but there were only two other rooms on this floor, half what the other floors had. Thankfully, the residents looked after their little bathroom well. It was fairly clean and usually smelled fresh and rarely had bugs.

While thinking about how fresh the bathroom smelled, and considering his desire to pee, a rodent scurried down the hall. He'd left his door open and worried the thing would dart in there, but it didn't. It must be cold, too; it ran along the baseboard and stopped a few inches from the radiator. Together, they warmed their feet and noses.

Finally feeling warm, Charlie gathered his boots and headed into his room. The rodent, it seemed small for a rat, but had that long, scaly tail. It twitched its nose, but otherwise didn't move.

Inside, with the door closed, the room felt warmer. Charlie touched the radiator and thought some steam might come up, but it certainly wasn't as hot as the hallway.

Out he headed, to the bathroom. It was freezing cold inside there, too. He quickly peed, washed his hands and face, and brushed his teeth. He'd shower when he woke up in the afternoon when it might be warmer. He longed for a bath in a real tub.

Once more, he lingered near the radiator to warm himself, before heading into his room. He searched haltingly for the rat, but didn't see it anywhere.

After changing his clothes for bed, Charlie gathered the

money from all his pockets. Coat, pants, shirt, jacket. So many little hiding spots. He organized and sorted and counted. One-hundred thirty-seven dollars and a heavy handful of change—nearly three more dollars in quarters and dimes. Nice to be ahead. To have a cushion. If they didn't fix the heat, he'd decided to pay his weekly bill in coins. He'd been saving up the daily handful of quarters and dimes just in case.

At that moment, he wished he still smoked. That last smoke of the night had been his favorite. Seconded only by the after-a-meal smoke—that one he rarely missed now. He'd quit a few years earlier because he'd grown winded walking up some subway stairs in Grand Central. He was astonished how much smaller his daily nut needed to be without the expense of smokes.

He counted the money again, pleased. He would buy a new set of strings the next day.

Charlie owned his life. It wasn't what he'd envisioned when he was a kid. Not really. But here he was, making money nearly every day. Not beholden to anyone. He could play and get paid and live without a day job or a boss or debt. He could do what he was good at every single day, what he loved. He didn't owe anyone anything beyond the two-hundred and seventy dollars a week for this freezing little room.

After stashing his cash in various hiding places, Charlie hung his guitar on a hook on the wall, hoping to avoid the rodent who might find its way inside, and slipped into bed. His one major investment: a heavy quilt from the thrift shop. His second investment: having the quilt properly cleaned. If he stayed in New York, he planned to spend the winter snuggled under that quilt. If he headed south, he'd give it to an unhomed person—there were plenty of them in his neighborhood and the nights were getting cold.

With no television or radio, with no cell phone or electronics, his silent space offered no escape. He stared into the darkness, imagined the long crack that ran across the ceiling, imagined that hanging fixture with the bulb that didn't work, thought about the old couple in Times Square who danced. He'd never have that. Long-term relationships weren't really possible when you lived in an SRO hotel and your second biggest investment was a used quilt—no matter how clean and warm.

Not having any media at his fingertips, he had to work to discover new music—which is why his repertoire so heavily favored older songs. When he could, he'd slip into a library and listen to music. Or, while having a beer in a bar, he'd tune into the house music or juke box tunes, storing them in his memory to sort out later. Occasionally, he'd see a Broadway show if they were papering a house.

In the silence of his room, he worked on the chords and fingering for "Hey Ya!" with its brilliant beat and easy melody. A perfect park song to get a crowd invested and singing. When they sang along, they dropped more in the case. Always the goal. Plus, it was fun to play. The challenge: getting that driving rhythm without drums or click track. Charlie, both a strong rhythm player and an excellent lead guitarist, was certain that came from not having a television. Not getting too comfortable. Needing to get out into the world for stimulus. However, if he were going to stay in the city for the winter, his next investment would be a radio. It was a good way to stay current on all the new music. He could afford a radio, but hated spending money on things only to have to abandon them when he moved on. He thought then about one of his foster mothers listening to the Top 40 on Sunday nights while she ironed their clothes for the week—he wished he'd been with that kind family longer.

He imagined he could hear the rodent wandering around and chills ran through him. He tugged the quilt tighter to his chin. It wasn't just about investing in the quilt that mattered. The harder thing would be to eventually leave this one behind. Soft from years of use. Some old woman, maybe her mother had made it, slept under this quilt for a generation. Her energy secure and safe. She'd raised children and snuggled grandbabies under this quilt. She'd dried nightmare tears and made love and died under this quilt. Charlie could feel the energy of her life; it gave him great comfort—even if he'd only crafted the whole story.

As the sun began to push into the cold morning, Charlie finally gave in to sleep, another song firmly placed in his repertoire. The repertoire: the true investment that never got left behind.

FOUR

Charlie took up one of his favorite Eastside afternoon spots, in a doorway about a block from the Guggenheim Museum. The doorway, in a derelict building, blocked most of the wind and lightly amplified his sound. The museum foot traffic, constant all day, gave him plenty of passersby to come upon him, listen for a moment, drop a buck or even some change, and move on. He liked that flow, that energy.

No one was there when he finished "Hey Ya!" for the third time. His career allowed for lots of practice. He could play the song all day if he chose, few would ever hear more than a few bars. He'd figured out how to transition into the last refrain and how to get a great rhythm sound, too. He still didn't have the lyrics right, but he'd play it tonight in Times Square where there'd be a crowd.

He tugged on his scarf, getting it positioned properly around his neck and under his coat. Once more, he tuned the E-string. It really did need to be changed. Charlie checked his watch and realized he wasn't wearing it. Wondered where it might be. In the room. Lost. Stolen. It must be mid-afternoon. He looked to the sky for a clue, but the clouds covered the sun. He packed up and headed east. Brothers would be open and he could slip in, buy a set of strings, maybe change the E there, and be back out on the street, playing again in no time.

His case had two quarters, a dime, and some coin from a foreign land, along with three rather limp dollar bills. Not a great take for the past hour. It had been practice.

When he entered the music store, he envied the wall of guitars. He liked his instrument, a Seagull he'd discovered in a pawn shop. Gotten it for a song. Well, not literally, but very cheap. He'd now had it for a long time, and it sounded great, but years of playing outdoors and banging around on the road from town to town had left its impact. He could certainly buy something new, but it would eat up his savings and he liked having enough money tucked away to get out of town in search of something new, or warmer weather, or to escape whatever. Still, he kept his eyes open for sales or some stray in a shop window. There used to be lots of pawn shops in Times Square and Midtown, on the Eastside, in The Village. They'd gone away. It didn't really matter. Living like he did, he could really only have one guitar at a time. He wasn't ready to part with his old Seagull.

"Hey," said a young guy behind the counter. "Can I help you find something?"

Having a guitar slung over your back when you entered a music store elevated you and got you better service. Charlie pointed into the shop. "Need strings." He continued walking toward the display.

"Sure."

He debated just getting the one he needed, but it was cheaper over time to buy a set of strings. And if this E had gone, the others might follow. One night, six years ago, in the cold of winter, with his pockets empty, all six strings broke within twenty-four hours. Better still would be to buy a set and change them all to keep the instrument's sound even.

Charlie chose another set of Martin Retros because that's what he had on the guitar now. Sticking to the same brand and style would be better for sound if he only replaced the one wonky string. He again contemplated replacing them all, he could choose something different. He wanted a little softer sound, but didn't want to waste the good strings he still had. His choice, middle of the road, would keep him playing in the cold for at least a few weeks. Maybe he'd upgrade on the next round or wait until the spring or if he decided to head south. A long bus ride to get to warmer weather, a great time to change strings.

New Orleans flashed through his head. Picking a good spot on any street in the French Quarter yielded great results.

Especially on the weekends. But he'd been mugged twice the last time he was there.

At the counter, the guy rang up his purchase. "Need picks?"

"Nope, just the strings." Charlie paid the bill with change.

"Thanks," said the guy. Based on his tone, he wasn't thrilled.

"Money is money and quarters weigh you down," said Charlie.

"Sure," said the clerk as he recounted the mound of quarters, dimes, and nickels.

Being close to his hotel, Charlie headed back with his purchase. He'd see if the manager was there, he usually was in the afternoon, and find out about the heat. Then, warm up while changing his string, and head out for the evening.

FIVE

Normally Charlie entered the Hotel Mostar through the side entrance—the door opened into the stairwell, and he was three flights up. Today, Charlie used his key to open the front door. His best odds of finding Jank, the manager, would be in the lobby where he often napped between smoking cheap cigars.

As expected, Jank sat in one of the threadbare, wing-backed chairs, haloed by rank cigar smoke, a *New York Post* spread out on the table before him.

"Ah, the musician. Why here? Rent not due for three day." He turned a page of the paper and flattened it down dramatically.

"Heat."

"The heat on. Feel how warm?" He indicated the lobby with a sweep of his arm. "Too warm now." He tugged at his collar.

"Not in my room. It's freezing." Charlie shoved his keys into his pocket. Two keys. One for the outside doors. One for his room.

"You mess with radiator? Don't mess with radiator." Jank didn't move.

"No. I haven't touched anything. No heat in my room." He didn't know why he mimicked Jank's speech style. It certainly wasn't meant as disrespect. But he did it. Every time he spoke to the man. He began dropping articles and even verbs from his sentences. Even being aware of it, he still did it.

"Okay. Let's have look see." Jank pushed himself up using the table. He set his cigar in the dirty ashtray, where it continued to smoke. He led the way to the stairs and the men walked up to the third floor.

Charlie followed the lightly wheezing super. He should mention the rodent from the previous night, but decided to stick to a single issue, the heat. The priority. The goal.

Without waiting, Jank used his master key and opened Charlie's door. "Hm. Cold."

"See?" said Charlie.

"Neat boy. Good." Jank touched the radiator. "Cold."

"See?" repeated Charlie.

"Da. You no touch?"

"Haven't touched anything." Charlie took his guitar off his back and set it on the bed.

"You play?"

They'd been through this before. If Charlie engaged the manager in conversation, he'd never have any heat. "Da," said Charlie, not sure why. He didn't speak the super's native middle-European tongue.

Jank nodded his head, bent, turned the valve near the floor at the base of the radiator. "Need to bleed."

Charlie didn't know what that meant.

"I come back."

"Now?"

"Yes. Can't have boy musician freeze. I fix. You play?" His tobacco stained toothy smile charmed Charlie.

"Of course."

"Good. Five minute." Jank headed out of the room, the super's footsteps fading on the creaky, wooden side stairs.

While waiting for Jank to return, Charlie stripped off his coat and scarf and went to work changing the uncooperative E-string. By the time the super returned, Charlie was tuning the new string. Already, the instrument sounded better. He decided he'd change all the strings, expense be damned.

With a wrench in hand, and an odd-shaped bucket that fit perfectly under the valve, Jank went to work on the radiator. Within moments, brown, rusty gunk seeped from the pipe into the container. "Play," he said.

With the string tuned, Charlie strummed a few chords. It sounded good. He appreciated the Seagull, it's tone full and rich and warm.

"Something sweet," said the older man.

Charlie admired the super, knowing how to fix things. Admired, too, that he was older, but in good shape. “Something sweet…” he strummed again. “How about this…” he played “Better Place to Be” by Harry Chapin. One of his personal favorites. Not exactly sweet, but a sentimental story song.

By the time Charlie finished, Jank had the valve replaced on the radiator. The unit started to clunk and clank. “It be warm soon,” said Jank. “You good.” He pointed at the guitar.

“Thanks.”

“Why here? This place. A good musician. You should play Broadway or band.” Jank wiped his hands on a dirty rag.

Many before the super had asked that question. Charlie didn’t have an answer. He’d tried some things. Played in a few bands. For short periods. It’s not like he didn’t play the same songs over and over. That was his bread and butter. He liked playing alone. He didn’t write music. He’d never thought his voice unique enough for a solo career of albums and tours. Yet, he also wanted his anonymity. His freedom.

Jank stood up. “Okay?”

“Thank you.” Charlie pulled a precious twenty from his pocket.

“No. No. I take tips from others. Not musician. Especially musician who pay rent on time.”

So strange that he emphasized “especially,” but didn’t generally have all the necessary English words for sentences.

“You need something? You tell Jank. You need break. Come play song.”

“Thanks, Jank.” He decided not to mar the moment by talking about the rodent. He’d save that for another time. Another song.

The radiator banged again.

“See. Now.”

“Thank you.” Charlie waited for the man to leave and close his door. Once alone, he went to work replacing all the strings. He now wished he’d chosen a different brand or style, but he had what he had. He’d spent the money and would play these until he wore them out.

While he changed the strings, the heat came up. By the time he'd tuned all the strings and had a good sound on the instrument, the room was too hot.

"Be careful what you ask for, for you will surely get it," rang through his head.

Out in the hall, he heard a strange noise. A banging. Charlie opened the door. A very old man, thin and tall, nearly transparent, sprawled on his back like a long ancient turtle. "Gosh, are you okay?"

"Fine. Tried to stomp on a mouse and lost my..." he indicated his situation.

"Can I help you?"

"I wish you would." The old man had translucent, white-blue eyes, like the rheumy eyes of a blind person. They watered, but not really like tears.

Charlie positioned himself and, with great effort, the two worked together to get the man onto his feet.

"Thank you, young man."

"Charlie."

"Thank you, Charlie." He dusted himself off. He didn't introduce himself.

"Anything broken?" asked Charlie.

"Nothing new is broken. Damn mouse. Do you keep food in your room?" The old man eyed Charlie suspiciously. He stretched his neck to try to get a glimpse into Charlie's room.

"Nope." Which was true. He rarely had leftover food. He chose to eat on the street or in the bars. Although he did sometimes bring back a six pack if he'd had a prosperous day. "How about you?"

"Well..." the old man smiled. "It wouldn't be a good day without a cookie."

"Um hm."

The two stood staring at each other for a long moment.

Finally, the old man turned, walked down the hall, and into the bathroom they shared. Before he closed the door, he said, "Thank you for being neat in here."

"You're welcome," said Charlie.

SIX

Even on cold days, if the sun shined, there were people in Central Park. Walking, exercising, meeting, playing games. The paths were strewn with crunchy brown leaves. Most of the trees were approaching bare. One gold-leafed tree, a Ginko maybe, showered little, obscure shaped leaves on all who passed beneath it, magical, like a fall blessing.

Charlie headed into the park and set up under that tree. He had several places he liked to play. Near the Children's Zoo, although those benches were more likely to attract tourists, who would ask questions about entrance fees and feeding times and where the restrooms were, like he was an employee of the park. He could answer them, but that wasn't why he played there.

He enjoyed watching the polar bear in the Children's Zoo, so he would hang out close to the reflecting pool. The coffee folks on the café side were older and more likely to drop a dollar in his case as he played something from the seventies or eighties. He also liked the Alice statue, but that attracted children and young mothers or nannies. Great if he wanted to play something silly for an audience, but the odds of getting a tip of some sort were rather low. Instead, he'd end up with a sticky instrument from the little exploring fingers and hands. Depending on the weather, there were great curves along the paths near the boathouse. Lots of foot traffic of all sorts, so the odds were good that people would stop for a moment, listen, and drop some change or a buck for his efforts. The curves created little performance spaces, so those who stopped wouldn't block the rest of the foot traffic.

Under the tree, he pulled out his instrument and quickly

tuned. It would be a few days until the new strings settled, but they sounded crisp and fresh as he strummed.

"It's the guitar man!" shouted a little kid who rushed toward Charlie, his father, Charlie assumed, walking behind him with a baby in a carrier on his chest. The dad had a handsome smile, a scruffy, close-cropped beard of stubble that framed a strong, square jaw. "Guitar man, play the paddy whack song!" The little boy bounced in front of Charlie.

"You got it, little man." He strummed a few chords and sang, "This old man, he played one..." On the choruses, the little kid tried to sing along. His father smiled and swayed while gently patting the back of the baby at his chest.

By the time he got to seven, there were half a dozen kids singing along and dancing while their parents or nannies or caregivers all stood and smiled and enjoyed the moment of a break from having to keep track of their young charges.

At the end of the song, the kids all clapped and shouted, "More" or "Again." A few coins dropped into his case. This was the problem with children and young parents and underpaid nannies.

Charlie played "Playmate, Come Out and Play with Me," one of his own favorites from childhood. As a kid, he liked the idea, the image of swinging on a garden gate. He'd grown up moving from family to family in the city, in the system. Mostly in tall apartment buildings with lots of other poor kids, surrounded by rats and roaches and drug addicted parents, and other scary things that went bump in the night, and the day. Having a garden gate, a garden, a rain barrel, a place to play and have fun and friends; that appealed to him.

He lost time then. As he started singing "The Bear Song." Some of the kids sang back the call-response lyrics, but he didn't pay much attention as his elementary school memory, stronger than the chill afternoon air, stronger than those young voices, cascaded over him.

A man had come into his school one day. A guitar on his back. No case, just a guitar on a thick strap. He visited the classrooms. Charlie could hear the music in a nearby room. A song about a rain barrel and a garden gate and his compatriots singing along and clapping loudly.

Visitors didn't happen often. Music didn't happen often. They had no band or choir in that elementary school. They had no concerts or movies. They had old, haggard, tired women of all shades in front of classrooms so full some of the kids had to sit on the floor. They lectured and argued and shouted and did their best with a mob of unruly kids whose bellies were empty. Those rooms filled with bullies and inappropriate knowledge. With kids who didn't know how to read or count, but who knew how to spot a plain clothes cop at a hundred yards. Kids who were willing to fight for a scrap of anything, because the alternative was having nothing.

That visitor came to Charlie's classroom. He played a song about meeting a bear and all the kids were supposed to repeat the lines back as the music man sang. He was a big man. Furry like a bear. Big and burly with kind eyes. Most of the kids didn't sing. They talked or ignored the man. Charlie watched the man's big hands. Black on the top, blacker than his, and the man's palms were almost pink, the same color as his. Those big, thick fingers knew where to go on the guitar to make the sounds, the music. He didn't even look very much. Just smiled and sang the silly song about the bear and jumping in the air.

At that moment, Charlie knew what he wanted. He wanted to play like that big man. He wanted to sing songs and play and not have to look at his fingers. He didn't even know then that it was a job that could make money. He just wanted to learn how to do that. He sang out with all his voice and the man looked to Charlie and smiled warmly and fed him the next line to sing.

And now, standing in Central Park, with a gaggle of children all around him, Charlie played without looking at his hands. He sang out the last line, repeated it like that man did so many years ago, "And so I met that bear once more/And now he's a rug on my bedroom floor." Kids clapped and laughed and jumped up and down as a few more coins and a folded bill dropped into the case.

Charlie didn't want to spend the rest of the afternoon playing kids' songs. The memories were too difficult today. And the money sucked because kids don't have jobs and don't have dollar bills in their pockets. He said, "Here's one for your parents," and played a few chords and quickly retuned his guitar before playing "Are You With Me," the hit by Lost Frequencies. The kids immediately danced and shimmied to the beat and finger pattern.

Before the end of his latest song, most of the parents had gathered up their kids, dropped a few more coins into the case on the ground, and moved on down the path. New people stopped for a verse or a few measures of the fingering pattern.

At the end of the song, Charlie gathered up the bills, leaving the change in the case. He shoved the bills into his jacket pocket. For another hour, he played random tunes from his repertoire. He worked out the chord progression with many repetitions to a riff for "Strangers" by Kenya Grace—a current Top 40 hit he'd heard at a bar—he needed a library visit to learn all the lyrics.

And so, the afternoon passed in the chill of Central Park—his new scarf keeping him more comfortable in the weather than he'd been over the past week. He didn't earn much, but enough for a slice, a cup of coffee, and the subway fare to get him downtown for the evening. He'd decided to play that night in The Village. For some reason, Thursday nights in The Village had been good for him since it had turned cold.

SEVEN

Charlie slipped into the bank lobby and quickly made his daily deposit. Living off the grid and functioning in the modern world was a challenge, to say the least. He loosened the scarf around his neck. Such a useful gift.

Well, he wasn't really off the grid. He had his savings account. He chose this bank because they had branches all over the country and their ATMs took cash, he didn't need an envelope or any other paper form. Just slipped his card into the machine and fed in his cash. He'd tried to live a cash-only life, but he'd been robbed and mugged many times over the years. Anything he needed to save up for, like travel, that cash needed to be safe. Once, he broke a toe and was thankful he had a bit of savings to help him through, not just the bills, but not being up to performing and moving around the city for several weeks. His songs kept him eating.

Not having a regular address was a challenge, Charlie never stayed long in one place. A few weeks. A few months at the most. But when you opt out of paper statements, Charlie discovered an old address could hold up for a year or even more. He just had to keep track of his ATM card.

He'd given up on keeping a driver's license about a decade before. You had to have a regular address for that, too. Instead, he carried a passport. He had been able to use his hotel address for that. Bought him ten years of not needing a permanent address.

For now, it all had lined up. He had a place to live, had a little money in the bank, and had an ID. You had to have identification these days. If a cop stopped you for any reason and you didn't have ID, you could end up being arrested for vagrancy and spending time in jail. That got you robbed. He'd lost a guitar because of that twice.

Having savings gave him comfort. His thoughts had been changing about stuff like savings and comfort and home and relationships as forty approached. The bank account, after that day's deposit, had enough that he could take a bus just about anywhere in the country. As winter approached, a train south held appeal. But he loved the city and its holiday decorations. Had since one of his foster moms stood him in line to look at the windows on Fifth Avenue. He couldn't for the life of him remember what shop, but they had the most wonderful and magical windows with lights and mechanical figures.

Back out on the street, into the chilly early evening, he tightened the scarf around his neck and headed a few blocks south to the little triangle park in the West Village. He'd been playing on Thursday nights for a while and hadn't been bothered or harassed. He'd earned some cash, and had met a few interesting guys who later turned into easy tricks. He never charged for sex. Not his style. Charlie never paid for it either, unless you count buying someone a drink or receiving a drink from a new friend a payment.

The only problem with the little park was that it lately smelled like piss. Some unhomed person or drunk had certainly marked their territory. On the upside, the fence, trees, and bushes blocked some of the wind. The benches were usually clean. And there was a lot of foot traffic.

While he played Pink's "Walk Me Home," a song he loved for the hard rhythm, not to mention the popularity—people always paused to listen to the song—an older queen stopped, smiled, listened, dropped a five in the instrument case before the song was finished.

"Want to get out of the cold?" he asked in a soft, effeminate voice.

"What'd you have in mind?" Charlie asked. He wasn't into or opposed to older gentlemen, and remained open to interesting offers no matter where they came from. What he really wanted was a cup of coffee and some time out of the cold. Unfortunately, he'd only brought in thirty-two dollars so far, including the queen's five. The park had been something of a bust financially, although the memory of the big guitar player from his childhood had made the day worthwhile. He wondered still who that big man was and what had happened to him.

"I'm headed for a cup of coffee. I'd be happy to buy you a glass of something if that's of greater interest...or need." He looked familiar.

Charlie blew warm breath into his cupped hands. "Coffee would be great. At the diner?" He nodded his head in the direction of the diner on the corner.

"Oh, that would be nice. I haven't been in there in ages," said the man. He held out his hand, "Quinn."

"The Eskimo?"

Quinn laughed. "Haven't heard that in a while. His blue eyes sparkled. "I don't think the young people remember that song. It followed me my whole life." The lilt in his voice comforted Charlie.

Charlie played a chord and sang the lyrics. Someone stopped to listen, so he continued the song. By the conclusion, old men were singing along and several dropped cash money into his case. It had already turned out worthwhile, this meeting. To light applause, as the little band dispersed as easily as it had formed, Charlie collected his money, got his instrument stowed and flipped onto his back, and he and Quinn walked toward the diner. Another seven dollars. Not enough for real food, but maybe a donut or pastry to go with his coffee. The best part of the old diners, bottomless cups of coffee and you could sit for as long as you wanted, especially on a weeknight, without being harassed.

It would be nice to have some company in a warm place.

EIGHT

Inside the diner, the air steamy and warm and thick with the scent of burnt coffee and something overtly sweet—maple syrup?—a hostess quickly seated them, leaving heavy menus with leather covers and laminated page after page of selections. Charlie pushed his instrument into the corner of his side of the booth, but he left his coat and scarf on. He didn't open his menu once he sat.

"Already know what you want?" asked Quinn as he turned laminated page after page. He'd left his coat on, too. A worn, brown leather. Classic and aged well. Rather like the man himself.

"Just coffee for me. I want to warm up," said Charlie.

"You should order whatever you want. It's on me." Quinn looked over the top of his menu. "Really," he added.

"That's kind." He liked the chicken parmesan dinner at this diner, but wasn't ready to be in debt to this handsome stranger.

"Really," Quinn said again. "Unless you're not hungry."

On cue, Charlie's stomach grumbled. Neither man said anything.

"Something to get you started? A drink? Appetizer?" asked a waitress.

"Coffee," said Charlie. He flipped the heavy ceramic cup upright on its equally substantial saucer.

"Me, too," said Quinn who added, "to start." He flipped his own cup.

"Just made a fresh pot. Cream?" she asked.

"Yes," said Quinn. He turned his attention to Charlie. "Are you from the city?"

"Yes. You?"

"No. I've been here a long time though. Must be thirty-five years. Gosh, forty. It goes by fast."

They sat silent as the waitress poured coffee.

"I've seen you there before, in the little park," said Quinn, pointing a long, manicured finger toward the window.

"It's been a good spot." The coffee smelled bitter and burned. Charlie poured some sugar into his cup and stirred. He licked his spoon for a taste before adding more sugar.

The air between them awkward. If he were attracted to the man, really attracted, talking would be easy. He'd be working the guy, hoping to get him into bed. He realized quickly that wasn't the case. Not that Quinn wasn't an attractive man in his own right. He was. Trim and tall with those arresting blue eyes. Yet, something about the man, something created a distance, an odd energy. Charlie didn't question energy with people. His whole life he'd trusted his gut with strangers; he'd never been misguided. He sipped the bitter coffee. At least it was warm and warmed his mouth, throat, chest, and stomach. He needed that warmth to get down to his toes. His next purchase would be some thick wool socks. New. Maybe from one of the camping stores.

Quinn sluffed off his jacket. All the time, he watched Charlie.

"What?" Charlie asked. He sipped more coffee. It was terrible, but he hoped if they finished their cups the waitress would be forced to make a fresh pot.

"I feel like I know you. I know that's hokey, right? But..."

The waitress returned. "Ready to order?"

She and Quinn looked expectantly at Charlie.

"Chicken parm dinner. Salad. Italian," Charlie blurted, his stomach taking over his brain.

"Spaghetti or fries?"

"Fries. Crispy."

"For you, handsome?" she asked.

"Cobb salad."

"Blue cheese?"

"The way it comes." When Quinn smiled at the waitress his eyes sparkled. "And more coffee?"

"Got another pot brewing." She walked away. "Few minutes," she tossed over her shoulder.

Charlie hoped folks found him attractive in another twenty years.

"I'm glad you ordered a hearty meal. You look like you could use some real food."

Despite finding the comment rude, Charlie didn't say anything. People, strangers, were always making assumptions about him. Thinking him homeless and hungry. He'd learned long ago to let them assume because it usually meant more cash in his pocket. They'd give him money. Buy him food. Attempt to care for him. Quinn buying him dinner at the diner would save him twenty or thirty dollars—money he wouldn't have spent here, not tonight, he was way too far below his daily nut. A bottom line much improved by the Eskimo buying him a meal. He wouldn't need to eat again until the next day.

"I really do feel like I know you," Quinn said again. "I have no idea from where. I don't think we've actually met before."

"Probably some past life thing," said Charlie. He mostly half believed.

The room grew close, warm. He took off his scarf, unwrapping it from his neck, round and round, careful to tuck it into his guitar case strap.

"That's a nice scarf. It brings out your compelling eyes," said Quinn. He lifted his coffee cup only to discover it empty. He set it back down. "That's why I feel I know you, seen you before. I remember your dreamy eyes."

"Thanks. A gift from a friend."

"Your eyes?" Quinn laughed a little. Picked up his empty cup, set it back down.

"The scarf."

"You have friends in the city?" asked Quinn.

More assumptions. He'd just said he'd grown up here. Although, he didn't really have friends in the city. No one from his childhood. Milo was an acquaintance. Everyone he knew lived on the surface of his life. He'd probably spent as much time away from the city as in it. No parents. Never any siblings. No BFF from school. He'd dropped out early. All those horrible fosters.

"Sorry. That sounded rude," said Quinn.

The waitress returned with coffee. Refilled their cups. "Just a few more minutes on your dinner." She headed off and filled other cups around them.

Charlie wanted to leave, but there was a big plate of food coming. Such a tradeoff. "I don't have many friends."

"Oh, sorry. We all lost so many."

"It is what it is," said Charlie. He was certain Quinn was talking about the AIDS crisis. Charlie was a bit young for that to have affected him in that way.

"Did you grow up…" Quinn didn't finish.

"I was in the city through high school." He didn't finish his senior year. That was when his last foster mother died. He'd never been formally adopted. He knew very little about his actual history before being in the system.

"After that?"

The waitress slid a salad in front of Charlie. Plus, a basket of bread. Butter. A vat of salad dressing in a silver boat on a plate. He liked diner meals. So much food. He dug in. Offered the breadbasket to Quinn, who declined. Eating helped him avoid the questions. He didn't want to talk about his childhood. Over. Done. History.

Strange though that the day had been filled with those memories. That man with the guitar and the bear song. Now Quinn and his questions.

They sat in silence while Charlie ate. Hoovered is a better word. He consumed every piece of lettuce, every chopped vegetable, every piece of bread. Every pat of butter. He watched Quinn who was about to say something when the rest of their food arrived. Charlie's plate took up half the table. Heaped with chicken and fries and marinara sauce. Quinn's salad would feed a small family.

They ate in silence.

Halfway through his meal, Charlie's stomach hurt. He hadn't stretched it out this much in weeks. He wouldn't need to eat for days. Despite the pressure he felt in his middle, he continued to work methodically through the food before him, planning not to leave even a drop of sauce on the plate.

Across from him, Quinn picked at his salad.

"Don't like it?" Charlie finally asked.

"It's good. I…had a big lunch today. I'll take it for later." He smiled and his eyes crinkled in an interesting way. "You were hungry." He pointed with his fork at Charlie's plate.

With a full mouth he said, "It's good."

As they finished, their silence returned.

"Thanks for the meal," said Charlie. Quinn hadn't paid yet, but it was important to reestablish the agreement he thought they had.

"You're welcome. Do you want dessert? Some pie or something?" Quinn's question preempted the waitress's return.

"More coffee? Something else?" she asked.

Quinn looked expectantly at Charlie. After no response, he said, "Just a box for this and the check."

"You got it, hun." She placed the paper slip on the table. "Pay on your way out."

"Thanks," said Quinn.

Charlie slunk back into his coat. Wrapped the scarf around his neck a few times. But didn't stand. "I really do appreciate the meal." His stomach so full, if he moved too fast he might throw up.

"You're very welcome. I only wish…"

Charlie didn't take the bait.

The waitress returned with a to-go container and a bag.

Quinn smiled at the waitress and went to work packing up his salad. "I wish we'd talked more," said Quinn.

As far as Charlie was concerned, they'd talked plenty. Music. Songs. Even politics or religion, he'd talk all night. When the subject was him, he had little to say.

The awkward silence returned between them.

Finally, Charlie said, "Well, I need to get back to work.

The songs won't sing themselves." He slipped out of the booth, slung his guitar case over his back, twisted the long scarf once more around his neck.

"No, I guess they won't." Quinn didn't move.

So, Charlie didn't move.

"I..." Quinn started, but didn't look up, his eyes focused on his now empty salad plate.

The moment, awkward. All around them, people talked and laughed and ate huge portions of hashbrowns and French toast. The air grew close again.

"I gotta go," said Charlie. "Thanks. I appreciate the meal." He meant that. He liked to feel full.

"Sure," said Quinn. He still didn't get up out of their booth.

Another beat passed. Charlie gave a little wave and headed out. He'd planned to go back into the triangle park, but instead, turned the corner and headed down into the subway station. He didn't know where he'd go, but he didn't want to be out there, up there, on the street. He didn't want to be with Quinn or take the chance that the man would stand there all night listening to him playing, watching him, trying to get him to talk more about his childhood and past.

A train blew into the station, dragging cold air and the stench of urine and a flurry of paper and plastic trash on the tracks. The very end of a New York City summer. A flow of people came out of the doors, through the turnstiles, past him, and up the dirty stairs. Others flowed down, a few rushed to try to make the train as it pulled out of the station with door chimes and the electronic voice giving directions.

Charlie stood there, near the wall, in the cold station as two more uptown trains arrived and departed. His brain silent. Normally, a song would be in his head. A nudge to play something from the never-ending soundtrack of his life. Nothing. Silence. A switch had flipped. The machine turned off. Charlie swiped a MetroCard, entered the platform just as a train glided in. He got on, not sure where it was headed. He'd ride the trains for a while. Stay warm. Wait for the music to start again in his brain.

NINE

The music didn't start again. All around him, Charlie heard snippets, notes. The bing before the subway announcements, the bell before doors opening and closing. Notes floated out of a rider's headphones. Two girls got on the train, into his subway car, singing something street and wonderful. A man sat near him, humming a jingle from a popular restaurant. Nothing sparked him. He sat, his cased guitar nestled between his knees, watching stations pass, watching passengers embark and disembark. He didn't want to play. Didn't feel inspired. He rode the train to the end of the line, and back.

When the train returned to Times Square after hours spent traveling the length of Manhattan several times, Charlie got off, stood on the platform, watched the train leave him behind. All around, people rushed hither and dither. He stayed on that dirty platform for a long time, without knowing why.

He considered pulling out his instrument; considered forcing himself to play something. That had worked in the past, had jump started him a few times before. But during those times it brought no joy and that was the point of the gig, of life: having fun, being joyful.

At other times, Charlie had simply ridden the wave of silence in his head. He'd read. Gone to movies. Slept...a lot. Allowed his well and soul to be refilled. Those times, while also miserable, didn't take the joy away from playing, from learning music, from making music. Those times, he simply woke one day—sometimes a few days later, never more than a week—and wanted to play. On that reignited morning, he didn't think about the silence, instead waking with music in his head.

Without thought, his feet moved. He changed platforms, enduring the pushing and pulling crowds, adjusted his scarf to let his neck breathe in the too close bustle, got to an uptown train that would take him close to his room, and moved north. Without thought, he stopped at the bodega and got an orange and a piece of beef jerky, a six pack of beer. Without thought, Charlie arrived at the side door of his hotel, walked up a few flights, looked for the rat, but didn't see it, and entered his room.

Without thought, because there could be no thought, his head void of words or sounds or lyrics or songs, he hung his guitar, dumped his jacket, kicked off his boots, unwrapped the long, blue scarf, peeled his orange, and ate, in silence.

A hint of sunshine crept through the moth-eaten blind as Charlie snuggled down into his warm bed. As he pulled the soft quilt up to his chin. At least the heat worked.

TEN

The next few days passed. Still in silence. Charlie journeyed with the Seagull on his back to the bodega for fruit and beef jerky and beer. He walked a little farther down the avenue for a roast beef sandwich and a bag of chips. One day, he headed into a little local coffee shop, a mom and pop place: Coffee Haus. He sat drinking a cup of coffee for several hours. He liked the place, a storefront that had been a wine store when Charlie was a kid. It smelled of rich, roasted beans and brews. It didn't have lines like the big chain with the green logo, a place he avoided shopping at, but would frequently play outside of. It did have a steady stream of customers. And more important, they played great current songs. Lots of alternative and grunge rock. Everything they played had excellent lyrics. Love. Strife. Angst. Songs about the journey of life. Songs Charlie usually found inspirational.

After several hours, his head remained empty.

Charlie had read books on philosophy over the years. He'd learned about meditation. He'd done some yoga. So many of the people talked about wanting a silent mind, a quiet mind, mindfulness. Charlie hated it. Having no thoughts, no sounds, no music created a personal hell he didn't want to be in. Others spoke of the voice in their heads being their hell. That was not Charlie's experience. Not at all.

When he put his coat on to leave the coffee shop, a young, handsome barista said, "No guitar today?"

Charlie studied the man, so trim with a coating of hair on his face and arms and at the V of his blue and black flannel shirt. His name tag said: "Jasper." Handsome. At least a decade younger than Charlie. "Not today." He wrapped the blue scarf around and around his neck.

"I like your scarf. You'll need it, it's gotten cold," said Jasper. "Your eyes look amazing."

There were no other customers.

"Thanks," said Charlie.

"Something for the road? I've got to dump this Italian roast in a few minutes. I'd be happy to give you a cup."

Was he flirting?

Charlie enjoyed the flutter of butterflies in his stomach. He liked being flirted with. "Ah, sure." He accepted the cup.

Jasper brushed his fingers with Charlie's as he passed over the paper cup with its cardboard sleeve.

Definitely flirting.

"Thanks," said Charlie.

"You're welcome." He released the cup. "Listen, if you ever want to sit in here and play, I'd be open to that."

"That's very kind of you."

"Well, it's getting cold and that's no way to make a living, standing in weather hoping someone will drop money in your hat." Jasper so cool, so confident with his perfectly aligned corn rows and his crisp apron. "I'm Jasper, and this is my shop."

"Nice to meet you." It was strange he'd never seen this man before. He'd certainly seen Charlie. Knew about him and his guitar. "I'm Charlie."

They shook hands; the handshake lingered. Jasper had long, strong fingers. Charlie imagined how those fingers would feel exploring his body. In his head, he heard the chime from the start of the *Hairspray* song, "I Can Hear the Bells." Only the chime. He strained deep in his head; the song didn't come.

"Maybe tomorrow," said Charlie.

"I'd like that," said Jasper.

ELEVEN

Charlie, beneath the big, leafless, Central Park tree, sang a Plain White T's song. He sang about love. He sang about loss. He sang because that's what he did. A young man stopped on the path across from him, sat on the bench, adjusted his shoe, retied it, and took off once more at a quick pace. No passerby seemed interested in Charlie or his singing.

At least the music had returned.

Often, the moms and nannies pushing strollers stopped here in the late mornings to listen to him. This was his spot. He came whenever he found himself up before noon. So not a daily experience. Once, maybe twice a week, in this natural alcove near the big tree. Maybe a poplar? He didn't know. And he usually sang new material.

Just a week before, the tree next to this tall tree dropped most of its leaves in a single morning session. Golden and transparent, they drifted down in a light breeze creating a remarkable effect. That morning, many people stopped to listen. Several dropped dollars into his instrument case. Before he packed up to move to a different location, Charlie had to sort the money out from the pile of leaves. Magical.

Not today.

Like most of the spots he chose to work, there was a good flow of foot traffic. People would stop, usually for a chorus or a few moments, rarely for a full song. They'd listen, if they liked him they'd smile, perhaps nod along, and eventually drop a dollar or some coins into his guitar case before moving on.

With the leaves gone from most of the trees, Charlie could see beyond the path, up the little climb to the stone wall and onto the street where buses and cabs and bike messengers whizzed by.

He finished the song and immediately started the same song again. He almost had the whole thing under his fingers. If he practiced it enough, he could play and sing it without having to think about it, he thought, looking at his fingers. Once he reached that level of performance, he could play this song and work on a different one in his mind. At the moment, he wasn't there—he still only had a song at a time—this had never happened before, not when the music returned.

What was there: a desire for food. His stomach grumbled so loud he abandoned the song, quickly packed up the Seagull, slung the case on his back, feeling the ever-present comfort of the guitar. Charlie often imagined this was what turtles must feel about their shells. He realized his thought might be wrong. Did turtles even know they had shells? Did they think about their shells? He'd never thought about that before, although he'd once looked into the eyes of a big sea turtle in a zoo and knew they must have deep thoughts.

After a hot dog from a street vendor and a bottle of water, which took most of his morning earnings, he headed to Times Square. Wednesday meant matinee ticket seekers would be in line at the TKTS booth. Afternoon bread and butter.

He traded the stark beauty of naked trees for the concrete canyon of Times Square. The theater district blocks had been altered. More pedestrian friendly. Some of the blocks closed to cars and buses and cabs. More walking area. More food vendors. More street performers, too.

He liked to play there before shows, and after shows. Tourists often filled the bleachers erected over the TKTS booth. Those in line for tickets a captive audience for a complete song cycle. The acoustics were for shit, but the square never lacked an audience. He could play there for hours and hours. On a good day, he'd need to sort and stash the cash that accumulated in his guitar case. Duffy Square, that little triangle of concrete, where his feet hurt from standing on the harsh surface, where the sun beat down, where the exhaust from the cars ruined his throat some days, was where he earned the bulk of his daily nut on Wednesdays.

As he did each time he entered the triangle of Duffy Square, Charlie patted Father Duffy's foot, chose his spot, close enough to the TKTS line for those waiting to hear him, far enough away to not get trampled by the folks working the line with their show postcards, close enough to the bleachers that he could turn to them and perform when a crowd gathered, but not too close, so he could pay attention to the general flow of foot traffic.

He'd built a new lover's lament playlist and the Plain White T's song from the morning rehearsal in Central Park, was the new lead entry. He launched into it for the crowd in line. "One, Two, One two three four…"

After the lover's series, which hadn't garnered much audience response, or cash, he shifted to the Broadway collection. He'd been working on and off for years on that selection of songs, finding good transitions that made musical sense. It started with "Put on Your Sunday Clothes" from *Hello, Dolly!* and traveled through more than a dozen shows, ending with "Comedy Tonight" from *A Funny Thing Happened on the Way to the Forum*. By the time he reached the conclusion, the medley took near thirty minutes to perform, his case was filled with one- and five-dollar bills. The audience on the bleachers and in the long, snaking ticket line, burst into applause like he'd never received before, not in Times Square at least. He bowed several times and thanked the crowd, and then quickly, in a well-practiced move, gathered up the folding money from his case and shoved it into his pants pocket. It was at least fifty dollars. Halfway to his goal in thirty minutes. Although, he'd need to make up for the silent days.

"Do you know 'If Mama was Married'?" the question came from a sweet-looking older lady who'd come around the exit side, holding two tickets for a show.

"Yes. Of course. From *Gypsy*. Can I play it for you?" said Charlie.

"Would you? It's my favorite."

Of all the songs in the American and Broadway song books, he couldn't imagine "If Mama was Married" being anyone's favorite number. Of course, he knew it. Charlie quickly tuned his guitar and launched into the request while he sang a second song. “Hey, Ya” ran in his mind. The group that had gathered for his long performance dispersed, and within a few minutes of playing and singing it was only him and the swaying grandmother in front of him.

He didn’t mind. It’s actually good to clear out the crowd. Especially if the majority have already given cash. They’re unlikely to give more. So, it’s better to please them and let them move away to make room for a new crowd. Here in Duffy Square at the TKTS, the crowd turned over every thirty to forty minutes once the booth opened. Some tourists lingered, but not for long.

The old lady got misty eyed as Charlie strummed the final chords and sang “…get married today.”

“Thank you, young man. I think you sang that better than Sandra Church and Lane Bradbury.”

Charlie wasn’t sure who she was talking about. “You’re so kind. I’m glad I could perform it for you.”

“Me, too.” She pulled a bill out of her pocket. The greenback folded tight, but showing the hundred-dollar numbers. “For you.”

“Thank you.” Charlie didn’t question anything. He took the money and tucked it into his shirt pocket. This was one of his daily goals, the one he never voiced, to have a single person enjoy him enough to provide his entire nut for the day. He was even now for today and most of the day before. He could do whatever he wanted. Even stop.

In his brain, “I Can Hear the Bells…” pleasantly played.

“You’re much too good to be singing in the street,” said the lady.

“That’s very kind of you.” Charlie was done with this woman. He began to tune his instrument, but didn’t need to, the new strings had stretched and settled and now held their tuning. He strummed a G-chord and then a C-chord, ready to sing something. He reveled in wanting to sing and to play. A huge relief after the previous day.

Quinn sitting across from him in the diner flashed. That crinkle of the eyes. He wondered why that stood out.

"I have a little place downtown. I'm always looking for someone to play in the lobby bar." She produced a thick business card, cream stock, gold letters raised off the paper.

Charlie ran his thumb over the name: Hotel de Chanson.

"I would think you'd be great for the cocktail hour. Happy Hour. Four to Six. I could pay you two-hundred dollars? We could try it once or twice and see how it goes." She looked into his eyes in an expectant way.

"I don't own a watch," said Charlie. He'd never found his last name. Even this moment of conversation about him needing to be somewhere at a given time drew sweat into his pits, tightened his sphincter.

"Charming." The old lady smiled and chuckled. "Well, it's up to you. I don't have anyone at the moment." She pointed. "There's a big clock right there."

Her smile infectious, Charlie found himself considering her offer. "It's very kind of you," he said. "We'll see."

She patted his arm, "You wouldn't need a jacket or tie or anything like that."

Now, Charlie chuckled. He strummed a Cm7. Then a G-chord. "Thank you for your kind offer." He didn't commit to anything.

"Well, you have the card, the address. I'm Patricia, but my favorite drunks call me Patsy. Hope to see you soon."

"I'm Charlie. Charlie Dillon."

"Like the singer?"

"I am a singer, but my name is spelled differently. Enjoy your show, Patsy," said Charlie.

"Thank you, dear." Patsy walked off into the crowds on Broadway.

Charlie strummed a pattern of chords, absently, then he sang, "Out there…" He hoped magic would strike, again…or within the next thirty minutes.

TWELVE

About three-thirty that same day, after making nearly four-hundred dollars on a matinee afternoon, two cops started hanging around near the statue of Duffy on the little TKTS island, about ten feet from Charlie. Charlie got that weird feeling in his stomach. He finished the song, leaving out two verses and a chorus, grabbed up his cash, tucked the guitar in the case, and headed toward Broadway, and then a block north, and a block west. He stopped for a moment before the corner. No one followed him.

It took a beat to get situated, his guitar over his back, his money tucked away in his pockets properly.

Four hundred dollars. He'd made up for the days before. Had a little extra. One block over he stopped in at a bank branch and deposited the excess. He'd hate to get mugged with surplus in his pockets. Hate to lose the momentum of the day. That had happened in New Orleans and he'd learned his lesson. On his way out of the bank, he shoved his cold hand into his pocket, ran his thumb over the raised letters of the card, envisioned the Hotel de Chanson.

The momentum of the day…

"Out there…" ran in his head. "There's a world outside of Yonkers…"

Patsy.

Perhaps she was a Dolly Levi. Or perhaps, based on her song choice, a Rose. Did he require a stage mother?

He could go down there. Check out the bar. He'd never been in Hotel de Chanson.

"I've always been a woman who arranges things…" ran in his brain.

As he thought, a southbound bus pulled to a stop and opened its doors.

The moment felt just like a movie musical.

Charlie stepped inside, swiped his Metro Card, found a seat by the window, watched the city pass as the universe moved him south to The Village.

THIRTEEN

"I thought I'd see you today," said Patsy.

Above her, in old-fashioned, gilt letters: Hotel de Chanson.

"Welcome," she said. "Do you want to play some? There's no one here right now. Just me. I think if you play they will come."

"Who will come?" asked Charlie.

She indicated the door. He didn't know if that was an invitation or an answer to his question.

"Could I get a beer?" Charlie asked as he followed her inside.

"Of course." She stopped in the dark room. "Wait right here."

Charlie waited, in the dark. His eyes started to adjust. There were cocktail tables. Round, with fancy, iron-backed chairs, perhaps from some French era. Two at each table. Light from somewhere, a hint of light, the idea of light, tinkled off of bottles. He assumed a bar.

Flash.

A little stage in a corner. A few feet, raised up about a foot. Enough room probably for a piano at one time, but there was nothing there now.

Flash.

The bar illuminated. Also, very small. Maybe six feet. Maybe eight? Behind it shelves of bottles. Dusty bottles.

Flash. Flash. Flash.

Little tiny lights, not twinkle lights, but small bulbs in the ceiling lit, placing hints of light over and around the tables.

In one iteration, this might have been a coat room.

A handful of tables. A handful of bar stools. The little stage.

"There might be a stool around here," she said. "These are

too heavy to move." She indicated the three stools that lined the bar.

Charlie remained standing just inside the entrance to the room. Her at the bar, holding out a beer bottle. A brand he'd never heard of. A label he'd never seen. He wondered if this was from the last century. Or maybe French?

He took the beer, the bottle cold in his hand; he screwed off the top, it popped from the pressure inside. He drank it down in one long pull. Cold and refreshing, a hint of hops, too much yeast. But good. He placed the bottle on the bar top. Quietly belched. He went to the little corner stage.

The room, warm; dusty. He had questions but didn't ask anything.

Scarf off. Jacket off. He pulled the scarf into the sleeve. Instrument out. He took his time tuning. Taking in the room. Quaint. The guitar sounded nice with all the hard surfaces.

She'd lied to him. There hadn't been a happy hour in this place for a long time. He could see his footsteps in the dust on the floor. Dust gently coated the tables and chairs.

He strummed a chord. A rich, full, C7th. The little room reverberated with the notes, the overtones. A small space with some echo. No need for amplification. Exactly the way he liked to play: acoustic.

Patsy brought him another beer. He looked at the label more closely. Something French indeed. He drank it down in a single swallow. Handed her back the empty. Wiped his damp fingers on his pants leg.

"I'll be sure to order more beer," Patsy said, her voice kind, her eyes bright. She went about the room wiping tables and chairs with a rag.

Charlie strummed another chord. Sang: "Des yeux qui font baisser les miens…"

"Oui."

Charlie sang "La Vie en Rose. " His one French song. He only knew it because of requests from Lady Gaga fans. Everyone wanted to hear that song after the remake came out. Most of them didn't know that Louis Armstrong had sung it decades earlier, a lifetime ago. And Edith Piaf before that. Somewhere along his journey, in one of the homes there were old albums, he'd heard a record, learned that song. He sang it now.

She stood there, hands grasped near her old, flat bosom, her eyes sanguine and misty, wringing the dirty rag in her hands. She did not breathe; she did not blink.

He finished the song.

"Good." She turned away. "I'll find that stool for you." Her accent prominent, heavy, thick with emotion. She might have said something else, too, but Charlie didn't know French. He didn't even really know what that song meant. Something about life.

Tuning again, the instrument sounded so good. The new strings vibrated beautifully. It hadn't taken long this time. Hours of playing in the heat of his room, in the cold on the street, now back in this warm room. It had done something, tempered the sounds, the strings. The old Seagull held up.

"What should I play?" he called into the shadows. "Any requests?" He chuckled to himself. He could play something just for him. He breathed, strummed a C-chord, went to adjust the tuning, but stopped, the instrument sounded perfect. He breathed in the dust. Thought about the cold street. The beer worked its magic, loosened him up inside. His brain hummed. When had the last time been that his brain had hummed in a joyful way? The prospect of playing a song, anything he wanted, without the need to draw sad dollar bills from a stranger's pocket.

"What should I play?" he whispered to the empty room. The smile spread wide across his face. His teeth, exposed to the air of the room, cooled slightly. He played the first stanza of Harrison's "While My Guitar Gently Weeps," and then softly sang the next stanza, "I look at the floor/And I see it needs sweeping," and chuckled to himself.

"Oh, I love that one?" She carried another open beer and a tall wooden stool. "We'll get you something better. But for now," she said over his singing, over his playing.

He stopped the song. The moment had been about the single line anyway. He took the beer and drank it. She set the stool on the little stage.

"We'll have the guy clean in here tonight. It will be good for you tomorrow. Like new."

"Patricia, are we having happy hour in here tonight?"

"Oui. Oui," she said heading toward a man in the doorway.

Men.

Four men in tired old suits. They mumbled approval to one another and spread out around the room.

They didn't complain about the dust. They didn't acknowledge Charlie. He was in his usual state, invisible, yet heard.

He launched into "My Generation," as the men found spots, got drinks, settled in. They drank. They listened. They sang along. Old, single men. Each taking a seat alone at one of the little tables. One, because a table wasn't available, took an extra chair, but moved it aside, toward the wall, so he'd be alone, too.

In between songs, Patsy brought Charlie more beer. None of the gray-haired men requested anything from him. None of the balding spoke to him. Yet, they sang along to the old songs he chose. Music from the sixties. From the seventies. They nodded along and were joined by several more. All men. All older. All looking kindly toward Charlie.

And then, without anything being said, they all, there were nine of them when this happened, all nine of them stood, as one, almost as a single entity, and they departed.

Patsy came to Charlie, held out two crisp $100 bills. "Good. You'll come again tomorrow for Happy Hour? I think they liked you."

"Where have they all gone?" Charlie took the proffered cash, wondering why she'd given so much when there were only nine people. When he'd only played for about forty minutes.

"Happy Hour ends at six," she said.

"Happy Hour ends at six," Charlie repeated as he tucked the money into his shirt pocket. Intrigued by the scene, he said, "Tomorrow."

"Oui. Good," she said, patting his arm.

FOURTEEN

Charlie played "Cat's in the Cradle," while he sat on the comfortable, new stool. The men, a group slightly larger than the day before, men now forced to sit together or stand gathered and listened. They sat at the little café tables, singing along, drinking cocktails and beer, while Patsy moved from man to man, table to table serving the Happy Hour crowd. Charlie couldn't help but think about what she had told him just a few minutes earlier.

She had been sitting and talking with a woman in a doctor's office thirty-five years ago. The woman had been pregnant. Patsy had been there to have a mole removed. Luckily, it hadn't been cancerous, but there had been some concern that it might be. Her mother had died from that, from cancer, that had started or been discovered because of a mole, a large, fast-growing mole on her upper arm.

Why he now was so caught up thinking about Patsy's mother's mole...well, it was because of the rest of it.

Patsy had told him that the woman sitting there with her, it was only two of them in the waiting room, that woman had his eyes. Charlie's eyes. How could that be? Why would that matter? He'd thought he remembered his mother, but that woman died. He had no memories of his father. Yet, this woman, the pregnant one in the waiting room didn't sound at all like the mother he'd known, or her sister, who Charlie thought he remembered living with before the system, although there was a woman many years later who insisted he call her aunt.

But he reasoned as he sang the chorus, the woman Patsy described might be an aunt. Or some other relation. Even a sister, perhaps. Or perhaps just another unrelated story. Lots of people had blue eyes, although none he'd ever met with the brilliant, vibrant hue of his own.

Patsy said the day she gave birth was February ninth. Charlie's birth date. They'd stayed in touch. They'd become friends for a time, although after she moved, the other woman, not Patsy, they'd lost track. She'd put that baby up for adoption, that was what Patsy said. But he'd never been adopted.

Charlie's birth date. That was the same.

Why would she tell this story to him? How could any of this be true? After a lifetime, did it even matter? He'd become his own man. His past didn't really matter at all.

He sang now about a distant father. Two of the men listening were misty-eyed. This Chapin song did that to people.

How did Patsy know his birth date?

A woman Patsy had randomly met, who had a baby the exact day and place he had been born himself, who had the same eyes as his. How strange.

She'd told the story now because of her curiosity. She'd seen him playing in Times Square and couldn't believe the recognition of the eyes. She'd asked about his mother and he'd told her. She asked about his father, and he'd told her he didn't know him. So much of the two stories didn't align. It was New York City, after all, there must have been dozens of babies born that day in the city and the boroughs. Maybe a hundred. How could it be the same woman?

Patsy couldn't remember the woman's name. Just eyes. The date.

Charlie circled back into the song, that last chorus one more time. Several of the men were softer-faced now. Weakened by the song. How amazing to be weakened by a song. The power of music something that couldn't be fought.

During that chorus, he thought of the story once more. Patsy had met his mother, or a woman who she now thought must have been his mother. Charlie had never seen his birth certificate. Yet he must have one. That would be easy enough to chase down, right? He had identification. He had a social security number...somewhere. He hated the idea of showing up on the grid though. More than he was already.

And what did it matter? Knowing more would change nothing.

He finished the song. The men in the room applauded. He let the applause die down. He strummed a D-chord, randomly, checking his tuning. He launched into Clapton's "My Father's Eyes."

It should be his father. A revelation about his father. That's what he'd longed for his whole life. He thought he knew his mother. Thought he'd been raised by her until she died. Then the aunt. That was when he was thrust into the system. Thought he'd been raised by an aunt, who turned out wasn't an aunt or something like that. Then the fosters. So many fosters.

Patsy met his mother randomly in a doctor's office? Could that even be true? They had the same eyes? How could she remember eyes? After thirty-eight years?

Did any of this matter now?

He played the song. Dreamed about family. Imagined his mother who now might not be his mother. Had he actually been abandoned as a newborn? Been in the system from the very beginning? What more did Patsy know. They'd stayed in touch for some time. Until his mother moved away? Put up for adoption? He knew so little about his own life. Had all those people lied from the beginning?

All he knew now was that he could play any song anyone wanted to hear. He had a great memory, an ear for music and songs and lyrics.

Yet, he also wanted to know where he came from, who he was. Maybe it did matter.

FIFTEEN

On his second third, the barroom was full of men. Patsy brought Charlie a beer: La Fin du Monde. Men sat at the little tables. Men sat at the stools at the short bar. Men stood in the dark corners of the room. They hummed along with the songs. They applauded when songs ended. They smiled and engaged with Charlie in kind, supportive, and other mostly silent ways.

"Play my song," said Patsy.

He'd played it every afternoon, "La Vie En Rose." He sang it in French. He did Edith's version and Louie's version and Lady Gaga's version with the joke about French tips. A song that did its job, sat well in his register, that made everyone happy.

While he sang, he looked from face to face, man to man. Why so many men? Why no women? This wasn't a gay bar or a gay hotel; Charlie knew that even though he'd never talked about it with Patsy. These were middle-aged single straight men. Old, single, straight men. Mostly. Straight men. Charlie's gaydar was honed enough to know. Even here, the hotel on the edge of The Village. These weren't all gay men. Why were they together? Gathered here for Happy Hour?

This was of course another SRO, only a nicer single-room hotel than his. Well, perhaps not an SRO. These men might all have their own bathrooms, something he didn't have. But a men's hotel that had been a men's hotel for a very long time, possibly back to the twenties or thirties based on the architecture and some of the lobby furnishings. He'd never asked Patsy. He'd never talked to any of the men.

He'd assumed that Patsy had been running this hotel for

a very long time. And decided that she not only ran the place but probably owned it. Was one of these old men her father? Possible. Not likely. She never showed that level of deference for any of these men.

He transitioned into a Django version of the song, fast finger work playing the melody with a backbeat. He loved Django. He could turn nearly any song, old or new, into something with Django's style. He could mash up any number of songs, bringing in varied lead lines and laying them over the foundation of any other song. And after a long run up or down the fretboard, he could arrive just about anywhere, enter any other song. The beauty of the style; he could play a single song for ten or fifteen or even twenty minutes. He could transition a crowd in the park with this type of work, by the sound of his impressive vocal range, his ability to impersonate other performers, not just cover them, and finger work that rivaled the best players in the world. Listeners were happy and impressed. That translated into higher tips.

That was how he finished his Happy Hour set. As he came to an end, to a final chorus, the men stood and applauded and exited. Six in the evening. Like clockwork.

Patsy returned to him, several folded bills in her hand, another beer in the other. Charlie took the money and the beer, even though he had a full one sitting on a little table next to him. An addition since his previous day.

"Thank you," he said pocketing the money and upturning the beer. He drank the bottle down in a single swig and handed her the empty.

"You're welcome, dear boy. I love that song and all the ways you play it," said Patsy.

That's when Charlie realized all the men hadn't retreated. One man sat in the middle of the room. Now alone.

Quinn.

He thought he saw Quinn smile in the dark room.

"Hello," said Charlie. He drank down the other beer. Two swigs this time.

"Good evening. I see you have a gig," said Quinn, who now came to the little stage. "I heard you were here and thought I might buy you dinner."

Such a strange offer.

"How did you know I was here?" Charlie tucked his guitar into the case.

"I was thinking about a little Italian place nearby. How does that sound?"

Why hadn't Quinn answered his question?

Charlie didn't know if he wanted to sit through another meal with this man. He had money in his own pocket. He'd been making money—a grand a week on Happy Hour alone. The regular nightly gig added substantially to his bottom line. In addition, wherever he played the past few days, people shoved wads of cash into his hands and pockets and instrument case because he'd played their "favorite song." This happened sometimes, this cascade of riches. He'd learned it best not to question or talk or even think too much about the phenomenon. Just play and take the money and sock some away for the inevitable rainy day that always followed when, like the monsoon season, the deluge ended as easily and quickly and unexplained as it had come on.

"Or there's a nice old Greek place?" said Quinn.

Patsy returned to Charlie, "No Happy Hour tomorrow or the next day. We'll see you again on Monday?" she asked.

Charlie didn't know about Monday yet. He still didn't own a watch, either. He nodded.

"Good. Good." She touched Quinn's elbow. "Happy Hour is over." She must have tugged on him because Quinn led her to the door.

Quinn pointed to the street and was out the door before Charlie could respond.

He wondered if there was a back door. Trust your gut, he thought to himself. He turned the bottle up for another drink, but the beer had been drunk.

"Another?" asked Patsy from behind the bar. She moved as if by magic.

"Yes." Charlie came down off the little stage, hung his guitar over his back, and bellied up to the bar. The room had been cleared of empty glasses and bottles. The bar top gleamed in the light from the back wall of bottles. The dust now gone.

Patsy placed another La Fin Du Monde before Charlie. "Thank you again. This has been a nice treat for my boys."

Questions bubbled up in Charlie, but he squelched his desire to ask them by drinking beer. Cold. Satisfying. When he studied the label, he discovered it to be Canadian, not French.

"You are avoiding that man?"

Charlie nodded.

"Good. I don't trust him."

"You know him?" Charlie asked over the lip of the bottle.

"I've seen him around over the years, but I don't know him. Don't even know his name. I don't like his energy."

Charlie wanted to say that's how he felt, too, but he drank a sip of beer instead. He thought of her phrase "my boys," and wondered over it again. He might become one of her boys if he wasn't careful...trust your gut. He finished his beer.

"Another?" she asked.

"No."

"If you go there, turn right, then left, there's a side entrance into the alley." She pulled her finger back from the point. "See you Monday, oui?"

After a long beat, Charlie nodded. He didn't know for sure if he'd be back, but at the moment, he thought he probably would return. Trust your gut, the little voice in his head said once more. He pulled off his guitar and tugged on his coat, shoving the scarf through the arm with effort.

"Charlie?"

He turned back to her.

"That scarf really brings out your blue eyes."

He didn't say anything, wrapping the scarf once more around his neck.

"Charlie?"

After a beat and another wrap of the scarf, "Yes?"

"Have a good evening."

"Thanks." He tucked the scarf into his jacket. It smelled like him now.

SIXTEEN

Charlie slipped out the side entrance, not really hiding, not really running, but doing his best to avoid Quinn.

Why?

He didn't know. The man had been nice. Had bought him a meal. Had offered to do that again. Yet, sitting with him that first night they'd met had been awkward and uncomfortable. Fine when he didn't have money in his pocket, but tonight he had some cash and could easily buy a meal for himself. He'd had beer, too, and enjoyed the slight buzz. This Happy Hour was a great gig. For maybe the first time in his life, he thought it nice to have a regular job.

On the street: people. Something one could always count on in New York City. People on the street. Lots and lots of people in The Village at this hour. A little after six. Rush hour. People leaving work. Getting home. Heading out for the evening. Everyone in a hurry. Women in skirts and sneakers. Men in suits. All headed into and out of subway stations, getting into and out of cabs, snagging the vacated cabs before someone else. Each person living their own private life in this incredibly public way. So many souls that mostly remained anonymous.

Charlie debated. He wasn't really hungry. Didn't feel like heading home. He didn't feel a drive to earn a lot of money, because his pocket was full. His bank account had a surplus. Another good day. Yet, he found himself longing to play. To play the music he liked instead of requests.

There were a lot of nooks and benches and alcoves in and around The Village. There were staircases of brownstones where one could sit for long stretches of time without being bothered or accosted. There were the little parks formed by streets coming together. And the more formal parks, too, with rings of benches and statuary and nearly naked trees.

How long would Quinn wait? Where would the man go next? If Charlie stayed in The Village, the odds increased that he'd be discovered and confronted and would have to answer to his choices. He wasn't in the mood for that. Wasn't in the mood for all the personal questions.

There, on the next block, a subway station. He could head downtown, toward Battery Park, although not his favorite place to be at night. The skies were already autumn dark. He could go up to midtown, and the theater folks, but that limited his song choices. They'd request hits and Broadway tunes. He could head further north to Central Park. Although, the days were so much shorter and the park grew dark too early.

What he wanted was to sit on a bench and just play for a while. To enjoy his buzz and watch the people and sing what he wanted to sing. Maybe some Joni Mitchell or Peter, Paul, and Mary or his near namesake, Bobby Dylan. He found himself in a sixties mind set for some reason and wanted to embrace the folk music pull. He'd never understood why those sounds, the messages through tight harmony had ever fallen out of favor. The times they be a changin'.

And he didn't want to be cold.

He watched the people around him, expecting Quinn to be standing beside him at any moment. Would that simply be a choice he had to make?

A group of women power walking in sneakers and headbands pushed past him. The snippet of an eighties tune popped into his head, but he couldn't grasp the whole of it. "What a Feeling," maybe.

In a circuitous way, Charlie arrived at the little triangle park. He sat next to the statue on the bench. Pulled out his guitar. Tuned quickly. Played "Lemon Tree." One of his favorites. People rushed past. People dumped dollars and coins into the guitar case. No one stopped to listen. He finished and sang "Both Sides Now." That got people to stop, to listen, to drop bills into the guitar case.

When he finished, a skinny old man said, "I heard her play that song live, right over there," he pointed off toward the buildings. "A coffeehouse used to be right there, and they all played on that stage. I heard them all. Joni and Bob Dylan and The Kingston Trio and Peter, Paul, and Mary, and...I was a waiter then." His eyes glistened. He sang along, out of tune: "I really don't know clouds..."

Charlie loved this moment. Loved when people connected on a deep emotional plane with his songs; they had the experience while he sang. He'd never had a desire to write his own music. He didn't have that skill. Didn't even dream of it. The work had been done. All he needed to do was learn it, like painting by numbers, and share the results.

When he looked up toward the old man, he was gone, replaced, there, before him, as he played the opening chords of "Blowin' in the Wind," was Quinn. Not angry, his look curious. He dropped a five-dollar bill into Charlie's guitar case and then sat on a nearby bench. He didn't speak, just nodded along with the rhythm of the song.

SEVENTEEN

Charlie played song after song. Dylan. Baez. Peter, Paul, and Mary. Seger. Mostly protest songs. Folks didn't stop, yet dropped money into the guitar case. Normally, Charlie would sift out the bills between songs. Too much in the case invited a snatch and grab. People pretending to drop a bill, but instead taking money out. He'd had it happen many times. Tonight, he didn't care.

The temperature continued to drop while he played. He kept his scarf wrapped tight around his neck and played. There were lots of protest songs. No need to slip over to other music from the same era, like the Beach Boys or The Mamas and the Papas. He loved their songs, too, but for some reason he had an urge for protest.

While he played, Quinn remained, across the little park, nodding along. He had to be cold, sitting there, not moving. Did Charlie care? He did, but didn't know why.

Why protest songs? It was an urge to play them. An internal drive that motivated him through all of those songs, here, near where so many had been first played, had become popular, had built careers. Changed the course of history.

There were things Charlie wished for in his life. One of those wishes was that he'd been alive in the '60s. He'd been a guitarist then. It seemed to matter then. Protesting the war, the government. Fight for Civil Rights, human rights. He'd read biographies and histories. Young people were arrested, often in huge groups. They'd sing in the cells. The songs bouncing between the groups of men housed together and the women housed together. The songs were not just protest, but communication. They were support. They were an acknowledgement that the singers weren't alone in their ideals and their convictions. Young people stood up to power and authority. Young people challenged the norms and expectations. From what Charlie had been seeing lately in the world, they needed people to stand up. They didn't seem interested in changing the world in the old ways.

Charlie wondered sometimes if he would have had the balls to be a Freedom Rider. To challenge the corruption and hatred in the South, or anywhere. The idea, while romantic, didn't seem honest or realistic. He didn't feel great conviction about anything. He'd never had much. He worked for what he did have. He had some talent, some skill. He had music on his side, and that was useful and important. He also had a fear of pain. Emotional and physical.

Would he have burnt his draft card? Dodged the draft all together? Gone to Canada? Without money or education, would he have simply gone off to war. Fought for something he wouldn't believe in and been killed or come home to the humiliation those boys faced. That's where the odds were.

Sometimes, he wondered if he had died during that war or during World War II. During World War I. He knew all that music and loved it all. Especially the lyrical, sad ballads from the Second World War, the protest songs from Vietnam. He'd done the math. He could have served and died and been reincarnated to serve again. Could it be the reason he knew this music so well, learned it all so easily, was because he'd lived during those eras and had found a way to bring the music along with him to the next life. That might explain why learning current, popular music was sometimes a challenge for Charlie, harder than learning the old songs.

How long had he been sitting in the cold and not playing? That was new. He bent down, scooped up the bills, righted them, shoved them into his pants pocket. He gathered up the change, shoved it into his coat pocket.

When he looked up, Quinn was gone.

Relief followed.

His stomach grumbled. He was cold. Tired. Hungry.

What time was it?

He found he wanted a bath. Not something Charlie craved. There was nowhere to do that. His apartment only had the shared shower.

"Do you have somewhere to go?"

He looked toward the speaker. Patsy.

"Yes," he said.

"I've been thinking, if you needed a place, I have a room available. It's small. But clean. Warm, too." She looked kindly at him, her eyes honest. "Would you like to see it?"

"I have a place," said Charlie. He zipped up his instrument case.

"Okay. I could show it to you," she said. Patsy didn't press. More an invitation. A kindness.

"Okay," he found himself saying without knowing why.

They walked together, around the block, to her hotel. The windows glimmered in the nighttime, like some old-fashioned scene. The glass not exactly clear, as if it had dripped a little. Old glass, lead-lined panes, that captured and held the light. Charlie imagined candles or gaslight.

Inside, they took the little elevator up to the ninth floor. The top floor. Down the narrow hall. Thick carpet, old, warn, an antique floral pattern in what might have been reds and browns originally, sturdy beneath their feet absorbing their footsteps. The place silent. The walls wood paneled. Opulent in a turn-of-the-twentieth-century way.

"Here." She had a little skeleton key and opened door 903.

The room wasn't small at all. A big bed against a wall. Wood headboard. A pair of pineapple finials topped bedposts at the foot. A desk and high-backed wood chair. A second chair, upholstered and oversized—a chair you could spend the day reading a book in. Charlie tried to remember if the furniture would be called "Empire." The floor covered in rugs, not carpet. Two narrow doors.

Patsy opened a door, a full-length mirror on the backside. "It's a very small closet."

It wasn't small, but rather a narrow, walk-in room with

empty racks and cubbies.

The second door opened to a private bath. A massive claw-foot tub, a shower above. A pedestal sink, something from the twenties. Old white porcelain. Tiled floor and walls in a black and white checked pattern. A toilet in the corner. Lush towels on the racks.

"This is all lovely, but I'm sure it's well out of my price range," said Charlie, longing to fill that tub with hot, hot, very hot water.

She named a price.

"Is that weekly?" he asked. It was more than triple what he spent weekly.

"No, a month. That includes maid service twice a week, but doesn't include meals." She held the key out to him.

Her price for all this space and luxury was less than he now spent for the SRO. How could that be? "That doesn't seem right."

"It's right. I run the place. I should know." She stepped closer, the key now within his grasp.

Would it be making a deal with a devil if he took this room?

"What if you fire me from Happy Hour?" Charlie asked.

"Why would I fire you?"

"Or hired someone else?" He wanted to snatch the key before she rescinded her offer.

"The two things are mutually exclusive. Play or don't downstairs. So long as the rent is on time, you can live here. Some of my men have been here for decades."

Was that a threat? It didn't sound like one, but something in him said it might be. Some of her men.

He listened deeper for that voice.

Silence.

He took the key.

"Good," said Patsy. "Good, good, good."

He took off his guitar and placed it in a corner. His stomach growled again.

"Oh, dinner is over, but I might be able to scare something up," said Patsy.

"No. I'll go out. I'll need to move my things."

"As you wish," said his new landlady. She framed herself in the hallway door. "You need anything, you just dial zero." She stepped into the hall.

As Charlie closed the door, he heard her repeat: "Good, good, good."

EIGHTEEN

Charlie had been traveling light for many, many years. A small canvas duffle bag and his Seagull guitar. He picked up clothes in thrift stores, wore them, washed them out in the sink, and then, after a while, released them back into the world, replaced by new thrift store finds. In New York City, there were always trash bins filled with discards, so much of it in great shape. The trick, he'd learned as a kid, was to visit upscale neighborhoods on trash night. He'd learned to dumpster dive early in life, too. So much good food went to waste daily in the Big Apple. And if he hit the neighborhoods around NYU or Columbia at semester breaks, he'd often find designer clothes and other useful items.

It's easier, he'd also learned, to release something back into the world, when it came from a trash can. When you paid cash there were different expectations.

So, moving from the SRO to Hotel de Chanson the next day was an easy trip. His guitar, the quilt, one small duffle, a key dropped with the manager, done. Charlie thought about springing for a cab, he was flush, after all, but then swiped his Metro card and traveled downtown by subway instead.

He rode the elevator up to the top, feeling like an impostor or a thief or something. But his key worked and he entered his room. His room: 903. He locked that door behind himself. He hung up his scarf, stowed his guitar in a corner, stripped out of his clothes, turned on the hot water in the tub, and trimmed his toenails while the claw-footed monster filled.

There were little soaps and little shampoos and little conditioners in a basket on one of the two cubby shelves next to the sink. The room filled with steam and that, in itself, created luxury: to be naked and to bathe and to relax in the privacy of his own rooms. His rooms.

Of course, a tub that size took a very long time to fill.

Charlie uncased his guitar, tuned, and strummed a few chords. The new strings were well seasoned now and his Seagull filled his space with mellow sounds. He'd heard a hint of a song on the subway. He didn't know what it was. A passing rider in the moment. No headphones. It wasn't exactly hip hop, but it had a beat. Yet, it sounded more melodic, a ballad by one of those strong women who dominated the charts. He played the notes, the line he'd heard. He didn't know it, but now had it better situated in his head, in his mind. He'd listen for it.

He shifted to an etude, and then to a baroque piece he loved. Something by D-minor Bach cello suite he'd transcribed in his head after hearing it in a restaurant.

There was an app. You could hum a few notes or sing a song and it would tell you the title and artist. You could hold the app open to a song playing overhead or nearby and it would identify the song. Of course, phones cost money and phone plans needed a commitment. And then every step you took was available to someone else if they wanted to know where you were or what you did. Although no one would want to follow Charlie. Why would they?

Charlie didn't believe in conspiracy theories, well not most of them. He believed men walked on the moon and that the world was round. He wondered if the government would eventually fill the citizens with microbots. He also worried about the growing number of surveillance cameras. Facial recognition bothered him. He recognized that anyone who carried a phone had already embraced having a tracking device and chip in their life: no need to get something surgically inserted, everyone willingly carried their personal tracking device around with them because they wanted to play Candy Crush or make words in a game. So, there was something to being off the grid: the network, really. He did have a bank account and that was traceable. The activity logged. And when he traveled, ATM transactions showed where he was. He didn't really know why that mattered to him, others not knowing his comings and goings. On some level it did.

He'd read an article about a group of people in Arizona or maybe Southern California who lived totally off the grid. Big brother couldn't track them. Charlie liked the idea of that.

He didn't know why.

He'd never visited there, either.

The tub was only half full. Charlie tested the water. Way too hot. He added some cold to the tap. Dried his hand. Played a few chords. He'd discovered a new way to form an F#7. Discovered it by chance making a change between chords. He liked that he could move one finger—

The telephone rang.

He didn't know the sound or its source at first. It was on the third ring that he picked it up, tentatively. "Hello?"

Patsy prattled on about joining her for dinner and meeting some of the other men who called the hotel home. Normally there'd be a charge for dinner, but seeing as it was his first night and all, he would be her guest.

His stomach grumbled.

"When?" he asked.

"Thirty minutes," she said. "Every night at six."

He agreed to dinner.

A wave of sadness washed over him. He'd planned to luxuriate in that big tub until the water turned cold. And then planned to add more hot water. A tub of his own. He couldn't remember the last time he'd been able to enjoy a long bath.

Still. Twenty minutes in the tub would be wonderful. Hopefully, he'd feel warm for the first time in weeks.

After lining up the soap and hair products, he slipped into the still slightly too hot tub, slipped in and down as the hot water prickled and irritated his skin. Down and down and in and under. He held his breath until he felt scalded like a lobster.

He surfaced and stretched himself out into the tub. He didn't have to bend his knees, the tub so massive. He imagined an opportunity to share this luxurious experience with a man.

How nice it would be to do such a thing. It had been a long time.

Would he be willing to bring someone back to this room? To his room? Probably not. However, the idea of sharing this tub with someone. Of bubble bath and bath oils and softness mixed with physical hardness held an appeal he wouldn't deny.

For now, he soaked and soaped and shampooed and conditioned and soaked a bit longer as the water began to cool. He'd have to drag himself out if he were to arrive at his dinner engagement on time.

NINETEEN

There was no Happy Hour on Sunday. Instead, it was Sunday Lunch, even though it happened at the usual supper time. Charlie walked into the dining room to find white tablecloths and sparkling crystal on all the little four-top tables. Like walking back in time.

The men there, for it was all men seated at the tables, wore jackets. Most wore ties. Charlie felt underdressed—a rarity for him to even notice how he fit in the fashion world—in a long-sleeved flannel shirt and jeans, his usual cold-weather wardrobe. Sometimes, if he found one he liked, he'd wear a sweater. In the heart of winter, he always looked for cable knit sweaters, like the fishermen wore, well, it's what the Old Spice guy wore, and the Gorton Fisherman. He did own a sweater now. He loved it, even with the stretched-out holes. The bath had rendered him warm, so he hadn't thought to slip it on.

Patsy greeted him at the door and escorted him to a table. He sat there, alone for a few moments while she flitted around the room. Waiters, for the entire staff seemed to be Patsy and a group of young men, carried in plates of food, serving everyone at the same time. Dishes of steaming pot roast and carrots and scalloped potatoes. A hearty meal for a cold Sunday.

A nerdy looking waiter, with glasses held together with masking tape, set a plate before Charlie and a second plate at the empty chair next to him. The guy didn't make eye contact, but said, "Enjoy your dinner, sir."

It was the first time Charlie remembered ever being called "sir." Maybe one other time in a fast-food chain where the kid behind the counter really was a kid and a thirtysomething Charlie probably seemed like an old man. This waiter guy, he wasn't that much younger than Charlie. Maybe late twenties?

"Thank you," said Charlie as the guy moved away.

Patsy joined him. "Hello, dear. Oh, this looks wonderful. I do love a good pot roast for Sunday lunch."

"Yes, nice." He pondered a moment longer the use of sir. Maybe it was simply Hotel de Chanson protocol.

"Is everything in your room working properly?" She took a bit of her food and made yummy noises.

"Yes." He now ate, too.

A different young man, early twenties, trim, handsome in an emo way, poured water into their glasses without comment. Behind him, a fat guy, bulging out of his black and white uniform, poured red wine into the glasses.

They enjoyed their meal for a few moments: the food excellent. He didn't have to pay, making it even better. Around them, men in pairs and quartets and even two solo diners ate food off fine bone China dishes with a delicate rose pattern around the edges. Ate with polished silver utensils and drank wine from shimmering crystal glasses. The room remained mostly silent. No one talked. That surprised Charlie. He wanted to ask about the silence, but also didn't want to interrupt it.

Generally, he slid easily through the world, whatever it offered or presented. He went with the flow, quickly figured out the customs or expectations, and basically fit in. That's how he'd survived a childhood in the foster system.

He ate in silence.

"You can join us for dinner any evening. The charge will be added to your monthly bill," said Patsy as she wiped her mouth. You can join one of the others, or sit alone if that is your preference. You'll find most of my men have their places and return to them night after night. So, just don't sit in someone else's place."

"Okay." He didn't ask the cost. He'd eat in the dining room once when he wasn't playing for Happy Hour and he'd check his bill to figure it out. There might also be some notice or price list in the room. He hadn't checked all the drawers yet.

"We have a very nice chef. He makes all the meals from the

best ingredients. A different menu every day, but there are some seasonal favorites that return again and again." Patsy indicated her nearly empty plate. "Like the pot roast." She smiled kindly. "I'm so glad you've joined us and hope you stay with us for a very long time. Most of my men here have done just that."

In the back of Charlie's mind, the place where gut reactions registered, he heard ominous, horror music playing and he wondered if that was just his brain getting the best of him.

"If you're interested, there are other amenities available for rent or hire." Patsy smiled in a mischievous way. "Televisions. Radios. Other useful things."

Again, he thought there was much more to this statement, more inuendo perhaps to that lilt in her voice.

She added, "Any charges are simply added to your monthly bill. Of course, you can also pay as you go."

"Good to know." A rented radio seemed like a silly choice when he could purchase one cheaply at one of the discount places on Broadway. He finished his wine.

Patsy raised a hand and the fat guy returned and refilled their glasses. After he left, she leaned in and said, "Wine is charged by the glass, but you are my guest tonight, so feel free to drink up."

It was like meeting a drug dealer and them offering the first fix free. He'd tried drugs, but didn't want to waste his money. Getting him hooked on the trappings of his new world. Around him, few men drank wine.

Charlie found himself longing to be out on the street playing his guitar. Being anonymous was the true perk of his life. He came and went and no one knew anything. Now, he'd agreed to be in a place where he realized, or at least surmised, that he would be seen. Watched, even. How could he not? Being the nightly entertainment ended his idea of anonymity. His stomach tilted and he swallowed another mouthful of wine.

He wasn't in deep. Not at all. He could walk away, right? No harm, no foul. Would he lose his gig if he checked out of the Hotel de Chanson?

The Eagles' song lyrics about The Hotel California rippled through his head.

TWENTY

The air turned unseasonably warm. Charlie, sitting on a stoop in The Village, playing softly, ever so softly, love songs from the seventies, mostly, overheard a passerby talking about Indian Summer and climate change. People strolled by, their pace slow, taking advantage of the time outside in a different way. People had taken off their jackets, rolled up their sleeves. Some boys in shorts and T-shirts rode by on skateboards leaving a wake of marijuana smoke. The atmosphere festive and inviting.

Occasionally, someone would notice him there, slow even more. A few dropped coins in his case. He hadn't made much money that night. Frankly, with Happy Hour, there wasn't a strong motivation to really sing for his supper.

The other new and recent phenomenon: the men who lived at the hotel had taken to buying him dinner. It turned out that was a thing, too.

"No need to reciprocate," they said.

"Better than just buying you a beer," others said.

"Just being neighborly," still others remarked.

Sometimes, the dinner companions would let a hand linger on Charlie's arm or even knee. He saw it as the price of the meal and remained good natured. A free meal was a free meal. He'd done far more for much less in his life journey.

While having dinner with the men, sometimes alone with them, sometimes in groups of three or four, he learned that some of the other items on the available ala cart menu included the waiters.

That explained their youth. That explained their varied and diverse appearance, no two young men looking alike.

"Are all the men living here...gay?" he'd whispered to a solo dinner companion one evening. His gaydar had originally said no.

The man smiled a sparkling smile, his light, cataracted blue eyes came to life when he said, "Yes, Baby." He drew out the word "baby" in a southern way, a New Orleans way. That one word sent Charlie right back down to Royal Street in the French Quarter where he liked to play in the afternoons and evenings when he spent time there. He made good money in NOLA, but the cash money always smelled of sweat and beer and sex.

An older man who Charlie had seen around the neighborhood, but who didn't live in the Hotel de Chanson, stopped to listen to Charlie as he sang Chapin's "I Wanna Learn a Love Song." Charlie liked Chapin's songs. They told stories. This song had been an anthem of his, even if it was about straight people. Sometimes he changed the pronouns. No one noticed or commented. He also liked Chapin's songs because they were long. Listeners often came and went during them. They knew the lyrics, would walk away humming the song in progress. He liked the songs because they were beautiful, too. That was really the important reason. He loved lyrical, gorgeous melodies and loved songs that told stories.

While he hadn't done it in a long time, there were whole days he'd sit on a bench in one of the parks and just play Chapin songs, hour after hour. He'd wished many times that he were older and had gotten to see Harry live. There were times when he played Chapin marathons that he imagined himself channeling the great singer/songwriter. Actually, could feel the man enter his body and play through him. That cello sound in his head, in the background.

As a kid, one of the homes he'd lived in, the woman there, a nice lady who didn't feed the kids she kept much at all, played Chapin hour after hour. Charlie would sit in a dark corner, in the shadows, away from her and everyone else in the house; this was before the guitar became part of him. Years before he'd heard the guitar man at school. He'd sit for hours, he must have been five or six. Before school. All day long he'd sit just out of sight of that foster caregiver and listen to Chapin's albums over and over and over again.

Other days, that same woman played the Mamas and the Papas. All day long. Sometimes, the same album over and over. Or Janis Joplin. Or Peter, Paul, and Mary. Or Dylan. Or…she had stacks and stacks of old, crackly albums. Each one had a little sticker with a name and address on it. Her last name never changed. But there were many different addresses.

For several years he'd lived there. It was the second home. Before he ended up with the woman who said she was his aunt. Charlie questioned that now, that claim. That relationship. At the time, he believed her.

Tonight, playing Chapin on a stoop in the West Village, thinking about other times recent and distant, the old man stood and listened. The song ended and he said, "I got to see him once. Right over there." The man pointed toward Broadway. He could have meant anywhere. Funny how this man said the same thing about Chapin that a different man had said weeks ago about Dylan. The old men in The Village remembered everyone.

"What would you like to hear?" Charlie asked. He checked the tuning of his instrument; it remained true.

"Do you know 'A Better Place to Be'? That one always reminds me of a woman I met when I was young." He got a far off look in his eyes. Funny how music and memories often merged into that look.

"I do," said Charlie. As he started the song, with it's beautiful and iconic opening and repeated riff, the old man sat down on one of the lower steps, his back to Charlie. Of course, the song is a true story. Over nine minutes in length. It rarely showed up on the radio. Most of Chapin's songs didn't play on the radio because they were too long. Imagine your life's work being too long for the radio.

He sang about the waitress in Watertown, NY. People stopped for a few bars to listen. Charlie played softly, sang softly, but beautifully. All the while, the old man near his feet rocked to the music, to the story.

When Charlie finished the request, he sat for a moment. It was just him and the old man. Others had passed. A few had even dropped money in the guitar case, but none had stopped and really listened. This old man had listened, sitting there, his ear not far from the soundboard of the instrument.

"Thank you," he said. Or Charlie thought he heard. The man used the railing to hoist himself up. Tall and old-man thin. He rooted around in a deep trouser pocket, took out a wad of bills, peeled off a twenty, and went to drop it in the case. He stopped. Looked Charlie in the eyes. Held out the money to him. "Thank you."

This time Charlie heard the words. Experienced the words. "You're very welcome." He stashed the bill in his shirt. "You're very kind."

"You, young man, are very good. You shouldn't be out here playing for just me." He smiled.

"I like being here, loved playing for you." He meant it.

The two looked into each other for a long moment. The man took a step away. Stopped, but didn't turn back. After a beat, he walked down the block.

Charlie watched him until he turned the corner, out of sight wondering what thought he'd had or what words he contemplated saying to Charlie. If Charlie were older, or the man were younger, perhaps he would have propositioned Charlie. Perhaps.

Life in New York City.

Life in a song.

TWENTY-ONE

Charlie closed up shop. He could always return to the same stoop on the edge of the West Village tomorrow. He could play whenever he wanted. One of the whole points of his life. After gathering the few singles from his case, he slung his guitar over his shoulder and headed in the opposite direction. He wanted to be with men. He wanted to smell them and be in their presence and drink a beer or two or three and imagine himself with them. Maybe even…

He entered the closest bar with a rainbow flag. They were everywhere in The Village. Loud, but at least they weren't smokey. Overly hot. The radiators were still on high even though the evening had turned warm. Charlie pushed into an empty spot at the bar, near an end, away from the service area, where he could see down the long bar toward the windows and door. No one would bump into him and his instrument. He could watch the men come and go. He ordered a bottle of beer.

"Two for one tonight," shouted the bartender over the pounding house music. "Want both?"

"Sure," said Charlie. He knew he'd drink the first one fast.

There was barely change from his twenty. The New York prices had Charlie longing for somewhere else, a place where you could have a beer for a few dollars, or a six-pack for less in the stores. He drank off one of the beers in a long, slow, easy swallow.

The pounding music annoyingly loud, overwhelmingly, pulsed through the bottle into his lips.

Charlie placed the empty bottle on the bar, pulled the second one closer, counted his change, all in singles, and pushed two back toward the bartender's well. He'd play nice.

The old man.

The old man had played nice. And he'd played nice for the old man. Now, he'd spent the old man's twenty.

"Do you play?" a guy whispered wetly into Charlie's ear.

"Yeah," said Charlie. "Do you?" His attempt at flirting went pear shaped, of course.

"No," said the stranger. "Will you play something for me? Maybe naked?"

He enjoyed that line. He'd heard it before. "Maybe."

The stranger cupped Charlie's ass. "Nice."

That could certainly be taken several ways.

Charlie drank.

"I live close," hissed the guy in Charlie's ear.

One of those guys.

How many tricks would they hook up with in a night? These smooth talkers would roll a series. Sometimes it actually was for sex. Sometimes, well, you'd wake up with empty pockets. Your shoes might be missing. Your coat gone. A lump on your noggin and a headache for days. "I don't think so. Not tonight." He turned toward the stranger. Thin hips. Hungry eyes. Handsome, but hollow. An addict for sure. Not Charlie's type. Well, not anymore.

"Asshole," said the stranger. He walked deeper into the bar.

"Good for you," shouted the bartender. "Making good choices." He pushed a fresh beer in front of Charlie. "On the house."

"Thanks." Charlie liked the look of the bartender. Shirtless. Hairy chest. Manscaped. A little beefy. Leather vest. Hairy armpits. He wanted to make a joke about two-for-one but felt it would be misinterpreted. Nuance and subtlety were difficult in a loud bar.

The bartender moved closer, stretched some so his head came close to Charlie's. He tapped a finger on his cheek, turning that cheek toward Charlie. Charlie leaned up on his toes and just as he was about to kiss that stubbled cheek, the bartender turned, his lips now against Charlie's. Charlie was ready for it, took the bartender's chin in his hands, and really kissed the man. Shoved his tongue into the guy's mouth. Kissed him hard. Tasted the bourbon on his lips and tongue—the liquid courage tasted great. He flashed on images of the two naked in a ratty futon bed, drinking right from the bottle, kissing until sunrise. He liked the image.

The bartender didn't pull back but leaned hard into the kiss, his own tongue pushed past Charlie's lips, forcing Charlie's tongue back to home base, exploring the real estate of Charlie's mouth—a boilermaker between the two of them. And fucking hot.

When the bartender pulled back, they both needed to breathe at some point, he whispered, "I'm off in an hour if you want to hook up."

Charlie smiled and nodded and the bartender's deep brown eyes sparkled in the dim light. Without missing a beat, he moved to the guy next to Charlie, "Another?"

The guy nodded. "I'll have what he's having."

The bartender ignored the comment and returned with two mixed drinks.

After adjusting his dick in his jeans to a more comfortable place, Charlie finished his second beer. He'd move on to the third once he caught his breath, the music pounding to match his pumping heart.

TWENTY-TWO

On the street, the bartender tried to push Charlie against a wall, to kiss him hard, but of course the guitar was there, at Charlie's back. He turned to avoid damage, but the guy tried to shove Charlie into position.

"Whoa! Cowboy. Take a breath."

"Don't you want it?" the bartender asked.

"I do, but I've got an appendage back there."

"A what? Are you one of those guys with a tail? I've heard of that but never fucked anyone with a tail before. This'll be fun." Now, the bartender tried to turn Charlie's back toward him so he could see.

After an uncomfortable laugh, Charlie once more stopped the guy from manhandling him. "Listen, I don't think this is a good choice."

"Come on, baby. You're the one for me tonight."

Charlie didn't mind the tonight part at all. He was comfortable with one-night stands and hooking up as tricks. He was happy to use condoms, even if most of these guys weren't. He went with the flow of life. He'd bottom. He'd top. He'd try just about anything. Because of that, he'd had some outrageous and incredible experiences. He'd met amazing and outlandish guys. He'd tried things in bed he'd never even imagined people did together. He liked most of it. However....

The Bartender had his tongue back in Charlie's mouth and the guy was an incredible kisser. But once more, he tried to shove Charlie back against the wall of the building where they stood.

He pushed the bartender away. "Nope. Sorry. Not working for me."

"What the fuck, asshole?"

He'd been called worse. He knew he needed to get away quickly. There probably wasn't an opportunity to diffuse this one fast enough. The bartender was big, too. More muscled than Charlie.

But why was this happening? He stopped for a moment to consider the question. Something was off. Drugs probably. When he felt this way, the guy he'd hooked up with was on something. Had taken or snorted or injected some crap that altered their mood. Probably right before they'd left the bar. Sometimes that could be fun; usually not.

And…the aggression. It was one thing to be a little rough. It was something else to…

Charlie shouldn't have waited. Shouldn't have pondered. The Bartender now had him by the throat. He was actually choking him. That. It had become a thing over the past few years. It had probably been around longer. Most things were as old as humanity. Charlie hated being choked, repulsed by the possibility of losing consciousness during sex with a stranger. Feared damaged vocal chords.

Without further thought, Charlie kneed the bartender in the crotch. Hard. Connected. Probably broke the bartender's erection. He felt it there. Hard and stiff, as he connected with his knee.

The bartender doubled over, and that caused him to release Charlie's neck. Which now hurt. There'd certainly be a bruise. He hoped the cold weather would return so he could cover what would be there with his scarf.

Without any further thought or contemplation this time, Charlie stepped away from the bartender. "No means no, asshole," he hissed out and quickly walked away. He turned the first corner, then another, and after a few more steps found himself at the bodega on the corner near the hotel. He stepped inside, bought a fifth of bourbon, because after the last kiss, he had that taste on his tongue and wanted more. More of the drink, not the tongue.

Charlie picked up a six-pack, a bag of pretzels, and at the

counter requested the alcohol. The guy obliged. Charlie paid, mostly with the change. The bodega clerks appreciated that. He took his bag out onto the street. He looked both ways, certain he hadn't been followed or that fate hadn't brought the two back together. That had happened to him more than once, the guy he'd left turning up a few blocks later. Most places were nothing more than small towns. Even New York City.

Up the block, he turned into his new home: The Hotel de Chanson. He nodded at the desk clerk before hitting the elevator button.

One of the men joined him there. Waited. "Nice weather."

Charlie smiled at the small talk. "Yep."

"Something untoward has happened to you." He reached out, but didn't touch Charlie's neck.

"A date gone wrong." Charlie swallowed. There was just the hint of discomfort. It made him wonder what that guy had been about. He wasn't really trying to kill Charlie. Maybe just giving him a taste of what was to come? An enticement? An invitation?

"Sorry."

The elevator still hadn't arrived.

"Can I buy you a drink and commiserate?" The man sounded kind. Most of these older men at the hotel soft spoken. Easy going. Kind.

Charlie held up his shopping bag. "Provisions."

The elevator door opened. A man with a cane nodded and exited. They got on, pressed their respective floor buttons.

"You could invite me in," said the man.

He'd pushed a lower floor.

Charlie did consider the offer. He liked the idea of company. "Maybe a raincheck?" For the first time he looked at the man. Saw his dark, handsome eyes. His soft jowls. His short, gray hair. A big liver spot on his scalp.

"That would be nice."

The elevator stopped and the door opened. The man exited. "I'm Charlie," he said.

"Me, too."

The door started to close.

"I know," the old man said in a flirty, come-hither way.

TWENTY-THREE

Charlie checked that his door had closed and locked. He put on the security chain and flipped up the little security bar. He stripped down, picked up the bottle of bourbon, headed into the bathroom, and got the water flowing into the tub.

He loved his tub.

While it filled, he drank a few shots of bourbon, then, after he couldn't stand it anymore, he looked into the mirror and inspected his neck. It might be worse tomorrow, but at the moment, it didn't look terrible. Obvious, but not terrible. Strangers would make assumptions; he couldn't do anything about that.

He grabbed a beer from the bag and wished once more for a refrigerator. One could certainly be rented, for a daily fee, he was sure. He popped the top and sucked it down. He sucked down a second, and when he topped that with a hit of bourbon, he tasted the bartender. He hated that boilermakers would probably always make him think of that hot, sexy, furry, aggressive guy. He forced himself to drink another sip of bourbon before opening the next beer.

The tub only had a few inches of water. He didn't want to pass out and leave the water running. Feeling the alcohol's effects, he'd begun to lose interest in the bath. He wondered what the older Charlie would be like. Would he want to talk a lot? Talk about books and politics and current affairs. Get his dick sucked. You never knew with older guys. It was easy to forget they had desires and fetishy inclinations just like every other guy in the world. For some reason, you see an old person and you don't see them as a sexual being. They are something else. Probably for the preservation of the species. A judgement hardwired into humanity. It might be nurture and society, too.

He sipped more bourbon.

A song had started to niggle in his mind. It irritated the shit out of him when he couldn't find a song. When a few notes sort of rolled around and around, but the whole thing didn't surface. Maddening.

He longed to drop a bath bomb into the hot water. Or a few caps of bubble bath. He'd picked up a small bottle of bath oil that slicked his skin in a meaningful way. That softness stayed with him for a long time, and he longed for that sensation. It was still too soon to get in. You had to wait. Wait until the water rose. Wait until you added a bit of cold. Wait until you were only moments away from slipping into the tub. That's when you finally added the thing that would make this bath special.

Charlie dropped his hand into the hot water. Too hot, of course. He turned on the cold water now, but didn't turn down the hot yet. Still too far to go.

It was a Bob Dylan song. Nudging. Niggling. Teasing. He could hear that grumpy, shadowy, mumbly voice. Not the original recording, which was clearer, but some concert performance or compilation he'd heard somewhere. Four notes roamed around and around his head, unique. The opening line. He knew those things but still couldn't find the song.

The water rose.

The furry bartender would not have made a good tub partner.

Charlie didn't think he would have been rolled by the guy, but he might have ended up tied up for several days, shitting himself. That had happened to him. Twice. The second time, he hadn't seen it coming. A sweet seeming man in San Francisco with a dungeon room. Charlie hadn't returned to the City by the Bay in six years because of that encounter. Freaked him the fuck out. He feared returning to San Fran and running into the guy while eating chowder in a bread bowl.

He dribbled bath oil into the tub. Not generous. This stuff potent. Now, two caps of expensive bubble bath, near the tap. He turned off the hot water while the top third of the tub filled with pure clear bubbles. He sipped bourbon, retrieved another beer, and set that on the ledge before slipping into the too hot tub. The pain excruciating and wonderful, his skin turning pink from the shock. In he slipped. Down he slid. Perfect. Perfection. He turned off the taps. Listened to those last drips of water. The bathroom so large and tiled that those drips echoed. Listened to the bubbles being formed and destroyed around his foamy ears. He dunked himself below the water. Fully submersed. His whole being fit under water in the great big tub. This would be the tub that all future tubs would be judged by.

"Lay lady lay," popped into his head. Fucking Bob Dylan. Perfection.

He wiped soap from his eyes, sipped beer, and listened to Dylan sing in his head.

Per-fucking-fection.

TWENTY-FOUR

Charlie lingered in the bath. The bubbles subsided and the water grew cooler, but it was still warm in that massive tub. He finished the beer he'd brought along, sipped more bourbon, not his usual choice of hard liquor, he liked the ride of vodka better than whiskey, but the taste of the bartender, it was worth reinforcing that tonight. Getting past the experience rather than ruin bourbon for the rest of his life.

For some reason, after he'd played through the Dylan song in his mind, saw the chords and the fingering, because, of course he knew "Lay Lady Lay," every guitarist of a certain age knew that song. Dylan was requested all the time. He had an image of sitting on the steps of Lowe Library on the Columbia campus, way uptown. He'd been dating a grad student and found himself forever waiting for the guy to finish classes or meetings or whatever. He sat on those stairs, watched the young, rich kids, for he assumed they were rich if they could afford Columbia. Certainly privileged. Certainly finished high school with an academic record that would give them the motivation to apply for the Ivy League…and get in. He hadn't been one of those students, one of those guys….he'd left high school early.

Huh?

The alcohol had taken over. The bath had grown chilly. His history had risen too close to the surface.

With cautious actions, Charlie used his toes to pull the rubber stopper from the drain. He remained there, submersed while the water lowered. Imperceptible at first. Then his shoulders were exposed. The little patch of hair at the center of his chest. He'd always longed to be furrier. Maybe not as hairy as the bartender, that fuck, but a nice covering of chest hair. Hair a date could rub their hand over and feel like they'd touched something erotic. His nipples were exposed now, and the slight chill of evening caused them to rise. Hard, flat pecs. Mostly from playing and being slightly under nourished. Food just didn't matter that much and he sometimes forgot to eat. Sometimes, he couldn't afford to eat. Pecs that recently felt a little softer than ever before. Age, he surmised. Or a life grown soft because of steady income.

With caution and effort, he stood, using the ledge and the side of the tub, you could reach around the cast iron and grab onto the edge with intention. His fingers were puckered. His hands were puckered. His calloused finger tips softer. He thought of that liver spot on the old man's scalp and wondered when those appeared on your body. What age did you need to reach to find yourself with a liver spot in the shape of New Zealand on your scalp?

Would he make it to that age?

The old queens in the hotel certainly had made it that far. Boy had his gaydar been wrong. He wondered why. Would he…

Fuck. He was living like those old men. Single. Alone. Having to carefully get out of the tub. Soon, he'd be paying for tricks who served dinner in the evening and then did things for money later in the night. That's what this was, wasn't it? He just knew Patsy was taking her cut of those blow jobs and hand jobs and who knew what else.

His stomach flipped and he wished now that he'd eaten something. It had been a long time since the pot roast. When had the pot roast been?

He stepped out of the tub, onto the folded towel. He'd asked the maid for extra towels. He suspected there would be a charge for those on his bill at the end of the month. He wrapped terry cloth, clean and fluffy and perhaps worth the extra charge, around his shoulders. Another he wrapped around his waist, not out of modesty, but to fend off the chill of evening. Had he left the little window open in the bedroom? Probably.

With luxuriously soft skin and brushed hair and cleaned

teeth and somewhat dried hair, he went into the bedroom, drank some of the remaining beer, now warmish, and then picked up his guitar and played the opening to "Lay Lady Lay." He thought of the bartender and wondered if he'd recovered. Charlie certainly wouldn't be going into that bar again. He wouldn't be playing on that block either. Not for a while anyway.

The odds were good that the bartender, after a few weeks, wouldn't even remember Charlie. That wouldn't be the case for Charlie.

He stopped playing at the knock on the door.

What time was it?

He went to the door, clad in those towels, holding the guitar in front of him, opened the door. "Yes?" He should have looked out the peep hole, but hadn't thought to until he faced a man he didn't know.

"Hi." He smiled.

"Was I too loud?" Charlie asked.

"No."

They looked at each other. The stranger eyed Charlie up and down. Charlie focused on the man's light brown eyes. Was that what they called hazel.

"Can I help you?" Charlie asked.

The man's smile hinted at lasciviousness. "Of course you could."

Charlie really wasn't in the mood.

"Sorry," the stranger said. "I heard you playing and thought 'oh, another night owl.' I decided to knock. See if you wanted company. I've got refreshments." He held up a bottle of whiskey.

All these men drank whiskey.

For the briefest of moments, Charlie considered the offer. The man wasn't horrible. He was tall and thin and in shape for an old dude. He had kind eyes.

"I've had a rough night," said Charlie. He hadn't ruled the company out.

"Listen, I don't plan to molest you or anything, although..." again the guy eyed Charlie up and down.

He was standing there in towels, after all. His stomach flat, although not chiseled.

"It's up to you. I'd love to hear you play. The guys were talking about the Happy Hour Guy, the guitarist. I'm assuming that's you?"

Charlie nodded. "Come on in. Just for a drink." He held the door for the stranger. "I'm Charlie."

"Derek."

Charlie closed the door but didn't lock it. He set the guitar on the bed, went into his little closet, pulled on underwear and a long T-shirt that he often slept in. He went into the bathroom and hung up the wet towels.

Derek sat in the desk chair and poured whiskey into two glasses.

"Did you bring those with you?" Charlie was surprised to see nice, crystal rocks glasses.

"I did." He handed a glass with dark liquor to Charlie.

He found himself hoping he wasn't about to be roofied. It had certainly been that kind of night. He held up the glass, "To world peace," and clinked Derek's glass.

Derek laughed. "Sure." He downed his glass and filled it again. "I love that movie."

Charlie sipped. Harsh. He'd seen the black label before and knew it was expensive. You'd think expensive whiskey would be smoother.

"I'm next door," said Derek. "Nine oh two."

Charlie hoisted himself into the bed, his back against the headboard. He pulled his guitar into his lap, sipped whiskey, placed the glass on the nightstand, and played a very soft version of "Hey There Delilah," by Plain White T's, one of his favorite songs. He sang softly and wondered why he chose all these songs by straight boys about girls.

There weren't many gay love songs to choose from. Romanovsky and Phillips were more satire than love.

Derek watched and seemed to study Charlie. He drank more. He listened in silence. Focused. Intense. Kind.

Why had he chosen a love song? Charlie sang the second

chorus. Did Derek do those things to him? Make him feel that?

No.

There were times. When he was drunk and relaxed from a great bath. He wanted to be in love. But love was messy. Love meant roots and cooperation. Love was something for others.

Although, a trick bartender wasn't always what it was cracked up to be, either.

He liked this song because young people liked this song. New York girls tipped when they heard it, thinking of the cute lead singer, seeing themselves as Delilah.

Charlie sang softly, "Oh what you do to me…"

Charlie drank whiskey. It didn't feel so harsh.

"Oh, you are good." Derek smiled kindly. "I didn't know that one."

Charlie thought he could explain it, where it came from. Instead, he started into "Good Riddance" by Green Day.

Derek got up, poured more whiskey into Charlie's glass.

Charlie thought the stranger would make a move, sit on the bed at least, but he didn't. Derek was a perfect gentleman. He returned to his chair, crossed his legs at the knees in a comfortable gay way that showed how flexible he was, how thin his waist. Charlie smiled into the song, into the bridge. Derek had already grown on him—and Charlie hadn't passed out from a date rape drug.

TWENTY-FIVE

But at some point, Charlie must have fallen asleep, or passed out, because he awoke with a start in the dark bedroom. He didn't know where he was for a moment. After a beat, he knew it was the new bedroom in the Hotel de Chanson. Quickly, the memory of playing for...what was his name? Yes, Derek. Room 902. Beside Charlie, his guitar rested on the opposing pillow.

With a tug of the chain, Charlie turned on the little bedside lamp. Alone. No glasses. No whiskey bottle. No Derek.

A gentleman.

For a moment he wondered if he'd been robbed. Decided to not even check. He trusted Derek although he couldn't say why.

He got up and peed. Brushed his teeth. Moved his guitar to its spot in the wingback chair, returned to bed, and slipped under the covers and his quilt.

How nice to spend the evening, or what was left of it, with a gentleman.

TWENTY-SIX

Sitting on his stool, Charlie played "I'm Yours" by Jason Mraz for the Happy Hour patrons. Always popular, and fun to play. Men swayed in the packed room. There, in the middle at a table, sitting alone, Derek from the previous night, drinking something neat from a crystal glass. He hadn't been cute or familiar. Just there. Just sitting and enjoying the music like the other old men. Killing time before dinner at six.

Charlie had a beer on his little table and several upside down shot glasses—the empty, upturned glasses chits for drinks the patrons had backed him up with.

He finished the song to applause and drank his beer down. He knew Patsy would replace the dead solder with a fresh one during the next song. He had to be careful not to drink a beer with every song. He'd be under the little stage before the two hours were over.

Next, he played one of his favorites, "We're Going to Be Friends" by The White Stripes.

Once more, the men in the room swayed to the music. They liked everything he played. No one ever complained and they'd stopped requesting songs and just let Charlie play what he wanted. The shot glasses kept coming, the chairs filled, Patsy bustled around the room serving everyone their favorite intoxicant.

He transitioned into "Banana Pancakes" by Jack Johnson. He embraced the rhythm. Modern, but informed by others. The squeak of the strings in the chord changes took him back to a childhood memory of the man who'd played for his grade school class so many years ago. The percussion of the strumming patterns took the instrument to a fun place. The

Seagull responded well, although it warmed up the sound—a cheaper guitar would be more wooden and percussive, his instrument augmented like a tympani instead of a base drum.

On and on he played his favorite rock songs, one popular, modern or modernish song after another. Music by straight boys.

What mattered more than the full room or the free beers or the money…he played the songs he wanted, the songs that were fun to play. When something became boring or tired or no longer enjoyable, he could dump it. With this older audience, he could play his favorites from any era. No one else mattered.

"Ain't no need, rain all day, can't you see can't you see, wake up slow."

He loved the song. He loved the applause. Charlie drank another beer down in one swallow. Fuck it.

Next up, "Budapest" by George Ezra. He appreciated the opening finger pattern, the activity kept him from touching his bruised neck. He'd chosen a high-collared shirt, but it didn't hide the marks. No one had commented, but Patsy's eyes held on his neck for a long moment when she first saw him that afternoon. She'd said, "You need a beer," and busied herself behind the bar without further comment while he took out his guitar and adjusted his body on the stool on the little stage.

Now, he played and sang and did his best to forget everything else in the world.

His neck had bruised even though it didn't hurt, at all.

He thought about his lack of banter. Many performers talked. They talked about the songs and why they played them. They told personal stories. They told showbiz stories. Charlie didn't do any of that. He didn't need the break of banter. He had plenty of material to fill a set.

He jumped to "Barcelona" by Sheeran, more of a dance number with great rhythm and a play on Europe. "Let's pretend we're dancing in the street in Barcelona…"

He'd never been to Barcelona. Never been to Europe. He'd been to Mexico; well, he'd been drunk on tequila and crossed the border into Tijuana with a guy he'd met in San Diego one summer night. Or, he'd crossed and then got drunk on tequila. That made more sense. A handsome guy. Sexy and so very skinny. The border guards searched his guitar case and his guitar with an expectation of drugs. They'd done a lot of drugs but hadn't brought any back with them. He was scruffy and the boy sketchy and he'd learned his lesson a few years before. They'd actually laughed all the way. Down and back and for about two weeks after. Then, the guy was gone, with what little money Charlie had had. Once more back on the street, busking for his supper, with a vow never to take drugs again.

That was his life. So long as he had a guitar he could survive. That was the fucking point of it all.

As he finished the song, Patsy was there, one more beer in hand. She said, "You're doing great, but you're over time. One more song and done."

The men didn't rush out at six on the dot. He'd become more important to them than dinner at six.

"You got it." Charlie drank half the Le Fin du Monde. There were even more shot glasses on the little table. He set down the beer and played a broad chord of Pink's "Just Give Me a Reason."

He loved the lyric, "We can learn to love again…"

The goal.

Get your heart broken and learn to love again. Get your neck wrung and pick up another boy in a bar. Take another chance. Another risk.

He sang from the heart. He sang from experience. He sang big and loud and happy. By the end, without realization, he'd stood, stomping while he played. The men rose to their feet, too. The song was an anthem in the bars. In the lives of gay men around the world.

He finished.

Silence.

Silence.

Massive applause. Whistles. Shouts.

"See you all tomorrow," said Charlie, quietly. "Thank you

for the beers." He picked up the latest beer and finished it. He watched the men file out, chatting among themselves. The songs he sang had changed the way these men reacted.

Charlie had never experienced a regular gig before. He'd played many of the same places, same benches or corners over and over in all the cities he'd lived and worked. But he'd rarely see the same people day after day. Sometimes he'd see people for a few minutes a few days in a row, but not like this. The same audience, or mostly the same men, returning night after night, four or five nights a week, to listen to him play.

He stretched himself to pull out songs he hadn't played in ages, to avoid playing the same twenty or twenty-five songs night after night. When you played day after day, even sitting on the same park bench or standing in Times Square, you could play the same three or four songs over and over and the people wouldn't know. They see you and hear you for thirty seconds, maybe a minute. Sometimes for a full song, three minutes or four. Then, they'd dump some coins in your case and you'd never see them again. These men kept returning. He wanted new material.

One of the challenges of being off the grid, of not having a smart phone or computer is that you didn't really have access to the world. And even if you had a TV, MTV didn't play music anymore.

It was time for a visit to the library. He could call the branch and make a computer appointment. You had to do that early in the day and hope you got on. There were all these rules about timing, but there was a reliable clock on the bank at the corner and he'd worked out the details. Once online, he'd have forty-five minutes to find music, listen to it, and learn it. He had some money in his pocket, so he could also print some chord charts out.

"Ready for another beer?" asked Patsy.

How many had he had? The pleasant buzz provided no real clue. Although he sometimes felt buzzed after he played... tonight was probably more about all the beer. "Sure."

"Come over to the bar."

Charlie packed up his guitar and slung it over his back. He picked up the shot glasses and carried them in a jumble to the bar.

Patsy pushed a few folded bills and another beer toward him.

"Thanks," he said.

"Thank you. You'll notice there's an extra twenty there for you."

He knew he could ask for more, but didn't. She was making a killing off his performing. They both knew it. Charlie had decided during his last soak that he would ask for a few free meals each week, or on the nights he played, instead of more cash. It would be cheaper for Patsy, but feel better to him. He just didn't think they were there yet. It hadn't even been three weeks. Charlie drank some of his beer.

Behind the bar, Patsy busied herself with the dirty glasses.

"Why don't you hire someone to help you out in here?" Charlie asked. He enjoyed watching bartenders perform maintenance tasks. They all had their own rhythms and methods—like performers, like musicians.

"I actually enjoy doing this. I've been tending this bar for a long, long time."

Charlie wouldn't ask how long; he knew a lady never revealed her age.

"I like running the hotel and there are many of the mundane chores I find enjoyable. But this one. Washing glasses. Cutting up the fruit garnishes. Emptying the metal box of bottle caps—I love that sound."

"Nice," said Charlie. He knew what it was like to enjoy life, and the routines of life. And the sounds of life.

"Now, stocking beer bottles in the cooler, that I don't like. I'm short and the coolers get gross. I have the guys do that for me in the morning. Washing out the sinks, that can be gross, too, and I have the cleaning folks take care of that for me. But wiping the counter. Wiping down the liquor bottles. I like that."

Charlie finished his beer and nodded.

"You can drink," said Patsy.

"Yes, I can." While he knew holding one's liquor was a learned trait, he'd also met enough drunks to know there was some genetic composition that probably helped. Some brain chemical or hormone production that encouraged it. More clues to his heritage and parentage, certainly.

She passed him another beer and took away a shot glass. Charlie drank.

"Are you going to have dinner here tonight?" Patsy asked as she washed another glass in the little sinks. Wash, rinse, sanitize in each station.

"I had planned on it, but after all this beer, I'm not really very hungry." Spoken like a true alcoholic. Should he be worried? Attend a meeting?

"Roast chicken. Very tender. Very juicy." She handled another glass.

That chicken line sounded like a line from a Broadway show, but Charlie couldn't place it. He hadn't seen many shows, that could be expensive. He had listened to a lot of cast recordings growing up and now. That was something else he could do at some of the libraries.

Patsy washed the last glass and turned off the rotating bristle thingy.

Charlie drank his beer.

"Hello, Derek," said Patsy.

"Good evening, Patsy."

"What can I do for you?" she asked.

"Well, I actually stopped back in to see if the troubadour here would like to join me for dinner. My treat."

"I was just telling him how good the chicken dinner is."

Charlie enjoyed being called troubadour.

"How about it, Charlie? Join me?" He placed a hand gently on Charlie's shoulder. "I sure would enjoy the company."

Patsy moved to the opposite end of the bar with her rag.

He considered the offer. He wasn't hungry, at all, but would be before the buzz wore off and the evening ended. "Okay. Let me take my instrument upstairs. I'll only be a few minutes."

"Excellent. I'll meet you in the dining room." Derek took a step back to let Charlie get up from his barstool.

"Thanks for the music, Charlie," said Patsy.

TWENTY-SEVEN

As promised, Charlie joined Derek at his table. On his way across the room, the men he passed nodded and waved and said hello.

"How does it feel to be a celebrity?" asked Derek when Charlie slid into his chair.

"I don't know about that." It had started to feel that way and he didn't like it. He loved playing to a full room, a larger crowd, but he didn't like being known by all those people and he feared in this moment that this might be a "Don't shit where you eat," situation—one of his foster fathers used that phrase. It would be the best idea not to get involved with anyone who lived in the hotel.

"Everyone knows you. And better, they love your music, your singing."

"That part is nice." When the guy came around with wine, Charlie pointed toward the bottle of white.

Derek accepted the red. "Goes better with Chicken, I think."

Charlie sipped his wine and nodded. It didn't matter. Drink what you like, he thought, but the man was buying him dinner and he wasn't going to argue.

Derek leaned in toward Charlie. "Thank you for last night."

Had he said it to be heard by a few of the others around them? To be known as a man who had done something with Charlie the night before? Something worth being thankful for? Something none of the others had been successful at? Charlie didn't like that game if that's what it was.

"Sorry I fell asleep." He touched his throat. "It was the end of a very long day."

"One minute you were singing and then you weren't. Right in the middle of a song, of a line. I hope you don't mind. I moved your guitar to the side."

"Thank you for that."

"I collected my glasses and bottle and headed out. I was worried you'd think I drugged you, or something." A sheepish looked crossed Derek's face.

Charlie had thought that might be a possibility. Not when he'd awoken, but when he took the first offered drink. He didn't say anything.

Plates arrived. A very handsome waiter with broad shoulders and narrow waist, with a charming smile and short kinky braids, placed a portion before each man with a slight smile and nod.

"Thanks, Andre," said Derek.

Andre nodded, said suggestively, "Enjoy your dinner, sir." He stepped back and away.

Questions swirled around Charlie's head, but he pushed them out. He wanted answers and, frankly, didn't want to know. He leaned in and smelled the food. Everything appealed to him. Vibrant broccoli and carrots. Roasted potatoes with crispy skin. And the chicken, his plate had two legs and a thigh, while Derek had a crispy skinned breast. The food made his mouth water.

"Tuck in," said Derek.

Charlie did as told, a few bites quickly leading to an emptying plate. He slowed himself down, drank some wine. "This is so good."

"Patsy makes great chicken."

"She cooks it herself?" Charlie asked, wiping grease from his lips.

"Well, sometimes she does." Derek ate more potato.

There were so many truths he didn't know about this hotel. "How long have you been living here?" Charlie tore into a chicken leg in a ravenous way.

"Oh, nearly ten years now."

"Ten?" Charlie whistled. "Shit." He couldn't imagine being

anywhere for ten years. He also couldn't remember where he might have actually been ten years ago. Realistically, it might not even be possible to figure that out.

"I sold my apartment when my building went condo. They wanted us all out and made an excellent offer. This was back when Chelsea was just making its second transition. I'd been in my place on Eighteenth Street for over twenty years. That's why my payout was so large. We got a dollar amount multiplied by the number of years we'd lived in the building. They were not happy when they wrote me a check. Actually backpaddled and tried to get me to buy into the new condo concept instead of paying me out. I took the fucking money and ran. Invested it. Now, I can live here, have maid service, nightly entertainment, no real overhead, great chicken dinners on occasion, for much less than the maintenance would have been on that condo."

While Derek talked, Charlie finished his dinner, wiping up the gravy with a piece of roll.

"Oh, would you like another plate?" Derek turned to signal the waiter.

"No. This was too much. I'm full and I've made a pig of myself, but it tasted so good."

"I want to ask you a million questions, but I got the feeling last night you don't like to answer questions." He thoughtfully ate a bite of carrot. Charlie wondered if he was modeling better table manners for him to learn from.

"No. Not a fan of questions."

"Why is that?" He ate a bite of crispy skinned potato.

Charlie let the jealousy wash through him. Imagine, being jealous over a bite of potato. It had been so good. He really did want a second helping. "I like to live in the moment. Answering questions usually entails living in the past."

"Hm. I see." He drank a sip of wine.

Andre came around with the bottles and Charlie accepted a second glass of red.

"What will you do tonight?" Derek asked.

"I haven't decided. Probably head uptown and find a comfortable spot in the theater district or Times Square to play for a while. Theater people are generally decent tippers if they had a nice time at whatever show they'd seen."

"Okay, not sure if this is a question about the past, not exactly." Derek set his silverware on his plate. He'd left his broccoli behind and Charlie thought he might reach over and pick up a crisp stalk. "How do you learn all the music?"

He got that one a lot. "I have a good ear. I can hear a song once and learn the music without even really thinking. Lyrics are a little more difficult, but once I have the melody and chords down, it's then easy to fit the words into the framework. I go to one of the libraries, usually once or sometimes twice a week, and listen to recordings or get online and watch YouTube videos or read the lyric sites, if I can get an appointment."

"Why don't you just use your phone." Derek tapped his device sitting face down on the table.

"Don't have one." If the questions kept coming, they'd be down the rabbit hole and he had no interest in being Alice tonight.

Derek changed directions. "Do you go to the shows? Or concerts?"

"Not often. I do sometimes sit in line in the summer for free tickets to Shakespeare in the Park. They usually do a musical in the season, but not always. I like that venue." Was he really not going to clean his plate?

A waiter came by, this one short and furry with dirty glasses on his face, and picked up their plates. "Apple pie tonight," he whispered.

Charlie was so grateful there would be more food. His stomach actually growled with the knowledge. "Did you work?"

"I did. I spent twenty-five years in public relations."

"Is that like advertising?" Charlie willed the pie to arrive. No one in the dining room had pie.

"Not really. Well, it can sort of be like that. It's all about getting people, consumers usually, to think the best of your client. We didn't run ads. Instead, we managed brands and perceptions. Got stories placed. Did media training for people who found themselves being grilled by the press."

"Storyteller?"

Derek nodded to Andre when he asked if he wanted coffee. Charlie declined. Then, accepted another glass of wine.

"I guess I was something of a storyteller. At least some of the time." The coffee arrived. Derek added sugar, but no milk.

Andre refilled Charlie's wine glass.

Finally, the pie arrived. Charlie's piece seemed smaller than Derek's. Without a comment, Derek traded their plates.

Charlie wondered what public relations paid.

The apple pie tasted like autumn. The crust flaked away. Charlie wondered if Patsy made it herself.

TWENTY-EIGHT

Frigid winds blew the city and Charlie had taken refuge at the corner table in Jasper's coffee shop: Coffee Haus—there didn't seem to be anything German on the menu or in the pastry case. He had his guitar out. Jasper silenced the music after Charlie ordered a cup of coffee.

"It's on the house if you'll sing a song."

"Who is your favorite singer?" Charlie asked.

The guy thought for a long moment, poured a cup of black French roast. "Do you know anything by Simon and Garfunkel? They seem to have been lost to the world."

"I do." Charlie smiled.

Jasper pushed the cup toward Charlie.

"You're very kind." He took in the place. Empty. "I'll sit over there." He indicated the corner.

"Great."

"Great." They had some intense eye contact going. Charlie's dick stiffened. Any harder and he'd need to adjust himself right there.

Finally, Jasper broke the scene when a patron came in, and he greeted them to take their order.

Charlie imagined the scrape of a needle on a record but didn't know where that image or sound came from. One of his foster homes, probably. He'd certainly never owned his own turntable. He picked up his coffee and headed into the corner. Too hot to drink, he set the cup down.

Like a lot of music from long ago, he'd learned it without realizing it. He knew the entire *The Concert in Central Park* album from 1981, released in 1982 as a double album set in a cool, foldout cover. He'd read the liner notes over and over while listening to the albums and wishing he'd been at the concert—a decade before he'd been born.

Charlie tuned his guitar, it sounded terrific in this space with all the hard surfaces—walls, floors, even furniture. Everything had a hard surface, although the chairs were surprisingly comfortable.

Under his breath, Charlie said, "Ladies and gentlemen, Simon and Garfunkel." He could hear the applause and launched into "Mrs. Robinson." By the time he was four tunes in, to "Me and Julio Down by the Schoolyard," the shop was full of patrons. Folks had trickled in for a cup of coffee or a pastry, but hearing Charlie, they stayed. They probably ordered more.

Before he started "Scarborough Fair," one of his favorite songs, a patron requested "something modern, anything modern."

"I'm playing this line up by request," said Charlie, taking the moment to once more tighten his tuning while again making intense eye contact with Jasper—he had these thick eyebrows that drew Charlie to Jasper's eyes. "You should have gotten here earlier," he scoffed at the heckler.

Several other people chuckled. Jasper smiled as he took someone's credit card, those crazy eyebrows raising and lowering with his laughter.

For the next hour, he played the line up of the album in perfect order. It had been burned into his brain through repetition. While he heard the original performance banter, the jokes about drugs and cops and neighbors of the park, he didn't speak them. Instead, he sort of fast forwarded the banter, wondering once more what the hell had happened to Garfunkel. He had a whole story in his head about the breakup of the famous duo, but had no idea if any of it were true, or important. Neither of them did comparable work after they split up. They both created stuff, but none of it had the magic that their brief time together had.

His case filled with small bills and coins. It surprised him that so many people still carried at least a little bit of actual money with them. Everything was turning to digital and people frequently asked him if they could Venmo him cash. He had a bank account but still hadn't figured out Venmo or Zelle or even PayPal. He'd managed to live his thirty-seven years without an email address or phone number and hoped that would continue.

Of course, living in the hotel, he probably had a phone number. The hotel number. They forwarded calls. His room had a phone.... He wouldn't be giving out that information to anyone anytime soon.

As he thought about the hotel, he imagined that tub and how nice it would be in a very short time when he'd be slipping into the hot, nurturing, oily water. He loved the bath oil he'd found and would need to buy more soon...already. And that thought had him wondering if Jasper liked baths. Had him then wondering what that handsome business owner looked like out of his apron, out of his skinny jeans. Would his hair smell like coffee after working all day? He imagined what coffee scented sweat, or better, semen, might...where the fuck was he?

A keen observer might have noticed the slight hiccup in his playing as he figured out what song he was singing. The middle of "American Tune." It sat in his voice in the same place it did for Garfunkel. High up there, a little awkward, yet sweet and appealing. Not a broken, cracked place, just at the top of the natural tenor range.

"American Tune," a song that gets lost by many. That many, if they were to recreate the list of songs, might leave out.

"Don't know a dream that's not been shattered..." great lyric.

Within the next few songs, Coffee Haus was standing room only. By "Fifty Ways to Leave Your Lover," the performance had become a sing-along. Charlie, while having a fantastic time, while wondering what the fuck was happening in his life that he had started to fill rooms, while considering the implication of so many people and the certain breaking of the fire code, he found himself enjoying the experience more than perhaps any performance he'd ever given. And he'd give thousands and thousands of performances around the country. He considered standing so folks at the back could see him, but he'd started this journey on his ass, and if he stood up, he might lose that comfortable chair. He'd already had to pull his instrument case under and behind his feet because people had been stepping into it, even as they tried not to, as they took up the other empty chairs at his table. He launched into the next song.

Finally, sadly, he arrived at the finale. "Sounds of Silence." The opening riff brought applause from the room. Just as it had in the live concert. And just like the live concert, the crowd grew rather quiet. They didn't sing along. They listened to perhaps one of the greatest songs ever written. It felt like a personal anthem. Charlie's journey on the planet.

Young people had their cameras out. Held up to him. That had been happening all night. He thought it rude, people watching through their phones. Recording him, no doubt. He didn't mind being recorded. He performed all the time. He was more comfortable singing a song and playing his guitar than talking to people. But he wanted them to listen. The people in the room or on the street to hear him. "But my words like silent raindrops fell…" he sang.

Words resonated deep inside. He heard the breaths of the people around him. Saw the tears in one young girl's eyes. Long, honey colored hair. He imagined her as a ghost of the late '70s. The concert was filled with the remains of the '70s. That's perhaps what makes *The Concert in Central Park* so important. It's the culmination of nearly a decade of war and fighting and drugs and protests. It's the last hurrah of a generation that would shortly be devastated by the AIDS crisis and Reaganism. Everything would change within a year or three. The energy of the '70s would be gone forever, a memory to the boomers who had so embraced it.

He strummed the last chord and let it ring until it died on its own. The crowd remained enthralled until silence took over the room. They burst into applause.

Charlie sat silently. He'd never publicly played the whole

album. Not in a single sitting. Never. He'd played at that. Played a few songs in order. It was a game sometimes. To play the album throughout the day. Moving from location to location, doing the next two or three songs, moving, picking the thread back up.

One stoned afternoon, he imagined that he played the whole album, but he was sitting in silence on a bus traveling for days from New York City west to San Francisco. It happened across Kansas or some other very long, very flat expanse. That was the trip when he also read Kerouac's "On the Road." Someone had left a copy on the seat next to him while he'd slept between two Indiana stops.

Now, people stormed him. Thrust money at him. Shook his hand. Asked his name.

All he ever said was "Thank you" or "Charlie."

Jasper shouted into the crowd. "Sorry. It's past closing time. You don't have to go home but you can't stay here."

Charlie played a few chords of that song, "Closing Time."

People started to sit back down.

"Charlie, you've got to stop. For tonight. I need to close."

He sang, "You don't have to go home but you can't stay here." Then stopped. He knew who he wanted to take him home. He wanted to sing that. It would now be their song, even if he never told Jasper.

"Closing time!" Jasper shouted again.

Finally, reluctantly, the crowd shifted. Everyone headed out onto the street, but many lingered there, talking, singing, waiting for the next miracle in New York City to happen.

This had been one of those moments. People would say they'd been there to their friends. They'd show the videos. They'd...

"Thank you," said Jasper.

Charlie found himself on his feet, in Jasper's arms, kissing him. Soft and kind and well-kissed kisses.

That was from some movie...

Their dicks were hard and pressing with all their might through denim on denim crotches pressed tight together.

"I live close," said Jasper.

"Uh, okay." Charlie once more imagined his big tub and the two of them together, but he also, usually, didn't take men home. Too complicated when people knew where you lived. They kissed some more. "Let's go," Charlie finally whispered.

"I need to finish up here. Can you wait a few minutes?"

Charlie let out a deep breath. He hoped it didn't sound like an impatient sigh. He hoped this guy wouldn't need to hurt him to get off.

"Okay." He sat down and adjusted his crotch and gathered up the money from the case and stored his guitar. He wanted to straighten and count his cash, a big wad of bills, but he felt too exposed. There was still a crowd, at least a dozen people lingered just past him, through those plate glass windows, watching him. Some still seemed to be filming him with their phones.

He released another deep breath before getting up and gathering the stray paper coffee cups and napkins and debris people had left sitting on the tables. He shoved the stuff into the trash bin.

Around him, lights turned off and others, security lights, came on.

"Ready?" asked Jasper.

"Sure." Charlie pointed to the people on the street.

Jasper went to the front door, pulled down an iron fence. Secured it with heavy knobs or bars or something into the floor. He pulled down another grate over the windows on the right. Locked it. Another on the left. "We'll go out the back. It's like a bat cave. Come on."

He waited while Charlie retrieved his guitar and swung it over his back.

Jasper said, "Thank you for doing that. I didn't think you'd..."

Charlie pressed Jasper up against a wall and kissed him hard. God, he liked this guy. He smelled the sweat on his neck, it was tinged with coffee just as he'd imagined.

That smell would forever be strung together for him with Simon and Garfunkel and *The Concert in Central Park.*

TWENTY-NINE

Charlie followed Jasper out the back door. They arrived in a service hallway. Doors to other businesses with block letters announcing a florist, a tailor, a candlestick maker. Unmarked doors to somewhere else. Concrete floor. Concrete walls. Concrete ceiling. A smell of dust. This didn't feel like New York at all. It felt more like being at a mall or…

"This way," said Jasper.

Down the hall, through a door, into another hall, this one more New York-centric with cracked tile floors and punctured drywall. An open ceiling with exposed pipes and conduit. Up a short flight of stairs. Another. Longer. Higher. The doors now apartment doors with letters and numbers 2F, 3N, up they walked to the fifth floor. An old five-story walkup. 5N. They kissed again in front of the door. Jasper ran a finger along the bruise on Charlie's neck but didn't say anything. He keyed them inside.

Modern. Another shock. Sleek lines. An open floor plan. More of a loft than a traditional apartment. The space huge and open. The windows avenue facing, nearly floor to nearly ceiling. The building across the way only two stories, so no direct view into them, but like watching a drive-in movie—not that Charlie had ever been to a drive-in movie. He'd seen Grease on television.

"Can I get you something? A glass of wine? A beer?" Jasper had become all business again.

"You don't need to wait on me," said Charlie. He wanted to be naked with this man.

"It's not that. Well, maybe a little. Service is in my blood. I live it. But…" he stopped and turned and went back to

Charlie and kissed him again. Parted lips. Darting tongues. Breathless. "Fuck, you're sexy." He kissed him again. Just a peck. "But I need a fucking glass of wine. It's been a long day. I've got a sauvignon blanc open. It's cheap, but good."

"Sounds great."

"Or beer if you'd prefer."

He didn't want a drink. He wanted a naked man. It had been a few weeks. If you didn't count the bartender. "Wine is fine."

"Make yourself at home." Jasper kicked off his shoes, hit a button on a device.

Etta James sang the blues, "I need a Sunday kind of love." So fabulous.

Jasper left the room.

Charlie could hear water running. He removed his guitar and placed it aside. Stripped out of his jacket. No scarf. Not cold enough for that tonight. He kicked off his shoes, too, glad he had on the pair of socks without the hole under the big toe.

Etta worked the song. Charlie had never heard this one before and wondered how that was possible. He loved James. Had seen her perform when he was briefly living in Vegas. Talk about a hard town to make a living without a permit. He hated filing paperwork for any reason. The cops were rather mean and ran people down and ticketed heavily those caught performing or earning money anywhere without a permit.

"Stormy Weather," came up next, one of the songs he'd heard live. The ticket was only $27. Imagine seeing a legend like Etta James for $27.

Jasper returned and filled two thick, heavy wine glasses with cold white wine. Crisp and fresh and lovely. They sipped wine, then kissed, their kisses now tasting of coffee and wine and…toothpaste.

"You cheated."

"Huh," mumbled Jasper over a sip of wine.

"You brushed your teeth," said Charlie.

"And it's ruining this glass of wine." He drank more, finished his glass, refilled it, led them into a seating area.

A pit grouping. The chairs big and plush, the couch long, the longest couch Charlie had ever seen anywhere in his life. They sat. They drank. They kissed.

Etta James sang “I’d Rather Go Blind.”

For a moment they drank wine and listened to the song.

“I love Etta James,” said Jasper.

“Me, too. I got to see her perform live once.”

“I saw her at least a hundred times.” Jasper drank off his wine.

“Wow. How did that happen?”

“I know, right.” He got up and went to the kitchen area, returned with another bottle, splitting the remains between his glass and Charlie’s. “I worked concessions at a theater here and she played there several times. Long runs.”

“You don’t seem old enough to—”

“I like you. I can’t explain it. It’s different. I mean, I see guys all day, right. They come in and flirt and spend money. Every day or even two or three times a day. Pumped up muscles. Big crotches. With you it’s…it’s so different.

“My crotch not big enough?” He laughed.

“No. That’s not—”

As if on cue, Etta sang, “Something’s gotta hold on me, it must be love…”

Jasper’s smile broadened, a dimple, very small, showed deep in the middle of his cheek. Charlie traced it with the tip of his left index finger.

“Ow.” Jasper took Charlie’s hand, kissed his fingertips. “Rough.”

“Playing. Calluses.”

“I didn’t think your fingers would be so rough.” He kissed Charlie’s palm. “Your hands are so soft.”

Should he talk about bathing with oils? With bombs? With bubbles? Were they there yet? Charlie didn’t think so. He wondered for a moment, what did he want to know about this guy? How big his dick was. What his ass tasted like. How his dick would feel pressing inside of him. His cock got hard. “Do you like it rough?” he whispered.

Jasper seemed to ignore him. "Do you love playing the guitar? It seems like you do."

Charlie went with the conversational flow. "I do." He sipped more wine, set his glass on the coffee table. Moved closer, kissed Jasper soft and long, his tongue probing, his rough fingertips exploring cheeks and neck and clavicle. Jasper accepted his advance. Charlie ran his hands up under Jasper's T-shirt, running his callused fingertips over one of Jasper's nipples. That brought a moan through the kisses. His nipples growing instantly hard and erect. They were long, so he obviously liked nipple play. But not pierced. No pierced nose or eyebrow or tongue or even ears. Charlie had little diamond chip earrings in his ears. Small and cheap and dull from him wearing them all the time. Small enough if stolen he could easily replace them.

"Want to get naked?" asked Jasper. "This is great, and I don't want to—"

"Yes. Since the first time I saw you," said Charlie. His voice had grown harsh, low, with a little growl. "Although…"

"I know, we just met and—"

Etta sang "If only you'd trust in me…" It was like the soundtrack had synced to Charlie's thoughts. That happened sometimes. If you played the right performers.

"It's not that," said Charlie. It's been a long day. I played for two hours then played for you for nearly two hours. I'm…well, I'm kinda gross."

"Shower? My shower sucks though."

Once more Charlie thought of the big bathtub in his room at the hotel. Should he invite him back there now? They could splurge on a cab and be there in what, twenty minutes. Thirty. Could he wait? He could. Did he want to? No.

"I'm really more of a bath person. I know that's passe," said Jasper. He drank the rest of the wine in his glass. "We could draw a bath, open another bottle of wine. I don't mind taking this a little slower, as much as I want you to fuck me."

Could this even be real? Everything Charlie liked? Everything Charlie wanted? Was this the power of Simon and

Garfunkel and French roast coffee?

"I'd love a bath. Is your tub big enough for us both?" Charlie reached for his glass, but realized it was empty. Had he finished it? Or, had Jasper?

"Follow me, kind sir." Jasper held out his hand. He helped Charlie up. "Bring your glass."

Again, called sir by a not much younger man.

They detoured through the kitchen, grabbing a cold bottle of wine from the old Frigidaire. The apartment vibe similar to Coffee Haus, cool and eclectic: a blend of modern and new and minimalism and old appliances. Music emanated through the unseen speakers, no matter where they went in the loft, even and balanced.

Through an industrial door, an enormous bathroom with a hint of peppermint in the air invited. A toilet sat alone in the middle of the room. A shower enclosure took up a corner. In another corner, but not up against the wall, a big old tub. It didn't have claw feet, but was built into an enclosure that created a lip all the way around the tub. And inside, even though the porcelain seemed age-stained, it also gleamed. Clean.

Jasper bent into the tub, placed a rubber stopper in place, and turned on the hot water. "It takes a while to fill."

Charlie nodded his head in knowing. Near one of the sinks, there were three of them side by side, which lined one of the shorter walls, was a baker's rack. Bottles of oils and bubble baths. A wicker basket was pyramided with round bath bombs each individually wrapped in soft white tissue paper. Shades of pastel showing through the thin paper shells.

Jasper twisted the top on the wine, poured more into their glasses.

Etta James sang "My Heart Cries" with someone else. The men danced together, they drank wine, they kissed. It was romantic and easy. Like they had been together forever. Of course, if they had been together forever, they'd no longer dance like this or drink together like this or kiss like this.

Charlie, turned on, come rising into his dick begging for release.

The song changed, but had the same rhythm, "Boy of my dreams, don't you know it's you..." she sang like punctuation.

They began undressing each other. Buttons. Zippers. One shirt off. More wine. Another sock off. More kisses. Clothes piled up around them. Money fell from Charlie's pockets.

"You're making it rain," whispered Jasper, amused. His eyes, grey, light, sparkled. Sexualized. Alcoholized.

"Oh."

Normally, under any other circumstances, with any other person he'd ever met in his life, he would drop to his knees and gather the flurry of bills that had released from his pockets. He'd worry about not having organized it early. Not having counted it. Not knowing what was there in case he got robbed or rolled. It had happened before.

He didn't care.

Instead, he kissed Jasper again, hungry for the taste of him. The smell of him. All the smells of him tinted with coffee. So exotic. His skin even. Smooth. Furred over in tight curly black hairs. Those nipples so big. Charlie dropped his head down and licked one. Licked the other. Sucked. Jasper pulled him tight to his chest, moaned with his hands tight on the back of Charlie's head. Like pushing a button.

"Fuck. You're gonna make me come."

Charlie sucked hard, nibbled and bit Jasper's rock-hard nipple. He dropped a hand down to the other man's dick. Found the head. Rubbed it through his boxers. Already so wet.

"Fuck. Fuck. Fuck." The wet seeped through Jasper's shorts.

Charlie raised a sticky finger to his mouth and sucked it, tasting Jasper. His come had a hint of coffee behind the salty pungentness. Charlie came a little in his shorts, too. "How's that tub?"

While Jasper adjusted the water, Charlie drank off the remains of now warm wine.

"What do you want in the water?" asked Jasper, his voice matching Etta James, who still sang to them: dusky and lusty and sex filled.

"Oil?" said Charlie.

"Right. Bubbles are awkward." He smiled; the dimple appeared, so sexy. He poured oil from a tall, blue glass bottle into the water. Set it on the shelf. Dipped his fingers into the tub. Adjusted the temperature of one of the spigots. He came back to Charlie and kissed him. "So fucking hot."

They sat now on the ledge around the tub. Strong and sturdy. The tiles already warmed by the steam and water. Charlie let his hand trail into the water. Perfect. He drank off his glass of wine, stood, and stripped off his boxer briefs—all that was left to remove. His dick was sticky and rock hard.

"Nice," escaped from Jasper's lips. He reached up and cupped Charlie's balls. Such an intimate act.

Charlie gasped at the touch. He hadn't been with anyone in a few weeks. He leaned into it.

Jasper didn't take Charlie's dick in his mouth, instead, he stood too, stripped his wet boxers off, and led the way into the tub.

Charlie admired his skinny waist, his lightly haired ass, his strong legs. Charlie followed and they got situated. The tub was big, but not as big as his clawfoot. They could be side by side if they were at Charlie's hotel. Here, one had to be in front of the other, or they could sit facing each other and one of them would have the spigots in their back.

"You in the back?" asked Jasper.

"Sure." Charlie kissed him one more time while they stood facing each other in the hot water. He lowered himself into position. A towel at his neck. Jasper followed. It took a moment for them to find their comfort position. Charlie's hard dick poked at Jasper's back.

"Like *Pretty Woman*," said Jasper.

Charlie thought he'd seen the movie, there was a bathtub scene or two or three. He didn't have a good response, so he wrapped his arms around Jasper and hugged him tight to him. They fit together well in the perfect-temperature water.

"I'm exhausted," said Jasper. It came out of him in a sigh. "Such long days." He leaned back into Charlie.

"Well, you run a business." He wanted to massage Jasper's head, feel the ridges between his cornrows. Such an intimate choice for this early date. Instead, he selected a luxurious, thick sponge, the real kind from the ocean. He submerged it until it softened and then rubbed it lightly over Jasper's chest, over his erect nipples. His cock stiffened to an impossible hardness, almost painful. "I can't imagine dealing with customers and employees all day."

"You perform." His voice a purr. "You deal with people every moment you're working, too."

"Yeah, but I don't really need to be nice to everyone. If someone's a dick, I can walk away or say what I think."

"Is that how you got the bruises around your neck?"

Charlie sighed. Decided to be honest, even if it meant looking for a moment at his past. "I got picked up by a bartender who was sexy as shit. Things got a little too rough for my taste."

"Been there." That was all Jasper said. No probing. No judgment. No advice. Just acknowledgement.

Jasper refilled their glasses with the remains of the bottle. They consumed more wine while exploring one another with the sponge, or what they could easily and comfortably reach of each other. The water hot and Etta singing and…

Charlie woke in a start. It took a moment to remember it had only been a moment of closed eyes.

"Ready for bed?" asked Jasper. "I've pruned up pretty good." He held his hands up. Entwined his fingers with Charlie's pruned fingers.

"Sure. I think I might want to sleep." He felt embarrassed by the statement. He had this sexy man, naked and slick, at his disposal. Charlie could have his way with him and all he really desired was to sleep with entwined limbs. Had they skipped the honeymoon and gone right to marriage?

"Me, too. I can be a little clingy in bed at first, but then like my space." Jasper got up, flicked the stopper with his foot, and stepped out of the tub. As Charlie followed, Jasper handed him a huge, plush, soft, thirsty towel.

"You've got the best stuff." He dried himself, then took a

few swipes at Jasper's back and ass.

"I work hard and make money and should have the things that I like. I love baths, and bubbles and sponges." Jasper turned around, the towel held to his chest between them. He kissed Charlie in a soft, sensual way.

Charlie's dick sprang up.

"I thought you said you were tired." Jasper gave the dick a gentle tug.

"I am, but you're fucking hot."

"Good answer."

With damp hair and damp towels, their clothes still in a messy pile, money everywhere, Charlie followed Jasper into the big open room, across it, and through a massive industrial, sliding metal door.

"What a place."

"Thanks. It would be hell to heat if it weren't for the radiators."

They got into a sprawling, oversized bed. He wondered where you found sheets for such a massive mattress.

Charlie wished he'd had a chance to brush his teeth, but he hadn't even thought of it until now.

They found comfortable positions, Jasper wrapped into Charlie's arms. They snuggled into the soft cotton of a heavy quilt with an intricate pattern of rich jewel tones. Like the loft, modern, yet traditional. It all felt like a made-for-TV movie where the boy gets the boy. Like some happy ending after a long struggle. But that wasn't how it had gone. Charlie had played some music for a handsome man, and they ended up in bed together. A tale as old as the tradition of troubadours. Definitely a perk of the job. No struggle involved.

Charlie breathed in hints of eucalyptus and coffee around him. Jasper's breaths had already calmed, evened. He already slept.

The end of a very long day, indeed.

Charlie took in his surroundings. How easy the night had been. The old man at dinner. The crowds in the afternoon and evening. Something had changed. He knew it. Like so many moments in his life, he decided not to question or analyze it any more than he already had. Instead, he breathed in the scent of Jasper—coffee and juniper—felt the heat from their bodies.

Jasper rolled away. Charlie shifted his hips until his softening dick found a good position at the curve of Jasper's perfect ass. He enjoyed the moment as sleep took him down the dark path.

THIRTY

Charlie woke in darkness, pressed against a man, nestled under unfamiliar covers. A digital clock read 3:59. As it clicked to 4:00 an alarm sounded. Beep. Beep. Beep. Beep.

Jasper reached out from under the covers and touched the clock. It stopped beeping. "Hey," he mumbled.

"So early," said Charlie. Awake. His dick hard and pressed into Jasper's back. Morning wood, plus blue balls from the unfinished activity the night before, agonizing.

"Work. I have to be down there to open. Usually four-thirty." He wriggled his ass up against Charlie in a pleasant way and yawned in a not sexy at all way.

They remained snuggled for another moment. The clock now 4:02.

"Sorry. I need to shower quick and dress. You can stay in bed all day if you'd like. It would be wonderful to return home tonight and find you here." Jasper rolled over and faced Charlie. He had terrible morning breath, tinged with bitter coffee.

Charlie kissed him lightly anyway.

"No. I'll gather up my things and head out." He stretched. Jasper patted his chest in a soft, pleasant way. Pleasant the perfect word.

"Okay." Jasper slipped out of bed. His dick mostly hard, beautiful. His pubes trimmed, but not shaved. His ass a perfect peach shape. He headed into the kitchen, pushed a button and the loft filled with the aroma of coffee.

Charlie followed out of the bedroom. "You make it all day, even at home?" He headed into the bathroom. It took a long moment for his dick to soften enough to pee.

"I like coffee. It's one of the reasons I do what I do." Jasper entered the bathroom and went to the shower, turned it on full. The glass cabinet sadly too small for two people.

Charlie flushed and rinsed his hands in the sink. Brushed his teeth with a wet finger. Rinsed and dried his hands. He found his shorts. They were stiff from precum but he pulled them on anyway, not wanting to go commando in jeans in the cold morning. Especially with a hard dick rubbing all the way home.

Home.

Was Hotel de Chanson home?

Part of him, deep inside, would love a real apartment. A real life like other people had. Like Jasper had. He sometimes felt that way after a satisfying encounter with a new man. Within a few days or a week, he'd let go of his FOMO emotions and once again consider his desire to head south or west for the heat during the winter.

He pulled on pants, shirt, and gathered up the bills that had scattered around their clothes. Picked up his socks. All the while watching Jasper in the shower. Wet and soapy and fabulous. "Should I come by tonight and perform a concert in your shop?"

"If you're going to do that, we could put up a sign or write something on the chalkboard." Jasper stepped out of the shower and toweled off. His balls bounced pleasantly as he dried his head. His abs rippled, too. "But only perform if you want."

He must work out or run or something, Charlie imagined. Of course, he was in nearly as good shape and all he did was play all day and forget to eat. "I don't like to make commitments like that." He knew he was talking about more than just playing in the coffee shop that night.

"Okay. If you decide to come by, that would be great." He stepped up to Charlie and hugged him tight.

They kissed.

Charlie reached down and cupped Jasper's balls. Felt the weight of them in his palm. Wanted them in his mouth.

Jasper pulled away, “Sorry, no time. Come on, have a cup of Joe before you go.” He headed into the kitchen, poured two steaming mugs, passed one to Charlie, all the while standing there naked and enticing as hell.

Charlie sipped. “This is amazing.”

“I know, right. I got it when I was down in Honduras a few weeks ago.”

“Honduras?” Charlie drank the coffee. The best coffee he’d ever tasted.

Jasper leaned against the counter, his dick soft, but still so big, a cracked coffee mug against his lips.

Charlie couldn’t help himself. He set his cup down, dropped to his knees, and took Jasper’s cock into his mouth. God, he wanted this man. Wanted him in a way he hadn’t wanted anyone for a long time. This went deeper than lust, although lust drove this moment. He bobbed his head, taking all of Jasper’s big hardening cock into his mouth. He tickled his furry balls. He ran a hand between his legs and pushed the tip of his finger into Jasper’s puckered asshole. It didn’t take long. Jasper tensed. Arched his whole body. Pushed as hard into Charlie’s mouth as he could, as deep as his dick would go down his throat, and exploded. Charlie stayed on him. Sucked him in. Swallowed the just as he expected coffee-tinged spunk. Stayed clamped hard and tight to him until Jasper begged, begged, begged for him to stop. Stayed anyway, sucking every drop of coffee cum out of his dick until Jasper, with his fingers laced in Charlie’s hair, pulled him off. “Fuck.”

Charlie stood, clamped his lips to Jasper’s, shoved his tongue into the other man’s mouth, wanting him to taste himself from Charlie’s perspective.

When they broke apart, Jasper said once again, “Fuck.” He breathed hard. “You’re fucking amazing.”

An alarm sounded on Jasper’s phone. “Work. Gotta go to work.”

Charlie nodded. Kissed him roughly, playfully. Stepped away. Took another sip of coffee. There was a drop of come on Jasper’s cockhead. Charlie reached his rough-tipped index finger down and used it to gather that drop of semen, and pushed that calloused fingertip into Jasper's mouth who sucked greedily. Charlie kissed him again. "I guess you should get dressed if you're going to work." The words a challenge. Playful. Their eyes locked upon each other.

Jasper didn't move, but nodded. "I need to." His phone buzzed. "Stella's at the door down there."

Charlie thought, too bad she doesn't have a key, but didn't say it. He stepped back. Picked up his mug. Drank a large swallow of excellent coffee.

Jasper rushed from the kitchen to the bedroom. Charlie pulled on his socks. Slipped into his shoes, once more considering that it was time for a new pair. Time for a trip to the thrift store. He looked around at the nice things Jasper had in his apartment. People had nice things for themselves. People shopped retail.

Charlie put on his coat. Slung his guitar over his shoulder. Drank the last swallow of coffee from his mug. Debated. He could just walk out. He could wait and they could go down together. He could…

"Ready?" Jasper returned, dressed in fresh clothes. A sweater. Interesting designer boots. He looked nice for a day of serving coffee to strangers.

"Yep." Charlie followed him out the door, down the stairs.

"I'll go through the back. You can go out there. The front doors are just around that corner." He stopped and they kissed again. "Hope you come by tonight. No pressure. And you should only come by to play if you want. I just want to see more of you. Finish what we started?"

"Okay."

"I'd just love to see you again."

"I'd like that, too," said Charlie. They kissed lightly, a kiss tinged with coffee and salty spunk.

On the street, in the early morning darkness, the bagel stands were opening. He stopped at the corner, bought a plain bagel with cream cheese, and headed down the stairs to the subway. He'd considered a cab. It would be faster. He had money in his pocket. But Charlie remained frugal. He swiped his Metro Card and entered the quiet station just as a downtown train pulled to a stop. He still tasted Jasper on his tongue as he entered the empty subway car.

THIRTY-ONE

Charlie stepped out of the subway station a few blocks from the hotel. He wished he had his scarf in response to the chilled wind. He hadn't eaten his bagel and hesitated at the cart on the corner, thinking of getting a cup of coffee, but the memory of the amazing coffee he'd just had stopped him. Jasper's coffee. Jasper. His heart fluttered and his dick stiffened.

Nice.

In the corner bodega, he got a bottle of cranberry juice and a fifth of Grey Goose. Not taking a cab made that purchase comfortable, well, at least possible. He paid with many small denomination bills. The proprietor liked that Charlie did that, paid in stacks of dollar bills. Even a pile of quarters made him happy.

As he stepped out onto the early morning street once more, he ran right into an old drag queen. She looked a little rough, but her lipstick remained pristine. Her red hair, obviously a wig, needed some attention.

"Sorry," he said.

"It's fine. Attention from a handsome man is appreciated no matter the circumstances," she said. "A man with a hint of sex about him. It's a walk of shame if the sun isn't up yet."

"Stride of pride." Charlie smiled. "Do you require an escort?"

"I haven't paid for it, well, not directly, in decades." She sounded like the old men in the hotel. Could she be as old as them? Older?

Charlie studied her eyes. "Not what I meant. Just an arm to help you navigate."

"Aren't you the gentleman. That would be nice. I'm just a few blocks over and down." She took his arm, placing her hand into the crook of Charlie's elbow. "A gentleman coming to my aid on a cold night. How lovely."

A gentle, sweet, flowery perfume enticed Charlie. Reminded him of something or someone. A pleasant memory, even if he couldn't retrieve it.

"Charlie," he said as they walked.

"Chris," she said.

Such a plain name for a drag performer, Charlie thought.

They walked together in the rhythm of Chris's heels, Chris guiding Charlie with barely perceptible tugs and pulls at his arm. He followed her lead.

"You're a musician?" she asked.

"Yes," he answered.

"Me, too. Coming from a gig?"

They waited for the light to change, even though there wasn't any traffic on the early morning streets.

"I am. Well, sort of. I played a gig that ended a long time ago."

"Me, too," said Chris. She chuckled. "I hope you were having more fun in the interim than I've been having."

"Not a lovely evening for you?"

The light changed and they crossed.

Chris gave a little tug, they turned right, then crossed the street in the middle of the little block. "I'm this way."

Charlie didn't push for an answer.

After a few more turns, they arrived at a metal door. "This is me," said Chris. "If you don't have anywhere to go, you're welcome to come in." The tone seemed resolved more than inviting.

"Oh, no. I live at the Hotel de Chanson. Not too far from here."

"You seem far too young to be living there." Chris turned, a bemused look in her old eyes.

"Well, I guess I am, but I'm currently the entertainment," said Charlie.

After a chuckle, still in the bemused category, Chris released her hold on Charlie's arm. "I see."

There was knowing and some inuendo in those two small words: I see.

"No," insisted Charlie. "I'm not for hire. I play guitar for Happy Hour. I needed a place to live, and Patsy offered me a great deal on a room."

"Oh, Patsy. That old cunt still running the place." Chris smiled through the salty statement—her perfume softening the edges of the comment.

Charlie nodded.

"Well, tell her Christopher Marlowe from Tamburlaine says hello."

"The dead British playwright?"

"The very much alive performer, thank you very much. And thank you for your arm, kind sir." Chris bent forward, kissed Charlie's cheek, left a hint of that scent, and, he suspected, a shadow of lipstick. Chris pulled back, offering a kind, bemused smile that brought a twinkle to her eyes. "Someone certainly has gotten lucky this evening." She pushed a key into a lock and opened the metal door. "Now, don't forget, tell that old cunt Christopher Marlowe from Tamburlaine says hello." Chris slipped inside and the door closed leaving Charlie alone on the dark, empty street.

It took him a moment to figure out where he was. They'd arrived at Chris's door in a circuitous way, but the avenue remained one block over. He could hear a bus screeching to a stop. He started in that direction, stopped at the T-intersection, looked at the burned-out building on the corner, and turned to the right toward the avenue. He'd be home in a few minutes.

Home.

Charlie lived in a hotel. The room was nice, but nothing inside was his. Once more he saw Jasper's apartment in his mind. That was a home.

THIRTY-TWO

Charlie entered the lobby and the night man nodded in a knowing way. He didn't speak to Charlie and Charlie didn't speak to him. The awkward moment lingered while he waited for the elevator.

He stepped into the ancient metal box with its iron gate and ornate interior walls. He shifted the bag with juice and vodka and the bagel from one hand to the other; he fished out his key and was ready when he arrived on the top floor.

Under the door, a note: "Stopped by. Derek."

A twinge of something, not really guilt, yet an uncomfortable emotional response passed through him and fluttered his stomach. Had he started to care for these men?

Inside, he undressed and poured a Cape Cod, even though the juice had grown tepid. He tossed the bagel bag on the little desk. His hunger gone. He drank the cocktail down in a long swallow, the alcohol taking the last taste of semen from his mouth, his throat. Had Christopher Marlowe actually smelled the sex on him? Probably.

After a second cocktail, Charlie used the shower for the first time. The water pressure weak, showering in the old tub, an awkward balancing act, dissatisfying. He brushed his teeth, and uncharacteristically, he slipped naked into bed as a hint of sun brushed against the blinds.

THIRTY-THREE

There's something luxurious in life when you wake up not knowing what time it is and not caring. Without a watch, without a phone, without a schedule your life is your own, time more of an abstract concept than a reality.

Charlie heard Croce's "Time in a Bottle" in his head. That wasn't the right theme for the moment though. He didn't really want to capture and keep anything. He liked living in the moment without a concern for past or future. Certainly much easier to experience when you didn't own a pit group couch or a coffee maker.

At this moment, there was something about the future that niggled at him. His FOMO over Jasper's loft apartment. His showing up every weekday afternoon at four to play for Happy Hour. He had more plans at the moment than he could remember since he dropped out of school. That first day he chose not to go, represented the last time he had somewhere specific to be. Even when traveling across country, if you missed a bus or train, another came in time.

He dropped out when he turned eighteen. Only a sophomore at eighteen. He'd missed a lot of school. Being in the system leant itself to missing school as he got moved around from house to house, place to place. He'd run away a lot during his teens, not willing to take the abuse. Some of the sexual encounters were actually okay. He was a horny teen and found ways to enjoy being sodomized, even knowing it was wrong, illegal, often gross. Getting off is important to all teen boys. No, it was the emotional abuse that hurt him. That lingered. Those people, the ones who shouted at you and said horrible things to you and about you, who tried to feel better about themselves...

See, this was why living in the past didn't work. It just brought all the old crap up to the surface. There's nothing he could ever do to change those things. They existed. Would always exist. Nothing to be done.

Moving now. Changing cities. Not becoming encumbered by relationships and people, and things that kept the moment, living in the present, possible.

He tried to turn his brain off. Tried to get a song going. Nothing came. He kept hearing that horrible loop. "You're a worthless bastard." The harder one surfaced when he shut that down: "Your parents didn't love you. If they loved you, they'd have made a plan for you."

There were no memories of them. His parents. He'd tried and tried and tried to find them. He couldn't. He'd simply been too young, too small. He supposedly lived with an aunt. His mother's sister. Something happened that he didn't know. He'd ended up in the system in New York City. Children don't get adopted. Only babies survived the system. Everyone who lived it knew that. The older you got, the less chance you had at a life with people who would love you.

Tears dripped from his eyes into the soft pillowcase. He let them drip and waited for a song to come, a song to take away the pain.

"Eyes Closed" by Sheeran popped out. That pizzicato turn of phrase. He hated it. He'd never sing it in public. Lots of people hated Ed Sheeran, and lots of others requested him. Loved him. "I'll keep dancing..."

At least the song had him up, awake, out of bed, peeing a strong stream, the sound of piss into the bowl echoing off all the tile that surrounded the room. Sunshine streamed through the dirty, narrow window. Not night. He hadn't slept through the gig. He held his head under the faucet.

"Dead Man," by Kushner entered his head. Another song he hated. The voice so low and dark, it didn't fit well in Charlie's range.

He feared this might be one of those days. He'd need to sit

it out, get drunk or stoned...he hadn't been stoned in a while... maybe not play today...or force himself to play through it.

Why had this happened? Why was he in this terrible place?

Charlie reached back to Simon and Garfunkel, but none of those songs would come out. He reached for images of being with Jasper, but none would come. He tried to smell coffee in his brain. Taste it in his mouth. Only darkness.

Boygenius's, "Not Strong Enough," came into his brain. "Not strong enough to be your..."

He sucked water from the tap. Swallowed some, spit some out.

His phone rang. Still wet and naked, he answered. "Hello."

"Are you coming down? The room is full. Henry said you got in late." Patsy didn't sound angry or judgmental. They didn't have a contract. "There are already four shot glasses lined up on your little table.

Maybe a flood of beer would help. "I'll be there in a few minutes." He hung up.

"Always an angel, never a god..."

The music in his head gave him a dance to the bathroom. He toweled off, dressed. Easy to dress when you always wear the same things. Clean jeans. A plain white T-shirt under an artistically stained sweatshirt. Socks. Shoes. Comfortable. He transferred some money from the dirty jeans on the floor to his pocket. You should always have a little money. He grabbed his room key, too.

He slung his axe over his shoulder and headed out. Ran his fingers through his wet hair, thinking he needed to get it cut. The last time he'd done it himself had gone horribly wrong. He needed to meet a hairdresser. That was the true key to gay life. Hook up with the people who can offer you something. Suck a cock, get a haircut. Fuck someone, enjoy a nice dinner.

For some reason, he thought of the old drag queen. Her red wig, slightly askew. Queens knew hair.

He entered the lounge. A few of the men applauded.

Patsy rushed up to him with a beer in hand. "Are you okay?"

"Fine." He took out the guitar, placed the strap over his shoulder, got settled. He took a sip of beer. Patsy stood near him. He thought of the queen's message, but decided to wait. The queen had called Patsy a cunt. Instead, he said, "Can I get a bottle of water? Not a glass, a bottle?"

"Of course." Patsy rushed away.

What the fuck would he play?

Charlie took a long time tuning his guitar. These were old men. They knew the old songs. He generally liked the old songs. He strummed a G-chord, then a D. He breathed. There in the middle of the room, Derek. Off in the corner, Quinn. What the fuck did he want? Charlie strummed a G-chord.

A.

G7.

The song came. The pattern rolled from his fingers. Ethereal. Magical. "Hold your breath," he said. "Count to three," he said. And he sang, "Pure Imagination," his favorite song from Willy Wonka. Although, other than the opening, he preferred Sammy Davis Jr.'s version.

That launched thirty minutes of Sammy Davis Jr. versions of other people's music. Charlie didn't imitate Mr. Davis. He simply liked those arrangements. As he sang, he transitioned from song to song. He didn't break for beer or applause or water. He sang, because stopping meant he might not start again.

That idea terrified him more than any nightmare he'd ever had.

That's what stopped the thirty minutes of Sammy. That thought of no more music and the result from that thought entered his brain and...made him happy.

Charlie ignored the applause. He downed the bottle of water. Then, drank off half a bottle of beer. He hadn't noticed, but more and more shot glasses filled the table. Took up the surface of the table.

The problem with shot glasses is that you couldn't easily stack them.

He set down his beer and a shot glass fell on the floor. Everyone ignored that, including Charlie.

He started it, one of the most requested songs of all time,

of his whole busker life: "A long, long time ago, I can still remember how that music used to make me smile..."

Applause.

People loved the song "American Pie" by Don McLean.

No rush.

The classic flowed easily from him. Molasses. It wouldn't be long before he had this whole room of old queens singing. Marilyn Monroe. Hell, everyone loved Marilyn Monroe.

The audience gave him the first chorus. After that, he provided the backup for them.

Nothing wrong with a sing along. Chapin built his concert career on sing-alongs.

He couldn't help himself. Charlie stood, leaned back, and in the process leaned into the song. He performed that song. Nearly nine minutes. This one a story, but not. It connected to emotions even for people who didn't know who it was about or why it was written. People who weren't even alive then responded to the non-sequiturs of the song.

After the song, he finished the beer and started the next. The music flowed. A mix of modern and classic. Time didn't matter and he played and sang and played and sang. Patsy might have signaled, but he didn't see her. No one left. They sang along. They applauded. They bought him beer. Maybe he should have a tip jar instead of taking all this beer. Banking beer didn't work. Of course, he received nightly pay for playing Happy Hour, so a tip jar might be inappropriate.

When did he start caring about appropriate or inappropriate?

He found a good moment. His fingers actually hurt, something that didn't happen often. Something that only happened with time. So, he asked, "Anyone have the time?"

Someone in the room said seven-fifteen.

They'd let him go over by more than an hour. They'd skipped their dinner seating—dinner started at six. It usually ended before eight.

"Sorry," said Charlie.

The men applauded.

"I guess I'll see you tomorrow."

The men applauded.

Charlie finished the beer on the table.

The scariest shit is the shit in your head.

He packed up his guitar, slung it over his shoulder. He watched Quinn slip out, alone, head down, no eye contact; no request. Derek waited there. Invited him to dinner with a hopeful smile.

“Not tonight,” said Charlie. He wanted to go uptown. He wanted to go sing songs for Jasper. Not for his patrons. For Jasper.

“Oh, okay.” He was hurt. “I stopped by for a nightcap, but you weren’t home.”

“No. I played late. Got in late.”

“Hope you made a lot of money.” He still sounded hurt.

Charlie remembered again that he never had counted the money from the coffee shop gig. He had no idea how much there was. Those jeans pockets upstairs were stuffed. “It was a good night.”

“Some other time?” He looked hopeful now.

“Sure,” said Charlie in a noncommittal way. When Derek left, Charlie headed toward the little bar. “Sorry for being late.”

“No apology necessary,” said Patsy. She handed him folded bills. She opened him another beer. “You’re free to come or not. Although the men would be disappointed if you didn’t show.”

He hated guilt shit. A foster mother while he was in high school thrived on guilt. That foster father…it was the first time he ran away. Went south on a bus.

“Oh, I ran into someone last night who said to say hello to you.”

“Oh?” She looked up from the glass she washed.

He practiced the line once in his head and said, “Christopher Marlowe from Tamburlaine said to say hello.” He left out the vulgarity.

“That old cunt is still alive.” She went back to her glass, but her face had changed. Something tight and rage-filled showed up in the lines on either side of her lips. She suddenly looked her age, or the age Charlie surmised she was.

"It might have been a ghost I met on the street," said Charlie. He drank down his beer and waved the empty bottle.

Patsy served him another, the bottle body coated in suds because she'd been elbow deep in the cleaning solution.

He wiped the bottle with a bev nap. He drank, a hint of soap in his mouth. He got the irony.

"I'll dance on her grave one day," said Patsy.

Charlie suspected Chris Marlowe felt the same way. He finished his beer but didn't push the bottle away.

"In a red fucking dress. Want another?" asked Patsy. She didn't move to get it.

"No. I'll take the rest on a gift certificate."

"How do you know that old phrase. I don't think you're old enough to have seen that series way back then."

"I don't know. I don't even know where it comes from."

Now Patsy studied him. "You have the mind and memory of a much older person. All the songs you know, so many of them, the bulk of them are from before you were born." It wasn't a question.

"Don't know," said Charlie. He flashed on stacks and stacks of vinyl albums in cardboard sleeves. He'd just got himself back to the present, he certainly wasn't in the mood to root around in that attic or cellar any more tonight. "I've got to see a man about a horse," he said, knowing it was the oldest line he could think of.

Patsy laughed. "Goodnight, Sweet Prince."

No one accosted him in the lobby. They were all late for dinner. He headed upstairs, tugged on his coat, added his long scarf, guitar over his back, then out.

On the street, at the corner, instead of heading down the subway entrance stairs, he hailed a yellow cab and gave Coffee Haus's uptown cross streets.

THIRTY-FOUR

At the counter, Charlie ordered a large cup of coffee from a barista who had a name tag: "Veronica." He added cream to the tall paper cup, something he rarely did, but was in the mood for the softness and richness.

Jasper wasn't there. Wasn't visible anyway.

The big clock on the wall, an oversized industrial behemoth, said the place would still be open for an hour. He took his coffee into the corner where he'd sat and played the night before. Like the night before, all the other seats were empty. It was only him and a room of empty tables.

He sipped his coffee and debated playing anything at all. Maybe the night before hadn't even happened. The beer still coursed through him, the buzz strong. He could leave the coffee. Slip out. Get some beer and go home.

There was that word again.

Home.

Life in the moment dictated that Hotel de Chanson was, in fact, his home.

Charlie pulled out his guitar, tuned it.

Veronica came to the counter, said, "Sir, I'm sorry, you can't play that in here."

"Oh, sorry," said Charlie. It certainly wasn't the first time he'd heard that. He'd been thrown out of lots of places. Been asked not to play in lots of places for lots of reasons. He bent to put his guitar back in the case.

Jasper came in from the street with a tote bag in his hand. "Charlie!" He came over. "Have you played, and I missed it? Damn!" He bent easily, kissed him lightly on the lips. "It's so great to see you," he said. "I've been thinking about you all day." He kissed him again.

"Nice asses."

"What?"

Charlie pointed at the bag.

"Oh, cool, right? From an Arizona artist. Brenda something or other."

"I've been thinking about you, too." Charlie leaned in. "Veronica said I couldn't play in here," he whispered.

"Oh. It's a rule. She follows the rules and that's why I like her. Please, play something for me. Your voice is incredible." He kissed Charlie again. A coffee-tinged peck.

The song, already in his head, begged to be released. "Veronica" by Elvis Costello. The upbeat tempo and the fun lyrics. Not to mention, it might annoy the barista who'd denied him. As he started the intro she came back, but didn't say anything. Jasper waved. The song wasn't as good without drums, without bass, but he got the percussion and rhythm going on the guitar, brought out the base line under the melody he sang.

If pressed, Charlie would eventually admit that he had a mixed love for Elvis Costello. There were a handful of songs he often found he couldn't stop singing. "Veronica." Sometimes Elvis tapped into Charlie's psyche and his songs drew something out of him, some amazing feeling. Pure joy to sing and play in the same way as "Big Yellow Taxi." He liked Joni Mitchell's rendition, but Counting Crows's version is the one that stuck in his head. He sang that.

Once more, the shop filled with people. A few at a time. A big group gathered before he finished the song. They might have been waiting for him, sending scouts. He could smell alcohol, some of those coffees were Irish. He smelled weed in the air. He loved the energy of drunkenness, right up until he didn't.

"Come Dancing" by the Kinks brought a sense of joy. All these joyful songs with a darker message underneath. A hint of sadness. But the parking lot connection is what bridged him from "Big Yellow Taxi" to "Come Dancing." Those connected to "Dance with Me" from Blink 182. Punk brought that strong beat, that head banging beat. Charlie wasn't a fan of metal head-banging songs. Too distorted. But punk music often had excellent lyrics. And if you slowed many of those songs down, sang them as ballads, listeners fell in love with them, not knowing the origin.

The big clock edged up to closing time.

He launched into "Shut Up and Dance with Me" by Walk the Moon. The crowd leaped to their feet and danced, hands in the air, a pop-up dance club.

The room, packed now, so many people the doors wouldn't close, allowing cold air to rush into the room from the street. The crowd attentive. Some sang along for a moment, then stopped to let Charlie sing. There were phones pointed at him, square lights in the masses of people. All of this new, it had never happened to Charlie before. Big crowds. Phones.

Amazing.

Finally, as he ended the song, said, "Last one."

Now, many in the crowd shouted out: "No." "Keep Singing." "More." "We love you, Charlie."

How did they know his name?

Like the night before he played Semisonic's "Closing Time." What a number. There are songs throughout the generations that are perfect last numbers. "Goodnight, Irene." "Bye, Bye, Bye." "Walkin After Midnight." "Closing Time" was one of those songs. A classic before the ink dried.

When he finished, his case bulged with money. Cash money. Lots of large bills scattered with the singles. As he gathered them into some semblance of order, as he shoved them in folded wads into his pants pockets, he noticed a lot of twenties and even a few hundreds. He couldn't believe it. No one had ever dumped so much cash into his case. Sometimes, someone like Patsy, acted liked a patron with a large bill. Usually, it was loose change and odd things from the bottom of people's pockets, and singles. Not large bills from a crowd. Like some cult figure, with followers ready to drink the Kool-Aid. Charlie shoved the bills into his pockets. He shook hands. He took selfies. He finished his cold coffee and longed for another beer. He longed for a hint of the foundation of sadness that beer brought him. It kept him even and human and connected to the earth in a way nothing else ever had.

When Jasper locked the front doors, when he pulled down the grates, twenty or thirty people, much younger than Charlie, loitered on the street, phones at the ready.

Charlie didn't pick up the trash. Veronica, still there, did that. She smiled at him from a distance. He held the eye contact.

"Sorry," she said.

"You were doing your job and can never be faulted for that." Charlie smiled at her as he wrapped his scarf around his neck. He didn't fully believe his own words, but thought he should take Jasper's company line.

"I didn't know it was you. You're famous," she said, dumping paper cups into the trash.

"Am I?" This information was news to Charlie.

"Well, yeah. Haven't you seen the videos? They're getting huge hits. You've gone viral."

Charlie didn't like the sound of that, at all. Viral wasn't something someone with a low profile and a desire to fly under the radar, off the grid, encouraged. "Show me."

She came to him with her phone out, queued up, she pushed play on a video of him singing Simon and Garfunkel's "The Boxer." He'd played that song the night before.

"Look. Nearly a hundred thousand views." She was no longer reserved, but instead, engaged, familiar.

"Don't pester Charlie," said Jasper. He had the asses bag in his hand again—were those donkeys laughing? "I think we're ready to lock up."

"Hold up," said Charlie. He scrolled with a finger on Veronica's phone. Six videos on several channels. "#Coffee House Charlie" accompanied the videos. Thousands and thousands of views on all of the uploads. His heart pounded.

Jasper hit switches that turned off signs and lights and turned on other nightlights. People continued to mill on the street outside the entrance and windows. The three exited out the back door. The hallway empty. The lobby empty.

Veronica waved goodnight and headed out, leaving Charlie and Jasper at the base of the stairs.

"I don't want to assume anything," said Jasper.

Charlie leaned in and kissed him hard on the mouth. They both tasted of coffee and desire.

THIRTY-FIVE

Charlie hung his guitar and scarf and coat on several of the long line of industrial hooks on the wall near the door. Although he felt like playing. He retrieved the Seagull and headed toward one of the couches. The main room open with tall windows overlooking the street.

Despite the massiveness of the space, Charlie found comfort tucked into the couch. He tuned his guitar—it rang out pleasantly because of the high ceilings and hard surfaces. He noticed the TV—so big it rivaled the billboards in Times Square. Thankfully, off.

"Wine?"

"Do you have a beer? I'm in a beer mood. I could run out if—"

Before Charlie finished his sentence, Jasper handed him an open beer, something foreign, Asian. A clean lager, probably a rice beer. He drank off most of the bottle. He set it on the coffee table. He strummed, tuned a few strings, strummed another chord. He finger picked the opening to "Hey, There Delilah."

"Oh, a private concert?" Jasper joined him on the couch with a big, very full glass of white wine. He unbuttoned a few buttons of his shirt and then picked up his glass and took a sturdy drink.

"Do you have a favorite song?" Most people only thought they had a favorite. Most people liked lots of songs.

"That's hard to answer. I mean, I love Etta James, but that's about the singer, not the songs. I love...a favorite? At the moment, I really like...you know, we listen to the Top 40 most days in the shop, or at least the Top 10. I hear lots of new music. I like a lot of it, but don't love it."

"I know what you mean."

"There's this Miley Cirus song that spent a few weeks on the charts—"

Before he finished, Charlie played a few bars of the refrain from "Used to Be Young." He stopped in the middle of the phrase and said, "I know what you mean. There's something almost good about this." Charlie drank some beer, the end bite of it growing on him. He played a few bars from "Barbie World," and they laughed.

"So, you listen to the Top 40, too?" Jasper drank more wine.

"I do, not every week, but it's a lot of the same songs week to week." Charlie didn't explain that he did that research in the library during one of his internet sessions, if he could get on the computer. He'd rush through the list, listen through to the songs he liked, and move on quickly over the others. Some things he liked, some of the rap and hip hop were amazing, but not his style to sing. He wasn't a white guy, but he was approaching middle age; he hated when those guys tried to be rappers. It came through as silly and insincere, mostly. He and Jasper were having a nice conversation, and he didn't want to get all philosophical and shit.

"I also am embarrassed to admit, but I mostly like older stuff and show tunes. I've certainly earned my Gay Membership Card." Jasper drank more wine.

"I love a lot of that, too," said Charlie. He finished his beer. "I've got a thirty-minute showtune set that I do by the TKTS lines sometimes. Very popular."

"I know. I've heard you do amazing stuff with seventies and eighties songs. Tonight, you played current stuff, too." He stood up. "Another?" He pointed at the beer bottle.

"Please."

"Good. I got a six-pack of this with Pad Thai a few nights ago. I didn't care for it." He opened a bottle in the kitchen and returned with it.

"So, dumping your discard beer off on me."

Jasper leaned in and kissed Charlie lightly. Charlie liked the move. He took the beer and drank some, this one bitter, but not unpleasant.

"You know it." Jasper laughed, drank more wine, and sat back on the couch with his feet tucked under him.

Charlie strummed a few chords, a pattern, played a bit of Garth Brooks's, "I Got Friends in Low Places."

"See, I like that, too. But not all his stuff. Although, he's so hot, even as he ages."

"Right. His ass in those tight jeans," said Charlie. He kept playing the music but stopped singing. "It's a good song. It works, the structure. Some of them don't. People don't know why they like and dislike a song at the same time, and I think it's the structure.

"Yes, professor," said Jasper. He drank more wine.

"Sorry, I get like that. I..."

"What, Charlie?"

"Well, I don't really do this very much. Talk to people. I mean, I meet a lot of people and sing for them and sometimes we chat, but it's just to get through to the next song, or to get them through to parting with more money, filling the space while they decide between a dollar or a five or a twenty."

"Man, people lined your case tonight." Jasper got up again, took his glass to the kitchen, returned with a full wine glass and another beer.

Charlie wondered if being around coffee all day made him overactive or antsy. "They did. It was like a game or something. People one upping each other with their tips. Should I give the house a cut?"

"Don't be silly. People love you. You're so good at what you do. Do you know that about yourself? The way you connected the songs tonight. The themes. Was that planned? Do you have a bunch of playlists built?"

Charlie drank beer while he thought about that, thought about being viral or not, going viral. "I guess I do. I mean, there are some things. Sometimes, as I'm waiting for sleep to come or the room to stop spinning or whatever, my brain starts pushing songs together. Themes or chord patterns or ending chords and starting ones, making for good transitions. Sometimes, I also know the whole album. Sometimes, those are built around a theme or idea. Bette Midler does that. Lots of those torch singers from the forties and fifties did that."

"Albums? You still buy albums? I guess they're making a comeback."

"No. I don't own any, at all. I still think of music that way. It's still sold that way. But when I like a Broadway show, I usually listen to the album, right? My brain stores it that way, mostly. So, I can play the whole lineup in order. I can also leave stuff out. When I'm lucky enough to see a show, I learn that there's incidental music and reprises that haven't made it to the cast recording. My brain inserts those. I don't have to really think about it. Just happens. Like, there's a wonderful little reprise piece in *Cabaret* that is only played by the bassist. It's not on the recording, but it's for a scene change or something. Anyway, it's called "Pineapple Pizz" and I play it sometimes when I'm killing time." As he talked, he played the brief piece.

"Oh, it's cute. It's from the 'Pineapple Song' with the old couple. I saw the last revival twice."

"Right." He finished another beer. "Are you really interested in this? I mean I don't want to lecture—"

"I am interested. Go on." Jasper jumped up, replaced the empty beer with a fresh one, got comfortable and drank more wine, focused fully on Charlie. "I'm fascinated, actually."

"Okay." Charlie felt his cheeks rise in an unfamiliar way. A smile. A true smile. Not one to get another twenty out of the crowd, not a fake smile for your picture with Santa, not that he ever met Santa.... "Okay, so, listen to the albums when I can and that comes in handy. And if I've actually played through like that, which I do sometimes when I'm alone, just to learn something new, I've got it down and can do it again, over and over. Like *The Concert in Central Park* the other night."

"Got it."

"I don't really perform like that very often. I do make up set lists, but they aren't for hours and hours of music. Usually, I group a block of songs together, two or three songs I like and think fit well." Charlie finished his beer. "These blocks can then turn into chunks of music. I can just pull them out and play them like a sequence. Don't even have to think. I use these a lot when I play on the street or in the park. Little sets. Since the crowd changes quickly, I can play a block of three or four songs over and over all afternoon."

"Nice. Don't you get bored? The repetition?" He was up, grabbing Charlie another beer, and back with a wine bottle, too. "There are two more of these before we move on to something else."

"Okay." That smile returned. God, he liked this guy. Handsome and charming and kind. He seemed genuinely interested in Charlie and what he had to say. "I don't get bored. I love to play. I love music. Plus, I've got lots of those little blocks. I mean, there are tens of thousands of songs. There're always new songs to learn. There are moments like tonight. I really like them because they're spontaneous and I find myself having fun. Putting songs together in a new way." He strummed a chord absently. "I play a song, usually something I really like, like 'Pure Imagination.' That, by the way, is one of my all-time favorites. Then, some idea within that song sparks the next song and the next. They come out in odd, new-to-me groupings. I end up with a new mini-set when that happens. I can use those over and over again in the future. I embrace when something new, something on the current top billboard or whatever list, blends well or aligns with an older tune. Those connections. Sometimes, usually, my brain makes those chains without me really getting involved." Charlie couldn't remember the last time he'd talked like this, nonstop, about himself and his process. Maybe never. He wanted Jasper to know everything.

"Coffee is nowhere near as interesting. What I'm always amazed by when I meet musicians is that they seem to love what they do. You sound passionate and sincere when you talk about your, what, your craft."

"I do love it. This is," Charlie indicated the guitar in his hands, "it's part of me, an extension of me. If I go more than a little while without it in my hands, I don't feel like myself. I can't remember the last time I've gone a day without playing.

I had COVID back at the beginning of the thing and spent a week in bed. Man, so sick. Anyway, even in my fevers and delirium, I reached for my axe. Even when I couldn't play more than a chord, I still found myself clutching it. Or, I'd wake up wrapped around my Seagull."

"Wow." Jasper stared at Charlie, tears in his eyes.

"What? Have I upset you? I'm so—"

"No, it's not..." He swiped at his eyes. "It's so silly. I just...I wish I felt passionate about something. Anything. The way you do about music and your guitar. I go to work. I like what I do. I make some bread, right. The place is popular. I'm feeding an addiction so there's a line most days. I charge a lot, but less than that chain. I search out interesting beans and blends from around the world to provide a curated experience. Though I'm not really passionate. I like being my own boss. I'm good at it. I treat my employees well. I'm good at hiring honest people, mostly. It's a job, you know. I don't feel strongly about it. If someone offered me the right price, I'd walk away tomorrow. Never pour coffee for strangers again. I've thought about building a little chain, but frankly, I'm not that interested although it would sell better if I had three or four locations. I just don't want to work that hard."

While Jasper talked, Charlie sipped his beer. Listened, as a wave of sadness washed through him. He wanted to strum a chord to make the noise in his head stop. Make noise instead on his instrument. That would be rude and distracting. His social skills sucked.

"So, when I hear people like you," Jasper continued, "passionate about your life, about your work, well, I find lately I'm getting emotional. It's silly. It's just that..."

"No. It's not silly." Charlie actually found it sad, but didn't want to say that. "It's you and where you are." He didn't know how to be a therapist for others...or himself. "I'm curious though, what would you do if you sold your shop?"

"Well, if I got the price I have in my head, I would move to Belize or Mexico. Hang out on the beach or spend my days drinking next to a pool."

"You'd do nothing?"

"Doing nothing isn't really doing nothing. I'd eat good food and have massages and stare out at the ocean."

Charlie tried to picture himself sitting on a beach staring at the water. Doing nothing. "That wouldn't be boring to you? After the first few days?" Charlie simply couldn't imagine a day without playing music for others, for strangers. Playing music for himself.

Even if he had all the money he needed forever, he'd still have to play, want to play.

"No. I'd read and listen to music and talk to people and take boat rides and maybe fish or something." Jasper looked sheepish now, he'd backed up a little, drank more wine.

"Sorry, I don't mean to sound judgmental. I just can't imagine a life like that. I've never thought about a life like that. I've never…"

Jasper leaned in again, interested in Charlie once more. "You've never what?"

"I can't ever remember thinking or dreaming about what I'd do if I had all the money I needed." Most days he generated all that he needed. The universe provided for him in the moment. Like a hummingbird, the nectar was there or he'd move to the next place it might be and find it. Sometimes that led him out of New York City, to NOLA, San Francisco, Chicago, Key West…and lots of smaller places in between. One summer, he went stop to stop on the train from New York to San Francisco, via Chicago. He traveled a few hours, got off at the next stop. Found a corner. Played. Sometimes made some cash, sometimes didn't. Sometimes found himself embraced by folks at a little local bar, sometimes was unceremoniously run out of town by the local officials. Back on the train and off at the next stop. He didn't earn as much in small towns as the bigger cities. But he ate a lot of excellent pie. He didn't say any of that to Jasper.

"Hmm. It's something I think about a lot," said Jasper, his smile melancholy, his eyes distant for a long moment.

Charlie broke the woeful mood with a chord, and another,

then a finger pattern that turned into "Fast Car," the Luke Combs rendition is what he heard in his head. So similar to the Tracy Chapman version, but sadder. The lyrics didn't fully fit the moment, but the emotion of the song did. He didn't sing, only played.

THIRTY-SIX

Before Charlie finished the song, Jasper said, "I would like a bath." He stood and stretched, a bit of his taut, flat, lightly haired stomach showing as his shirt pulled away.

"I love baths," said Charlie. "However…"

"Yes?" Jasper drank down the remains of his wine glass.

"My tub is actually better than yours."

"Really?" his tone high in skepticism.

"Well, I don't have the great towels or the wonderful selection of bubbles and oils, but I think, in my tub, we could stretch out side by side."

"Really." His eyes brightened. "Then, I shall grab some supplies, and we will hop in a cab."

"Really? Just like that?" It was Charlie's turn to be skeptical.

"Just like that." He dashed off to the bathroom and returned with folded fluffy bath sheets and a tote bag, this one cartoonish ostriches, full of bottles. "Let's go. Shoes. Coats. Guitar. Chop-chop."

They dressed and headed out, to the street, into a cab.

"You live in a hotel?" asked Jasper as they got out of the cab. "And you have a better tub than me? Frankly, I think I have one of the best tubs in the city."

"You have a great tub, but mine really is special," said Charlie. He held the front door, nodded to the night man at the desk, and steered Jasper toward the elevator.

"This place is so cool." He craned his neck to see the ceiling. "It reminds me of the old ships. Like images I've seen of *Titanic*.

Charlie saw the hotel through Jasper's eyes. Wood joists and tiny beams gleamed in a high polish. Great brass chandeliers, possibly once gas lit, now with antique bulbs like flickering flames, most of which flickered. Wood columns around the sides of the lobby were also polished to a high sheen. The wallpaper in a teal and black harlequin pattern. The rug a bit threadbare, but still amazing with its sharp angles in a rainbow of colors over an intricate parquet floor. Brass highlighted door hinges and the oversized front desk bell, not to mention the wall of room keys tucked into individual cubbies. Like walking back Victorian times.

The elevator door opened.

"It is a cool place," said Charlie. "A little sad, too." He punched the button for the top floor. He thought of that great ship's sinking. Would he go down with the Hotel de Chanson if it sank? Would he die in the freezing water while Jasper floated on the crate?

"Penthouse? Nice. Why sad?" He put his arm around Charlie's waist. Not his shoulders or his back, but his waist, under the guitar hanging there. He pulled Charlie closer to him, even with an armful of towels and bath beads, or whatever he'd put in the bird tote bag.

"Sad because all the men here are old queens. Well, old fags. Okay, old queers."

"Horrible word choices," said Jasper. "They paved the way for us, our elders, and we should revere them.

"They're old gay guys. Single. Alone. That's what I find sad. The alone part, not the queer part."

The doors opened.

"Wait," whispered Charlie. "The walls and doors seem to have ears here, too."

"Sure you're not being paranoid?" Jasper laughed.

"Maybe a little." Charlie keyed them into his room.

"It's small."

Was that disappointment? A hint. His loft was huge. It had conveniences.

Charlie locked the door, took off his guitar and jacket and scarf. "But…" he said, opening the bathroom door.

"Ah, fuck, it is bigger. It's fucking massive. Get the water going, it'll take forever to fill."

"It will. We should have stopped at the corner for beer or wine or something," said Charlie. He pushed the stopper into place and got the hot water flowing from the tap.

"It's going to take thirty minutes to fill this, right?" said Jasper.

"Right."

"Run out. Get us some wine. Maybe a snack."

"Snack?" Charlie snuggled into Jasper. "What might the kind gentleman like this evening?"

"Um..." he kissed Charlie. "A lot more of those lips on mine." They kissed again, soft, passionate. "Do you know what I'd actually like? If it isn't too late? A real deli sandwich. Roast beef and swiss with lettuce and globs of mayo."

"Oh, that sounds good. There's a deli not far. Let me run. You only drink white? Blanc something?" Charlie pecked Jasper's lips.

"Sauvignon Blanc. Only if it's chilled. The colder the better." He looked around. "No fridge?"

Charlie wasn't ready to talk about the rental situation here at Hotel de Cheapskate.

"No coffee maker?" asked Jasper in a clearly judgmental way.

For a daily rental price, he didn't say. "I only said the tub was better." Charlie laughed.

"And it is. Okay, run."

Charlie pulled his jacket on and traveled out to his errands.

THIRTY-SEVEN

Charlie keyed himself into his room. Cold from the food and wine run. He'd forgotten his scarf.

The tub full, Jasper sat naked on the tub lip pouring oil into it. Charlie's oil. "I love this. Where did you find it?"

He set his purchases down, took off his coat, stripped naked in a flash, and poured Jasper wine, into a water glass, the only one he had. He opened a beer for himself and set both, and the bottle, on the little shelf.

"Okay, here we go. The proof is..." Jasper stepped into the big tub. Slipped down into the water.

Charlie gently followed, careful not to step on him.

They settled in. They kissed. They drank. They kissed again... and again.

"Well, it's not Officer and a Gentleman, which is sexy and cozy, but this is luxurious." Jasper stretched his legs long and they easily fit with room to spare.

Charlie slid down more, his chin just above the water. He dunked under and came back up with wet hair, keeping his chin just above the water line, just high enough to drink his beer and not have the bottle fill with bathwater. "Nice, right?"

"Nice. I can't believe this big tub is here in this tiny hotel room. A hotel. You live in a hotel." He drank more wine. They kissed again. They touched each other's bodies, sensual, slippery.

"I found the oil in a thrift store. Unopened still in a holiday shrink wrap. At least a few years old."

"It's so nice. They used to sell this at Macy's. I haven't seen it for a long time. And you were worried you wouldn't have something nice enough. I can't believe I've met someone who loves baths like I do."

"All my life. Showers are fine for getting clean, and for fucking, but nothing beats this." Charlie ran his hand over Jasper's chest, a calloused fingertip over one of his elongated nipples. He wondered again if nature or kink the cause.

"Okay, so you've kind of avoided the hotel living comments. Should I be concerned?"

"No. Well, I don't know. The last place, where I was right before this, was an old SRO. I never brought anyone back to that room, or most of the rooms I've stayed in." He wondered how the rat fared. The old man. Jank.

"I thought those were illegal."

"There's lots of illegal in the City[LH1.1]." Charlie scratched his balls.

"Right."

"It wasn't bad. A bed in a private room. A complete room. Walls up to the ceiling. A shared bath. There were only three of us on my floor and everyone was very neat and tidy. It was affordable. Well, cheap. No paperwork. No questions."

"Now, I'm a little concerned."

"I live off the grid as much as possible. I earn cash and pay cash for everything."

"No bank account?" asked Jasper. "Trouble with the law?"

"I have a bank account and an ATM card and state issued ID. I've had a few tickets for things." Charlie turned so he could see Jasper's eyes, something they couldn't really do in his tub. "I got arrested once and spent three days in jail in Arizona. Vagrancy. To be fair, I was a vagrant. Passing through, I missed a bus, played some in a park, fell asleep. A cop woke me up. I'd been robbed. No shoes. My guitar gone—it was a beat-up old thing that I'd had forever. However, I still had money in my pocket. Not enough for bail, but enough to get my guitar back at the local pawn shop where the thief had already sold it. Small towns. I didn't get that instrument back, however. They had the Seagull there, too. I don't think they truly knew what they had, although with the internet, you'd think...anyway, I purchased it for a little more than a song.

I've always wondered if it was stolen, too. I know it was there for me to find, so I don't regret being arrested."

"And you got a great story."

"A story. Don't know how great it is. Not like a Harry Chapin lyric."

Jasper ran a hand across Charlie's chest, down to his stomach, to his dick. He cupped his balls in a pleasant way, but then ran his hand back up above the waistline.

They soaked together.

"No music?" said Jasper.

"No." Again, he thought about the rental options at the hotel. He didn't say anything about that. He had plenty of money now. He could buy a radio, but it would be another thing that would get left behind.

Jasper finished his wine for a third time, poured more. Emptied the bottle.

The water had grown tepid.

"I'm pruned up pretty good," said Jasper, holding his hands up and inspecting his fingers.

"We can get out or add more hot water," said Charlie.

"Out, I think. I'm exhausted and have to be up in a few hours. Plus, there's a sandwich waiting for us."

"Right. Sorry. We lead different lives, live on different timetables. You'll stay here tonight though, right?" Panic rushed through his chest. He didn't want Jasper to leave. He liked sleeping with him. And really wanted to fuck. Although, neither of them had established their advances.

"Gotta give your bed a try, right?" Jasper found a hand hold and stood, dripping and ruddy. He took a step and another, found his way out of the tub without falling. Grabbed a fluffy towel, one that he'd brought, and held it open as if for a child as Charlie followed him out of the tub. He allowed himself to be wrapped inside it.

The towel caused Charlie once more to want to buy some things. When you had a home, you could have nice towels that you kept for a long time. You weren't at the mercy of the thrift store find or the hotel room choices.

He considered all the money he'd made recently, but spending it might tempt the fates. His run was great at the moment, but it could turn south tomorrow.

They dried themselves, dried each other. Drank more alcohol. Kissed with their oiled, hard bodies pressed together. Their dicks hard and shoving into each other.

"As much as I want to fuck, I need to sleep," said Jasper. He didn't move from their embrace. "I'm also starving.

"Okay."

Jasper went to the sink; he brushed his teeth—he'd brought a toothbrush. He knew how to do a sleepover better than Charlie.

Charlie joined him at the sink. Together they brushed their teeth, naked, with towels over their shoulders. No modesty. Dicks hard, but not too hard. They hung up towels, turned off lights, pulled the stopper from the tub drain, grabbed the sandwich, slipped into bed under Charlie's well-used quilt, not new or crisp as Jasper's.

They each tore into their half of the big roast beef sandwich, not worried about crumbs; devoured it fast, fighting playfully over the last bit of mayo on the paper.

"Wait. Do you have an alarm?" asked Jasper.

"Not really." There was the nightstand clock, but Charlie didn't know how to set the alarm or even if it worked or even if the time was correct.

"I have my phone." Jasper jumped out of bed, found his phone, the screen lit up the room. He got back into bed while tapping at the screen face. "It's going to be a long day tomorrow."

"Do you not want me to come by tomorrow night?" asked Charlie, fearful of the answer he might get.

"Oh, I do. I really do. I can do my job asleep. I have a whole crew of employees to brew the coffee and deal with customers and make change. I just go in to open because I don't trust any of them with a key to the shop. I'll grab a nap at some point during the day"

"I thought you said you trusted your employees." Charlie pulled Jasper into a comfortable embrace, his arms wrapped around the naked man. He'd never spent so much time naked with a guy without them having sex.

Jasper belched softly and settled into the position they'd discovered the previous night. "I do. More or less." He yawned and immediately fell asleep.

Charlie held him; pressed into him; listened to the music in his head. Cheesy love songs and lover lament songs. A new playlist formed.

THIRTY-EIGHT

Charlie sat on stage in the Hotel de Chanson lounge. He played love songs. Two hours of love songs by Dolly Parton. Barry Manilow. Old 97's "Plain White T's." Etta James. The Temptations. The Righteous Brothers. Sade. The Postal Service. The Beatles. Alecia Keys. Boyz II Men. Shania Twain. Elvis Presley. Among others.

While he played, he thought about the previous night. He'd had a man in his tub. In his bed. They hadn't fucked. Two nights together and they hadn't fucked. What was that about?

There were guys who didn't like to fuck or be fucked. Kissing and blowjobs and dry humping. Those guys frustrated the hell out of Charlie. He rarely went back for a second date. Yet, he'd gone back for Jasper with only a single blowjob and precum soaked boxers between them.

He'd woken in the late morning. Alone. A note written in soap on the bathroom mirror. He should invest in a pen and pad. (Patsy probably rented them.) "I'll be thinking of you all day. J—" How romantic. A pain in the ass to clean off the glass.

He'd fallen asleep with love songs and woken up with love songs. All day long he'd heard them. Tonight, he'd played them. Some he'd planned. Others popped up as he went along. He ended with "Stand by Your Man." Two hours, on the dot.

The men in the room laughed and cried and sang along. They lined up shot glasses. Charlie drank lots of beer while he played, and afterward sitting at the bar. Derek invited him to dinner again; Charlie declined again. Patsy tipped him well above their agreed-upon rate.

After a stop in his room for his jacket and scarf, he headed uptown. He almost hailed a cab, the tip had been very generous, but he stopped himself. Taxis: a dangerous habit that came so easily and must not be indulged. Subway. A few stairs, a ride uptown, a train change in midtown, a ride further north, a few blocks walk. A savings of at least twenty dollars for roughly the same travel time.

Tonight, at Coffee Haus, he waited in line for his coffee.

Veronica gave him a large cup for free. “They’re here for you.” She indicated the shop. The last two nights it had been empty. The room slowly filled as he played and coffee drinkers stayed. Tonight: a mob scene.

For a long moment, he considered turning around and walking out. His anonymity had been compromised. But there behind the counter, Jasper worked. Not focused on Charlie, but the reason Charlie had returned.

His table in the corner had a “Reserved” sign, written in Sharpie on the back of a flyer for something else. No one sat there. The other tables, all of them, full. Not just one person here another there. Four tables had four and five people at them. They’d come in anticipation of Charlie. Strangers said hello while he got coffee, while he took off his coat, unwrapped his scarf, while he tuned.

He hadn’t decided what to play.

He wouldn’t be playing a night of love songs. Not here. These were young people. Hipsters. College kids. Cool kids. Some were even younger. High school kids, maybe. His head full of songs, full of possibilities, he tuned and waited for inspiration. For a spark.

People called out Simon and Garfunkel songs. They called out other requests. He ignored them.

Jasper came over to him smelling of coffee, his apron dirty. They kissed and got heckled in a polite way. “Is something wrong?”

“I don’t know what to play. Wait, I do,” said Charlie.

“Good.” Jasper kissed him lightly and went back to work.

Charlie drank a mouth of coffee and started the Old 97’s “King of All the World.” In his head, it sounded better with an electric guitar and drums and harmony, but it worked on acoustic. It took on a different quality, more like a ballad, even up-tempo. He liked the Old 97's. They made a living. They had a following. Yet, almost no one knew them. When he played their songs, people often asked if they were Charlie's songs. He never lied. He only covered other people, so there was no need to lie.

The crowd went a little crazy. Overzealous. So, he played another by the same band, "Question." One of his all-time favorite songs. He left the pronouns in place so as not to raise any questions. That one got calls for him to play it again, which is exactly how he'd responded the first time he'd heard it. Played it on repeat during one of his entire library sessions. Once more, he questioned why he loved so many straight love songs. Perhaps because there weren't any queer love songs.

"Feel It Still," by Portugal, The Man, came out next. Great bass line. And that led to a series of other favorites. They didn't tell a story as a set. They traveled nearly a hundred years of music history: A blend of ballads and up-tempo numbers. And after about ninety minutes, when the time was right, just before the clock struck ten, he launched into the familiar intro and finally sang out: "Closing Time."

The people stood. They sang along. They put away their phones. They dropped bills into his guitar case.

Coffee Haus was filled to the rafters. Charlie worried about the fire marshal or the police coming and giving Jasper trouble. Still, he sang through the chills that crept around his arms and legs and belly—another new sensation. Nervous? Ecstatic? They'd taken him viral. They'd come to hear him. Even better, just like the old queens downtown, they came back to hear him.

"Every new beginning came from some other beginning's end." He loved that line. Plus, he knew who he wanted to take him home again tonight.

THIRTY-NINE

They sat drinking beer in Jasper's loft. Charlie drank the last Thai beer, looking forward to other strays he'd noticed in the fridge. For most people, a refrigerator wasn't a luxury, just something you had, and it collected stray beers and leftover food containers.

"Why do you have all these different beers. You don't seem to like beer," said Charlie. Although Jasper was drinking a beer with him, his a Tiger.

"I like beer with Asian food. I buy a six-pack because it's cheaper. They get left over." He led them to the couch. "So, you played nearly four hours today? Not just played, but performed. Sang and played for audiences?"

"Is it really cheaper if you only drink one?"

Jasper shrugged.

Charlie set his bottle down. "Four hours is a light day. The coffee people are very generous. I don't have to play out in the cold if they dump all those twenties in my case." More twenties than singles again that night. He gathered hundreds of dollars and shoved them into his pockets when he finished.

"Light?"

"Most days I have to play seven or even ten hours to make my nut." He hadn't had to do that since he'd met Patsy. "Only playing for three and a half…I hope I don't get lazy and lose my edge." He drank beer, partially believing the joke he'd just made. He knew deep down it would never be true.

"You were terrific tonight. It amazes me how you have all these songs at your beck and call."

Charlie had worked hard his whole life, some of that work had happened before he knew it was work. But playing wasn't work. “It’s just what I do.” He kicked off his shoes.

“Listen. I really need to get some sleep. I hope you’ll stay here. I’d love for you to stay with me. I like sleeping in your arms.”

“I like it, too.”

“Good. But I have to be up early again tomorrow and last night I only got a few hours. I never got a nap. I can’t pull all-nighters anymore.”

“Why not?”

“You. The shop is busier than ever. People come in all day long asking about you, about Coffee Haus Charlie.”

Charlie wanted to ask Jasper his age, but didn’t. He thought the guy was younger than him, but he might be older. Charlie could never work the circus or carnivals, he was lousy at guessing ages. Either way, it would bother him. If younger, he had his shit together better than Charlie ever had. If older, well, he tried not to date older men. He’d trick with them for a meal if hungry. One-night stand with them. Never get serious. He—

“Charlie? I’ve lost you.” Jasper drank some beer.

“You did. Sorry. Did I miss something important?” His stomach clenched.

“No. Just me talking about my boring life.”

“It doesn’t seem boring to me.”

“Would you want to switch?” Jasper asked. Was that hope in his voice? Could they become a Disney comedy?

“Nope. I like my life. Most of it anyway.”

“What don’t you like about it?” Jasper handed Charlie a fresh beer. Sapporo.

Charlie wanted to walk into a store and buy new clothes. Clothes that had never been worn by anyone else. Shoes that he would break in to fit his own feet. He had the cash, but…. “I love my life,” said Charlie, back to living in the moment. Back to drinking the latest stray beer from Jasper’s clean fridge.

“You hesitated.”

“I can’t remember the last time I bought a pair of new shoes.” His toe stuck out of the hole that had grown larger.

“Your shoes are great.”

"I own this one pair and they came from the thrift store. When it rains, I end up wearing damp shoes for a day, sometimes two." That was something he would like to change. The trouble with owning things though, it made it so much more difficult to move in a flash. When you grew up in the foster system, there often wasn't time to pack. He'd lost several favorites when suddenly moving from place to place. To pick up and go. You had to make decisions, and he suddenly hated that. To live out of a small duffle that fit over his shoulder and didn't fuck with the guitar strapped to his back. Decisions. When you owned one pair of shoes, one coat, there weren't any choices to be made. And you were wearing the stuff, so you didn't have to carry it in a suitcase. Or make the difficult decision: carry it or leave it.

"So, buy a second pair of shoes," Jasper said.

Clearly, Jasper didn't get it. Charlie hadn't explained it. He'd tried with others. People with leases and mortgages and pit group couches and full refrigerators didn't really understand. That distance, the knowing that Jasper would probably never understand, deflated Charlie. "Maybe I will buy shoes." He certainly had the money to buy a second pair of shoes.

"I'm getting another beer. Want one?" asked Jasper.

"Yes. Then it's off to bed with you." Charlie downed the beer he had in a single gulp and accepted a Kirin.

They drank another beer together before brushing their teeth, Charlie still used his finger, getting undressed, and slipping under Jasper's incredibly comfortable, million thread count sheets. Their cocks hard, but once more ignored—that's why Charlie thought Jasper might be older, not younger than him. People fucked…until they got old.

FORTY

A kiss. A light, soft peck on his temple. He rolled over and Jasper stood above him, dressed, headed down to the shop. The loft smelled of fantastic coffee.

"Sorry, I didn't want to wake you. Sleep as late as you want. I made a pot of coffee for you. See you later?"

"Yes." Charlie reached out and touched Jasper's thigh. "Have a good day."

"My goal is a long break in the afternoon that might involve a nap." Jasper put his hand atop Charlie's.

"Good." He snuggled back under the quilt. Not as soft and used as his, but warm and safe.

When he woke again, he was alone. It took Charlie a moment to remember his location. He stretched out in the bed and scratched his chest and his stomach and his balls. He wanted a shower, but Jasper's shower sucked.

He smelled old coffee. That was strange here. Not the smell of coffee, but old coffee.

For some reason, he thought of the old drag queen he'd helped home a few nights before. Chris something? Why he thought of him he didn't know. Called Patsy an old cunt. Charlie laughed out loud. For a moment, he wondered if Patsy might actually be trans or living in drag. Anything a possibility in New York City.

An old song came into his head. The melody clear and sweet, but he couldn't find the lyrics. His feet touched the cold floor. His head pounded and vision lurched. The day would be rough, and he found himself relieved he had the Happy

Hour gig and the pockets of cash from Coffee Haus. He didn't need to spend his day on the cold streets of Manhattan unless he wanted to. At the moment, he didn't want to. Although, he did miss the rhythm of playing in Central Park. That flow of people, the mix of locals working out, and passing through, and tourists doing all manner of things. On the city streets, locals often became annoyed if people, and especially tourists, stopped around him to listen and blocked the sidewalk. In the park, that didn't happen.

After peeing for a very long time, one of the fallout effects of drinking copious amounts of beer, he washed his hands and face, rubbed toothpaste over his teeth with his finger, rinsing and spitting, and finally dressed, putting his socks on first because his feet were cold in the drafty loft. He contemplated his big toe sticking out of his sock. Funny how the space that appeared to him so amazing in the nighttime came across as cold and wanting by daylight. He hadn't noticed that before now.

This was the first time he found himself alone in Jasper's loft.

Charlie tasted the coffee, and after a sip, dumped it down the drain. That wonderful brew now burnt and dead and terrible. He washed his mug and the other mug and wine glass in the sink. He turned off the coffee maker so there wouldn't be a fire. But he didn't empty the carafe, some people liked day-old coffee.

Dressed, bundled up, scarf wrapped generously around his neck, he headed down the stairs. At street level, he first turned toward the long hallway that led to the shop's rear entrance, but then turned himself toward the street. He exited there and popped into the shop from the main entrance. He wanted a cup of fresh coffee for the road.

He waited in line, got to the front, ordered with a barista he didn't know, and paid for his coffee. He debated sitting there, waiting for Jasper to come out front or return from some errand, if that's where he might be, but after adding cream to the cup—when had he developed a taste for real cream? So good—he headed out. And without thought, he raised his hand in the air and a cab rushed over to him and stopped. Charlie had a pocketful of money. He took a cab home.

Home.

That word again. It rankled him.

And once again, the old drag queen flitted through his head. Christopher Marlowe. How could Charlie ever forget that name? The dead poet, he'd asked.

As the cab made its way downtown in a herky-jerky manner, the melody from earlier and a lyric came to him: "Life is just a bowl of cherries, don't make it serious." He worked in his head to find the words for the song. Everyone sang it at one point in the fifties or maybe sixties. He flashed on a little black and white television in the corner of some room he'd been in as a very little kid. One of the foster homes? Someone singing that song and a couple dancing together. A holiday? New Year's? A Tuesday night?

Who was that couple? None of the images worked with the memories he had lived with his whole life. He tried to tune in the image, to be clearer. He tried to focus on the faces of that couple. He saw his own hand, so small. Pudgy. That didn't fit either. Was it even his hand?

Black and white TV? He heard of those but couldn't remember ever actually seeing one except maybe in a movie.

"Buddy, we're here."

Charlie looked out the window and now saw the Hotel de Chanson. He looked at the electronic panel in front of him, shoved some cash at the driver. "Keep the change."

"Hey, thanks."

Once on the street, Charlie hoped he hadn't given the guy a wad of twenties.

"Mama." He heard himself say the word. Now. And in that image. A real life "Rose's Turn" moment.

Those people were his real parents. It wasn't yet "mama" but instead "ma-ma." Still two words. Two utterances. She reached out during their dance and touched Charlie's pudgy hand. Another hand, a strong hand that smelled of grease, automotive or maybe machine oil, sat on his head. The man's hair close-cropped, a beautiful smile. Charlie couldn't see the full faces.

Had he remembered his actual parents? Or, if he'd made it all up, he'd created a beautiful image. But why did they only have a black and white television? It must have been at least 1990. Maybe '91.

He rushed into the hotel, instead of waiting for the elevator, he took the stairs, two at a time. Then, after a few flights, regretted his choice and slowed down. He could have gone to a floor and pushed the elevator button, but obviously, he needed the exercise. Two weeks ago, he'd have kept running.

In his room, he pulled out his guitar before he had his coat off and played "Life Is Just a Bowl of Cherries." He closed his eyes and as he sang and as he played, he saw them again, that couple, his parents, twirling around the room, enjoying the song, and each other, and him. A remarkable memory. He came from somewhere. And the people he came from loved him.

FORTY-ONE

While playing for the men in the lounge that night, Charlie followed a litany of old songs. Fifties and sixties. Not the fun girl group shit, but more like "Life's a Bowl of Cherries." Rat pack songs. Dean Martin covers of covers.

The men bought him beers. They applauded. Some sang along. Charlie wondered if the music was too close to home. Songs the men's parents listened to. Songs they rebelled against.

In between numbers, he drank down a beer. A few of the men applauded his single-swig swallow.

In the corner, sitting on the last bar stool, Quinn. Charlie couldn't really tell, with a room of distance between them, Quinn backlit by the bar lighting, but he seemed disturbed in some way, his energy, his body language.

Charlie sang, "Never Grow too Old to be Young" Zoe Lewis. He didn't know where it came from. He had never performed it before. The easy melody. The hint of base line. It just came out of him. While he sang, he saw the image again: A couple dancing in front of him. A black and white TV. A record spinning. The image so strong, tinged by Pall Mall cigarette smoke. The smoke heavy in the air. The man—his father?—had two stained fingers. He danced with that cigarette smoking. He smoked, danced, smiled, spun the woman—his mother?—to a big finish. The image so damn clear. There in the corner, Quinn on his feet.

Shock? Disbelief? Anger?

Charlie couldn't read it, found it uncomfortable.

Without stopping, he played, "Life Is Worth Living." He knew it came next on the album. The parents in his mind danced, his mother's hips swinging. The voice of the singer special.

Black and white. Not the television. His parents. His father white. His mother Black. Yet, he couldn't make out their faces, not clearly.

There, at the opposite end of the Hotel de Chanson lounge, the old drag queen. Christopher Marlowe. She and Patsy had had words of some sort. Quietly, but animated. Now, the drag queen came forward, picked up the lyrics, and filled the room with her strong, old voice. Dark. A smoker's voice. Or a drinker's voice. Sturdy and sultry and deep.

Charlie played for her. Fun to play for her as she drove the line. He'd follow her anywhere.

At the close of the song, with applause ringing for them both, the old queen leaned into Charlie.

"'You're Nobody 'til Somebody Loves You' comes next."

Charlie knew it did. He could hear the little crackle of the empty groove on the album. He played. Chris sang. Quinn now stood halfway to them. Definitely in shock.

Chris continued to sing songs from the album. In order. While Charlie played them. In Charlie's head, his parents danced to the music. The whole album. But that black and white television continued to play in the corner. No volume? Could that be correct?

No.

An old hi-fi. A TV. A stereo. A turntable. All in a single cabinet. When you turned it on, green light glowed from the dials.

A record played.

Could it be Chris's record? Chris seemed almost old enough to have an album in the sixties. But it couldn't have been the sixties. Charlie hadn't been born until 1990.

None of it made any sense.

They arrived at the close. "A Hundred Years from Today." How did he know this song? This series of songs? He'd never played any of them except "You're Nobody 'til Somebody Loves You."

At the end. Six exactly. The men on their feet. Not for dinner or Charlie, but for Chris. This room of old men knew Chris. Christopher Marlowe.

Charlie drank his beer as the men mobbed the queen.

After a while, after Derek invited him to dinner and Charlie declined, using what had happened as his excuse (Chris didn't want dinner with the man, either), Charlie and Chris and Patsy were at the little bar. Chris drank bourbon, a triple. Charlie, one of his many banked beers. Patsy had her hands deep in the dishwater, washing glasses.

"So, I have to ask, how do you know Rusty Warren's album?" Chris asked. So sweet, her hair, brilliant red, perfectly quaffed. Her nails and lips fire-engine red. Put together. Not like their first meeting.

"I don't know who you are talking about," said Charlie. Something caught his eye, there, in the doorway of the lounge, Quinn, pacing in the lobby, looking into the lounge each time he passed the doorway.

"We just did the last half of her album, *Rusty Warren Sings Portrait of Life*."

"Honestly, I don't know her, don't know the album." Charlie drank down the rest of his beer and Patsy placed a fresh one in front of him.

"It's not possible to know that order of songs and those short arrangements from any other source," said Chris. She took a sip of bourbon.

That flash once more of Charlie's mother and father dancing, Charlie certain now they were his parents. "I have a memory from childhood. I was really young. My parents danced to those songs."

"Now we're getting somewhere," said Chris.

"I thought you didn't like Patsy," Charlie blurted out.

"Whatever gave you that idea?" asked Patsy.

The two stared at Charlie, waiting for an answer. He said, "That old cunt."

Both Patsy and Chris burst into laughter.

Once more that evening, Charlie had no idea what the fuck

was going on. He wanted to know, and he also wanted to get the hell out of there.

Quinn passed the doorway again.

Charlie wondered what would happen if he didn't go uptown to play at Coffee Haus. He liked the intimacy with Jasper but wanted more. So much more, physically. Yet, he didn't know how to ask for what he wanted. He'd tried many times to initiate sex with Jasper, and it just hadn't happened. Not since the blowjob he gave. They'd never climaxed together.

"Patsy and I worked together a very long time ago. There was a bit in the show. It was sort of a burlesque skit, in that style, and the punchline was 'That old cunt,'" said Chris.

"Very risqué," said Patsy through laughter induced tears. "We've been laughing about that for—"

"Give away our ages and I'll never drink your booze again," said Chris with a raised, empty glass.

Patsy didn't finish and instead filled Chris's glass with at least a generous double.

"You're very good," said Chris. "I play most afternoons at Tilde's."

"Around the corner?" asked Patsy. "Since when?"

"Since, well, you know Tamburlaine burned down. I started playing at Tilde's shortly after that."

"So sorry about your club." Patsy poured more bourbon into Chris's glass and some into a glass of her own. "And Elmor."

They toasted the old bar, the lost lover, a long-shared past.

Charlie knew these places. Tilde's and Tamburlaine were New York City institutions. Yet, he'd never noticed Hotel de Chanson before. To be fair, the entrance was a little tucked in.

"You can come in any afternoon you like, and we'll do some songs together. I haven't sung with a guitar in…well, a very long time." Chris drank off her bourbon and held out her glass. Patsy filled Chris's glass before opening Charlie a beer.

Charlie finished his beer, he'd lost count. He pushed one of his many empty shot glasses forward. What would Coffee Haus patrons think? What did it matter? They hadn't heard of him three nights ago. He accepted his beer.

"Charlie, you should come with me to dinner," said Chris. "I know a little Italian place nearby and I'd love to take you to dinner—a musician should always be paid."

"Is Salvatore's still open?" asked Patsy. "That's a place from the wayback machine. We are just a couple of old cunts."

"Yes, we are." They toasted again with the clink of crystal. "And yes, it is."

"Can I come along, too?" asked Patsy. I'll be done here in just a few minutes.

"That would be lovely. We can get caught up or tell old stories or hit on men like the old days," said Chris.

"To the old days." They clinked glasses and drank more bourbon.

Quinn passed by the doorway again.

"I think I need to take care of something," said Charlie.

"You can join us if your something allows." Chris wrote cross streets on a bev nap and shoved the paper into Charlie's pocket.

"It's really been great," said Charlie. He leaned over and kissed Chris on a powdered cheek.

"It has, dear boy," said Chris. "Always a gentleman."

Charlie slung his guitar case over his back, pocketed the bills Patsy shoved at him, and headed out of the lounge.

FORTY-TWO

As he exited the lounge, Charlie almost ran into Quinn who paced the lobby.

"We really need to talk," said Quinn. His eyes showed desperation…or fear?

"What? What is it?" Charlie held out his hands to keep some distance between them.

"Not here. Not in front of all these…people."

The empty lobby surrounded them. Only a desk clerk across the room, and Patsy and Chris in the lounge cackling together.

"Can we go up to your room?" asked Quinn.

"Ah, no. How do you know…I must have said something while on stage."

"Let's go have a drink. I know a quiet place," said Quinn.

"Okay. I need my coat. Wait here." Charlie reached for the elevator button as the doors opened.

Derek stepped out. "Change your mind about dinner?" he asked.

"Sorry, no. I look forward to dinner with you again, but I have something to deal with tonight." He glanced toward Quinn.

Derek nodded and he and Charlie switched positions. Charlie hit the button for his floor and returned to the lobby a few minutes later, his jacket on, his scarf around his neck, his guitar over his back.

"Do you go anywhere without that?" asked Quinn.

"Why does my life annoy you? No. It goes everywhere. It is me."

They walked out onto the street, the air biting into Charlie's fingers. He shoved them deep into his coat pockets and decided it was time to find gloves. Sometimes, he got lucky. Found a pair on a subway seat or left behind in a diner. There were often guys on the street selling pairs for a few dollars. Those frayed and fell apart, but they were cheap and easy to replace.

Quinn directed them, silently navigating around and through the people on the street. The bewitching hour in The Village. The last of the daily commuters returning home, the first of the night's revelers leaving Happy Hour, headed to parties and shows and events or dinner. The air wasn't exactly festive, but anticipation charged.

He touched his scarf. The cold gnawed into him.

He wondered when he'd eaten last? The roast beef sandwich?

After a few turns, Quinn held the door of an old, local, straight place, on the edge of The Village. Classic neighborhood place with a long, beat-up bar, lots of wobbly stools, floors seemingly clean, yet lightly sticky. They sat at the end, near the window, as far away from the other patron sitting near the register nursing a beer.

When the bartender approached, Quinn said, "Scotch neat." He turned to Charlie, "Want something?"

"Draft? Got Yuengling?" Charlie asked.

"Sure," said the bartender.

Quinn already had money out.

They remained silent; waited for their drinks.

Charlie's stomach flipped. What the hell was this about? He decided to do what he did, drink a beer, go with the flow, see what happened next.

The bartender delivered drinks, took Quinn's cash, returned with change.

Charlie sipped the beer. Cold. Little ice crystals on the frosty mug. A perfect head of suds. If he'd had a mustache, it would have left a bit of foam. He licked his upper lip. "Thanks," he finally said.

"What? Oh, you're welcome." Quinn made a cheers gesture with his glass and swallowed the scotch down in a single effort. His hands shook, his fingers long and splayed like Charlie's. "Another," he directed to the bartender.

Going with the flow, Charlie drank more of the cold beer. A

clock near the register read 6:37. He could still get uptown and play for a while before Coffee Haus closed.

Quinn sipped from his second glass. "You're okay?" he pointed at Charlie's beer.

"What is going on?"

"Listen. I wasn't really sure about this. When I saw you, that night in the little park by the Stonewall. I took you to dinner..."

What did Quinn expect? "Yes. I remember. It was like last week. Ten days?" Damn. Life could change in a moment. "It Only Takes a Moment" from *Hello, Dolly!* ran through his head.

"Well, I had a feeling then. When I heard you. When I saw your eyes." Quinn tried to drink more scotch from the empty glass.

Charlie drank beer, taking this ride as it came.

"I..." Quinn held his glass up in the air for another. The bartender there with the bottle. He sorted through the bills on the bar and took what he needed. Charlie pushed at his glass. Quinn drank some more. "Okay. Here goes. I...I think I'm your father." He let out a huge sigh and finally looked Charlie directly in the eyes.

He'd run into this kind of shit before. People wanting things from him. Playing him. Working on the street and living on the fringes of life, you met strange motherfuckers. He finished his beer. If he tried to leave, the guy might do something rash. Best to keep the movements slow and even. He was glad he'd kept his coat on, his guitar over his back. He could slip away without much planning or effort.

The bartender placed a fresh mug of beer before Charlie and took the remaining cash.

"I know it sounds crazy," said Quinn. "I know you probably have other stories."

Charlie nodded. Finished his beer. Pushed it to the well for another. The bartender responded without words. Charlie pulled out the fold of bills Patsy had given him, but Quinn shoved several twenties on the bar.

"I got this," he said. "When you played what you played tonight. When that queen sang with you, she sounded just like her."

Intrigued, Charlie asked, "Just like who?"

"Rusty Warren. She had this low, sultry kind of voice. A lot of women did in the sixties, early seventies."

"Who is this woman?" Chris had never heard of Rusty Warren before and now everyone around him was talking about her.

The words came out of Quinn in a rush. "The music you played, in the order you played it, it's from one of Rusty's albums. She was a dirty comic back in the day. She also sang in her act. Usually funny stuff. Like 'Knockers Up.' But she'd close her sets and some of her albums with the same stuff everyone else was singing then. A lot of nightclub performers sang, and they sang a lot of the same songs. Rusty made an album of those songs and your mother and I listened to it over and over. We'd dance to it when I got home from work. It's one of my favorite memories. You were there, in your playpen, you were just a baby, barely had any words. Barely could stand up on your own. You were just learning how to say 'mama' one of those nights. We were a nice family."

The words he spoke fit Charlie's memories, the images he'd had in his head. How could that be? Some psychic trick or magic trick? It made no sense. This old queen was his father? Maybe he wasn't a queen. Perhaps Charlie's gaydar was off about Quinn, just like it had been with all those older men at the hotel.

"I know it sounds…it must sound…." Quinn finished off his drink. The bartender returned with another beer, generously refilled Quinn's glass from the bottle. Quinn leaned back.

"But you're dead," said Charlie.

"Well, your mother is. She…" Quinn sighed again. "She had a tubal pregnancy and they couldn't save her. I went out of my mind with grief. Your aunt took you. Your mother's sister. It was just supposed to be for a little while. But she moved away with you, and I couldn't find her. She never liked me. We fought a lot. She didn't think I was good enough for your mom. Milo always said we shouldn't have married. Mabel harped on the interracial marriage…"

"Milo? Mable?"

"Your mother's parents. Milo and Mable."

"Wait. You lost me?" Tears dropped from Charlie's eyes. "How does that…" He stood up, his legs were wobbled, his knees didn't work, his feet numb. He attempted to wiggle his toes, but it was as if they weren't there. Charlie sat back down. He tugged at the scarf around his neck. Milo? It couldn't be the same Milo. The weight of the guitar on his back grounded him. The guitar. The only thing that made any sense in his life. Had ever made any sense. His love of music had come from that time…his parents dancing night after night to the same album of songs by the Warren woman.

"I…"

He'd never known his parents' names. Never seen a birth certificate. The state had created a new one for him. They had no idea who he was. They'd named him. At first, he was "Little Boy Doe." Later, because he loved Willy Wonka, someone had chosen Charlie. He didn't like Bucket for a last name, so he chose Dillon. He'd fallen in love with Bob Dylan's music and chose Dillon. He spelled it wrong, but only because he didn't know how Dylan spelled his name. He learned most things in life by hearing.

Charlie didn't know what to say.

"We could get blood tests, prove the DNA. They do that now." Quinn set his glass down. It wasn't empty.

"I have so many questions, but…" Charlie drank off his beer. "I think I need to not be here with you. Not right now."

"We should talk about—"

"You know where I live. You know where I play. Maybe tomorrow or the next day we can talk. I just can't…not right now." Charlie stood up once more and his legs worked, basically. "Thanks for the beer."

"Charlie, wait."

He turned back. "What was my name? When you…"

“It was Charlie. You’re Charlie Bellow.”

He repeated it: “Charlie Bellow.” He looked toward the clock by the register. Did he want to see Jasper tonight. There would be so many questions. They only talked and drank. He did want arms around him. But he wanted to forget the world and fuck. One-night stands provided more than this relationship.

“I like your choice of Dylan.”

“And my mother’s name?” asked Charlie.

“Farber. Mary Farber.

“Mary Farber. Mary and Quinn Bellow. Charlie Bellow.” Charlie headed out onto the street. A dead brother or sister. He stopped, looked back through the window. He studied Quinn watching him; Charlie wanting and expecting more, a lifetime of longing that had never been met or filled with anything. Here was Quinn’s opportunity: wasted.

His father’s opportunity to...what?

After a moment of searching Quinn’s face, seeing his father’s eyes, a less brilliant blue version of his own eyes—he could see that now—Charlie walked away into the brutally cold night.

FORTY-THREE

Charlie buzzed from information...and beer. He'd had a lot of beer. What did knowing his name, Charlie Bellow, change? What did having a father who was alive change? A father who'd abandoned him by choice. By choice, not death.

His own father had walked out on him. His mother dead.

When you're an orphan, you make up stories about who your parents were or might have been—Charlie flashed once more on the scene he'd found, a scene that turned out to be real, a scene that was now burned in his head because a drag queen had brought it to life, a scene that, of course, brought music into his life. The joy of that moment.

He saw, again, his father's greasy, cigarette-stained hand touching his own head. Love flowing between his father and mother, flowing from them to him. Ma-ma, he heard in his head as that woman singer sang and his parents danced.

A mother who died from a pregnancy. He'd have had a brother or sister. His mother was probably pregnant when they danced in his memory. Maybe they were celebrating in his black and white memory. Why black and white?

A father who dumped him with an aunt.

There had been an aunt. Not later, but in the beginning.

An aunt who had dumped him in some way at some point into the system in New York City. Without even a name. What had happened to her?

They'd chosen his first name. Was she still Farber?

The memories were around us, inside us, part of us whether we know that or not.

So cold. The air frigid and biting cold. Charlie tugged his scarf tighter around his neck before digging his hands deep into his pockets. He wanted to be hugged, but not by Jasper. God, he had to pee. All that beer.

Finding a place to pee in New York City: the ultimate challenge. Most places didn't let you pee unless you buy something. The savvy New Yorker knew there were places available. You just had to know about them.

Charlie took in his surroundings. He'd wandered north. He'd walked more than twenty blocks already. Chelsea. Not many choices unless he went into a bar where the bouncers were quick to kick you out. He could buy a beer. Seven dollars to pee?

A window of socks. Bright storefront. Charlie entered, selected a pair of dark blue, thick, wool socks. Paid. Sat on a display bench right in the store, changed his socks in front of an annoyed clerk, and headed out to the street where he draped the holey pair over the edge of a trashcan.

Grand Central Station, further north and a little east, had public restrooms on the lower level. Sometimes gross. Sometimes creepy. But public, and free.

There was also a good bar there. Tourist expensive, but an okay place to sit and have a drink for a moment. A place where no one would know him. He might run into a trick or someone in a Chelsea bar. But Grand Central? Only for tourists. He went deep into the terminal to the restroom and peed, washed his hands. Avoided his eyes in the mirrors. He came back upstairs, through the wonderful lobby with the backward constellations, and headed up the marble staircase, out onto Vanderbilt Avenue, and into The Campbell. A cavernous space.

"Good evening, sir, do you have a reservation?"

"No, hoping to have a drink at the bar," said Charlie. What was he doing here? He didn't know.

The young woman led him toward the bar, where there were several spaces open. She nodded. He took off his guitar and sat. A young bartender asked what he wanted and poured him a beer in a tall glass. Around him the room buzzed.

Again, he asked himself what he was doing there. In this swanky, expensive place.

Charlie had no answer for himself. He was there. He did like the energy of the room. The buzz and clamor. The big windows out into the night. Like a secret haven.

He'd been tossed from The Campell many, many years before. Not really tossed, just not admitted. The hostess tonight gave him the once over but allowed him in all the same. Age certainly helped with some things. Choosing good shoes. That was really the key he'd figured out. When he wore ratty sneakers, he didn't get into places. When he started buying sturdy leather shoes and boots that held up well and looked nicer, he got in places. And there was the fabulous scarf that brought out his eyes.

His eyes. He wondered if they amplified his sadness and fear and anger.

Charlie sipped his beer, didn't rush.

His father.

What the actual fuck?

He reasoned he could simply get on a train. He had money. He'd made a lot over the past two weeks and hadn't gotten to the bank recently. All that cash, from Happy Hours and Coffee Haus, was all wadded up in his pants and jacket and even in his guitar case. He usually didn't store money there. Too easy to have the thing stolen and he'd lose it all. But there was so much from the coffee shop nights and from Patsy.

Charlie could go anywhere. It was freezing cold now. Too cold. He wasn't getting what he wanted from Jasper. Not even losses to cut. For some unexplained reason, he felt used by Patsy and didn't trust her. Even if the room was nice and the bathtub wonderful. With the money she paid. The extra. The beer. He felt like, what? A house pet.

Horrible feeling.

Quinn and Christopher Marlowe and Patsy and Jasper and Derek…they all wanted something from him.

He sipped his beer and the bartender asked if he wanted another. He did, so he had one.

He could just get on a train. He had his Seagull, so there wasn't even a reason to ever return to the Hotel de Chanson.

Go south or west. Be in Florida within a day or two. He could be in New Orleans. Atlanta. Miami. Las Vegas. Phoenix. San Francisco. San Diego. Those other places would be better than Florida with their creepy governor and all the hate laws.

As he finished his beer, the bartender placed a fresh glass before him.

Charlie asked for a check and paid it before he'd finished his second beer. Although, at these prices, he'd sit and finish the second. Drink every expensive drop. Decide what came next?

FORTY-FOUR

When Charlie departed The Campbell, he didn't get on a train to New Orleans or Miami, or points west, even though a few weeks in Key West appealed to him. The politics in Florida didn't warrant his spending money there.

He snuggled into his jacket, wrapped the long scarf one more time around his neck, and headed north. The only comfort: the guitar pressed to his back, as his instrument braced his backbone, offered courage. No matter what happened, he could go anywhere and play anywhere and he'd be okay. He had money in his pockets. He had money in the bank. He'd be okay. He'd lived his whole life without a second pair of shoes; without a father; without a history. Why did he need one now?

Why indeed.

He found himself farther north, in Midtown, at the Milo's Pub. Charlie looked in the window. Milo was there. Could he really be his grandfather?

The steam tables steamed. It was late and there weren't many patrons. His stomach grumbled.

Charlie entered. Milo greeted him warmly. Tears rose into Charlie's eyes.

"What is it? Need a beer? Some food? That scarf looks terrific on you, brings out your eyes. Those intoxicating blue eyes."

Before Charlie could answer, Milo had a draft beer pulled and ready for him at the end of the bar. His stomach growled and Charlie tried to remember the last time he'd eaten. He pulled out a bill and set it on the bar. He heaped a plate with stuffed cabbage rolls and mashed potatoes. The real deal, lumps and all.

"Good. Eat. You have some money, good for you." Milo took the twenty and brought back change. "You okay, son?" The old man's eyes had progressed to dark yellow. Terrible looking.

Instead of asking questions, Charlie stuffed his mouth with food so he didn't have to answer. It tasted good. Hearty. Warming. This was all he needed. Some food from a steam table. A beer. A nice guy to remember him. "Do you have the time?" Charlie choked out through his swallow.

"About nine-thirty. Got a gig somewhere?"

"Something like that."

"Good." Milo went down the bar to get a drink for another patron.

Charlie ate more food. Filled his belly. He went back to the table for a third helping. No one stopped him. It was good to be full, especially after all the beer he'd consumed, especially after meeting his...Quinn. Food fixed something in his emotions. Well, if it didn't fix it, it smothered it with a layer of tomato gravy.

If he left now, took a cab, or even the subway, which was right below him, it rumbled the floor at that very moment, he could be uptown in time to maybe play a few songs, to see Jasper. He wanted arms around him. He wanted...

Something about that relationship had died and he didn't know why. The lack of sex. There certainly was plenty of intimacy. You can't bathe with a man and not feel intimate. But he wanted to fuck. Needed to fuck someone. He could go back to the hotel. Just about any old man there would gladly open their door to Charlie. No questions asked. Hell, they'd probably pay him without a word about it. It's what happened at Hotel de Chanson.

He didn't want some old man, not at this moment, not tonight. He absently reached in his coat and discovered the bev nap with the cross streets.

He'd missed the dinner invitation with Chris and Patsy, but that was okay. They certainly would have bought, but he'd have had to listen to old stories and the cackles of two old cunts. No appeal tonight.

What Charlie wanted...what did he want?

Answers.

Sure.

So what. He'd wanted answers his whole life. He'd gotten some and they didn't change a thing.

What he wanted...

To hit Quinn?

Sure. It hurt to know your father dumped you. Had hurt for thirty-seven years. Would probably continue to hurt even if he did pop the guy. He'd probably hurt himself and then what? Not be able to play? Let his father take away music, too?

He drank down his beer and Milo had another in front of him before Charlie set the glass down.

"What can I do for you, Charlie?"

"Milo, giving me this scarf is the nicest thing anyone has ever done for me. What more could I ask for?" Charlie sipped the cold cheap beer. It tasted good. Like home.

Home.

What the hell did that word mean?

"I have something that you might want." Milo went to the front of the bar, picked up that ratty Lost-n-Found cardboard box. "How about some new gloves?" He extracted a pair of very expensive leather gloves from the top and brought them to Charlie. "See if these fit."

They did. They were lined with fleece and very warm, but still lightweight and comfortable. "It's okay if I take these?"

"People lose their shit all the time. They are yours."

Charlie sipped beer, swallowing away the lump in his throat, as well as the tears that wanted to spill.

"Get enough to eat? If not, load up another plateful." Milo went back to the other patrons and served them.

Charlie flexed his hands in the gloves before taking them off and drinking more beer. He went back to the steam table and filled another plate with stuffed cabbage rolls.

He wouldn't be going uptown tonight.

"You're him," said a young guy walking by with a heaping plate of mashed potatoes. Only potatoes."

"Who?" asked Charlie, amused.

"The guitar guy." He snapped his fingers and snapped them again. "Coffee Haus Charlie." He pulled out his phone, thumbed the screen several times, and Charlie singing Simon and Garfunkel's "50th Street Bridge Song" blared through the tinny device speaker.

A moment of the song and two girls rushed him at the bar shouting: "Charlie!"

Less than ten minutes and Milo's Pub filled with people. Minute by minute passed and the place packed to standing room only.

Charlie considered walking out. His world grown overwhelming. He already had enough money to winter somewhere warm. If he got on a Greyhound, he could just ride in silence for days.

"What is this?" Milo asked Charlie. "They're here for you? Then you should play. We should charge a cover, boy."

Charlie unzipped his guitar case. He owed Milo a song.

FORTY-FIVE

The old bar filled with more people than Charlie had ever seen in it. All of them clamoring for Coffee Haus Charlie. He liked the alliteration.

Behind the bar, Milo smiled broadly and served up beers and cocktails and bottles of water. Charlie couldn't be certain, but from the overheard fragments, it seemed the prices had gone up by a multiple of two or three.

He unwrapped his scarf, careful to tuck it into his coat. He didn't want to lose it in the place he'd received it. He shoved the new gloves into a coat pocket.

Young people wolfed down the remains from the old steam table. Food like their grandmothers or rather great grandmothers must have made. Charlie, glad now that he'd gotten to eat the stuffed cabbage rolls, the lumpy mashed potatoes, the red sauce to his heart's content.

The cook brought out more and more food and the people, nearly all of them were young, ate heaping platefuls. None of them would have ever entered a dive bar like Milo's, but here they were, because he was here. Because they'd watched some online video of him singing Simon and Garfunkel songs as he tried to impress, or rather seduce, a guy.

But how did they know he was here?

For a moment, he thought of Jasper, but pushed the image away. Not ready to face it. He found himself tuning his guitar. Sitting on a tall stool at the end of the noisy bar. Glasses of booze picked up the harsh bright light from the dusty overhead fixtures. He wondered what to play for these people, these... followers. Amazed at how the world worked. That they'd seen a video someone posted of him and now followed the real him around like others had the Grateful Dead…or so he'd heard.

For most, the point of performing: developing a following, making money. Making albums those fans bought, giving concerts they purchased tickets for. Selling programs and merch. Charlie performed because he loved playing and could make enough money from it to live a life of anonymity. Not being chased around New York City on a frigid night. How had they found him here? In Milo's?

The Seagull now tuned, he strummed a G chord. Then D. He let his mind wonder. Normally, he'd have a song pop up. He thought about the afternoon. About his newly discovered father. About the old drag queen knowing every song he sang. All those old songs surfacing with a memory that caught him, trapped him. Maybe he should have gotten on a train south or west. Maybe he still would. He could certainly walk out right now and get on a train, but he feared if he did that this crowd, this mob, would follow him.

No song came.

Was this it? Was it over for good?

Every chair now filled, every stool wobbling under the weight of its occupant. People who drank and ate and waited in anticipation. This bar had no closing time, not like Coffee Haus. There was no out. By sitting in the back corner, he'd trapped himself in the room. By taking out his guitar, he'd given the sign he'd perform for these strangers.

Isn't that what he did? Who he was?

Why hesitate?

He liked to play, to sing. So much had happened in the past few hours. So much.

Charlie strummed an Fm7.

People applauded in encouragement. Others picked up the idea and also applauded, like when the conductor comes out onstage at a symphony. The audience appreciative, anticipation in the air.

He breathed in the scent of humanity. All those young, hyperactive bodies in winter coats, now sluffed off in the steamy room. Cabbage and bodies and beer and perfume and

Axe Body Spray.

He launched into, "Friends in Low Places." He sang and imagined a handsome, youthful Garth Brooks in those tight Levi's.

The audience quieted. Many filmed on raised phones. More content. Isn't that what people talked about. Content.

Milo placed a fresh beer next to Charlie. He positioned an old, chipped, glass, gallon beet jar with "Tips" written on it, on the corner of the bar.

While he sang, people started shoving money into the jar. Not just dollars, but fives and twenties. It made no sense. When he played on the street, he was lucky to make enough for dinner and a beer. Now, playing inside, because of a few videos on YouTube, people dumped money as if they were buying a concert ticket.

He wondered why the large sums bothered him. They'd paid for those expensive beers at The Campbell. They afforded him the luxury of a taxicab ride. They'd buy him a new pair of shoes, which he wanted and needed. He wiggled his toes. They'd buy a new pair of socks without a hole.

The raucous applause when he finished covered him drinking down half the draft beer. He caught a smile from Milo. So, Charlie sang Milo's late wife's favorite song: "Autumn Leaves." Not the best transition song, but he wanted to do something nice for the bar owner who had treated him so well. Who'd given him the nice gloves. Who'd given him his scarf. Who'd fed him when his day of work hadn't earned the price of dinner and a beer at the steam-table bar. And like the other song, like all the songs he'd been playing lately in front of these crowds, dozens recorded it. Some would post it. Some probably already had.

The tip jar filled: not a single coin.

The steam table once more emptied of food and the cook brought out more. Steaming cabbage scented the air in a not unpleasant way.

That tune led him into "Wake Me Up When September Ends." The Tim Hill song popular with this crowd, they went nuts, quieted, then about took the roof off the place when Charlie finished.

The tip jar overflowed with cash. Hundred-dollar bills now among the twenties and fives and singles.

Charlie breathed in the steam, joy bubbling up. Yet, he missed the anonymity of playing in Central Park all afternoon. Of barely being seen. Of thirty minutes of showtunes in Duffy Square. Now, all eyes and cameras and phones were on him. Coffee Haus Charlie.

His nickname would forever be paired with Jasper's shop.

Milo placed a fresh beer near him. "Play as long as you want. When you're done, be done."

The advice touched something deep inside Charlie. Milo had been more of a father to him than Quinn ever had. Perhaps his actual grandfather. Had been kind long before Charlie had gone viral. He thought now of the new leather gloves in his coat pockets. A gift from Milo. Of the scarf. Of his belly filled with good, hearty food. What had Quinn ever done for him but dumped him as a baby?

In deciding not to push Milo for answers, he'd decided to allow this kind old man to be who he'd always been to Charlie, a kind old man.

He found himself singing the John Mayer song, "Daughters."

People in the room softly sang along. This would be a good song to end—

Something drew Charlie's eyes to the front door, over the heads of the packed room, Jasper stared on, the look of hurt etched into his eyes, onto his face.

Charlie chose to sing Elle King's "Ex's & Oh's." He wondered what he and Jasper owed each other.

Because it had become something of a signature, a song the crowd would understand, Charlie played through the applause and began "Closing Time." There were groans from the audience because they did know the meaning. They swayed as he played, they sang along on the chorus.

When he looked up again, Jasper was gone from the door, replaced by two of New York's finest. Pain ran tight through

Charlie's belly. He feared he would puke up the mountain of cabbage and meat and potatoes right then and there. He had ignored his last ticket, although he now had the money to pay the fine. He just didn't want another one, didn't want a long record in New York. That would be held against him at some point.

He didn't know if he wanted to be taken home by anyone tonight.

Home.

What the hell did that word really mean?

He finished the song. People applauded like crazy. Charlie quickly cased his guitar. He couldn't do anything with the tip jar. People were still shoving bills into it. There were other things in there, too. Notes. Little cards.

Milo went to the door, he spoke with the police as patrons wormed their way past them and out of the bar. So much talk. So much chatter.

Charlie finished a beer and started on another full one that had grown warm, the glass slick with condensation.

People wanted selfies. Charlie hated the attention. He obliged, trapped as he was in the corner, while continuing to pack up and dress, coat, long scarf wrapped round and round, and finally, guitar case hugging his back. The walls closed in. He needed fresh air, air not tinged with cabbage and tomatoes and Axe Body Spray.

Milo patted the back of one of the policemen as they left the bar with the line of young people. Glasses and dirty plates and debris cluttered the tables. Milo smiled toward Charlie and gave him two thumbs up. Then motioned for him to wait.

Charlie wanted out.

"Want a bump, Charlie?" Milo had asked.

"Sure. Jack?"

Milo poured two shots. They each drank one. The alcohol burned all the way down to his toes and the burn felt good. He thought again of the drag queen and wished, on some level, that he'd gone to dinner with her.

"Anytime you need a warm place to play, you're more than

welcome here," said Milo. He refilled both their shot glasses.

They drank.

Together, they quickly sorted and counted the bills. Milo converted the small bills into larger ones. "I can use the singles," he said.

"I gotta go," said Charlie.

"Go," said Milo who downed a third shot.

Charlie made it out of the bar. The strangest thing, like a switch had been hit. One moment the center of attention, the clamor of attention, the next, everyone done with him. Charlie appreciated that. On the street, he thought he might stop by the TKTX booth and play a song or two. Then reconsidered. Not in this frigid cold air. Not with all this cash on his person.

He knew there was a bank branch nearby. He popped into the lobby and made a deposit. Not all of his cash, but the money he'd most recently shoved into his pockets from the beet jar, from Patsy, from the previous night at Jasper's. The machine counted it for him. Two thousand seventy-seven dollars.

His heart pounded in his chest, hard and fast. He again worried he'd puke.

Next decision: uptown or down? Home or train west or Jasper. Charlie pulled the warm gloves onto his hands.

"Great set," called a guy.

Charlie nodded. It wasn't his best set. It didn't flow. The songs weren't connected. He didn't talk and people didn't care. They liked him. They rewarded him with a mountain of cash. He'd offered some of it to Milo, who only pushed the bills back at him.

Charlie headed downtown. Three girls accosted him for selfies. He let them take their pictures and then hailed a cab. Inside the warm car, he thought again about what he wanted.

He had no answer.

The cabbie pulled away from the curb. "Where to?"

Charlie hesitated, then gave the downtown cross streets where he'd left her that first night.

FORTY-SIX

The cab slowed on the gloomy block. "Sure you want out here?" He stopped near the burned-out building.

"No, around that corner. About halfway down," said Charlie.

The cab turned and drove and stopped.

Charlie paid the fare, grabbed his axe, and jumped out onto the cold street. He watched the taillights fade and extinguish before pushing the button by the door.

He'd about given up on an answer, when he heard the now familiar voice: "Yes?"

"It's me. Charlie."

"Yes. The guitar player. Come on back."

The door buzzed and Charlie pulled it open. It swung easily. He went down a dark alley into a little patio where twinkle lights twinkled. A door opened.

"My boy! What a surprise. Come in. It's freeze-your-tits-off cold out here."

"That it is, Chris." Charlie realized he didn't know why he'd come.

"Would you like coffee or tea or something stronger?" Chris asked, already busying herself in the kitchen.

"Coffee *and* something stronger?" asked Charlie.

"My kind of man. Take off your coat. You can set your instrument down if you want. Oh, I love your scarf. It truly enhances your amazing eyes. Men must get lost in those eyes."

Warmth traveled through Charlie in an uncomfortable way. He stripped off his gloves and sluffed off his coat; he unwrapped his scarf and piled everything up on the kitchen chair he'd rested his guitar against. Above him, a turquoise cat clock with eyes and tail swiping back and forth, watched over him. He admired the walls covered with hundreds of *Playbill* covers.

"Well, the coffee will take a few, but here, let's start with this." Chris handed Charlie a tumbler with several fingers of bourbon from an expensive looking bottle.

Charlie took a sip of the smoothest whiskey he'd ever sampled. Worthy of sipping, not just getting through for the effects to come.

"Carry this right around the corner." Chris had mugs and a glossy white moo cow creamer and a sugar bowl with actual lumps of sugar and delicate cookies on a China plate circled with delicate flowers, all on a big wooden tray with handles.

That's when he heard it, one of the songs he'd played earlier that day: "You're Nobody 'til Somebody Loves You." A woman singing, a woman with a deep voice. That voice. The same one from the hi-fi in his black and white memory.

He carried the tray toward the voice and cups clattered when he placed it on the coffee table and took in the strange room. The walls like the set of a play, hanging from the tall ceiling by wires. The furniture stuffed and comfortable looking. He sipped more whiskey. On the wall, a little sketch he would have sworn was a da Vinci. And that woman sang.

"Sit, sit," said Chris. He carried the coffee pot and filled their mugs.

"Who is this singing?"

"That is Rusty Warren, my dear boy."

Again that name.

"She was huge in the sixties and seventies. Retired before the internet and all that. She was bigger than just about anyone in her day. Died not too long ago. All but forgotten now."

The song changed to "Life Is Just a Bowl of Cherries." He knew it before it came. The album of his memory.

"Why are you playing this? I mean we..." he sat down on one of the couches. "You sang these songs tonight." Charlie didn't often repeat songs, not close together. The exception had been his recent "Closing Time" buttons.

"I'm always listening to Rusty. This one and her comedy."

"Comedy?"

"Oh yes, that's what she's really known for. Do you want to hear some of it?" Chris had a remote in hand and changed what played.

An introduction. Then the woman talked. Talked about men being peacocks. Talked about peanut butter cookies and looking at boy's dicks. About sex. Her style casual. Easy. Comfortable. Funny.

Without comment or conversation, they'd listened to a whole routine about dirty pictures and cub scouts and a trucker and knockers being up and...a whole album worth of comedy. All the while, Chris had a wistful smile on her face, lost in the world. Short red hair. A colorful kimono. Slippers with bunny ears.

The coffee had grown cold. The bourbon bottle nearly emptied. The cookies, so delicious, little lemon shortbread cookies that melted on your tongue, eaten.

Together they drank and laughed at all the right places, as they listened to the famous woman Charlie had never heard of perform.

At the conclusion of the routine, Chris said, "That, my dear boy, is my favorite Rusty Warren album. Sexplosion. My favorite of her routines."

"I see why you love her so much."

"Love her? I admire her so much I became her. In a manner of speaking. Built my whole career imitating her. And have loved every minute of it."

Charlie sipped more whiskey. He still didn't know why he'd been drawn to Chris, a queen in waiting to the proverbial torch singer.

"What is it, Charlie? I'm sure this isn't a booty call." Chris laughed in a comfortable, charming way. "What can I help you with?"

"I don't know. I just wanted to be here, with you. I loved playing for you tonight."

"You're so good," said Chris.

Embarrassed by the compliment, Charlie didn't reply as

heat enveloped his ears.

"Patsy showed me some of your videos. Tens of thousands of views for Coffee Haus Charlie. I'm not a fan of the name, though."

"They made it up."

"They?" asked Chris.

"Whoever posted those videos."

"Well, people love you. You could turn all of this into your fifteen minutes."

Charlie had heard about the fifteen minutes of fame. He wished it would already be over. "I don't have any interest in being famous. I just want to play and earn my keep. It's really about the playing."

"I understand," said Chris.

"Maybe that's...I don't know why I've come to you. I appreciate your kindness...I think I should just go." Charlie made the motions of standing; he didn't stand. "I...I got some shocking news tonight."

Chris nodded. Her full attention focused on Charlie, almost like the hug he sought. Like a huge hug, even though they hadn't touched.

"My father who abandoned me found me. He didn't work to find me, but sort of came across me and decided to tell me." Charlie sipped at an empty glass. "I met a guy recently, a nice guy; it's not really working out." He leaned forward and Chris poured another generous shot into the glass. "Patsy has been nice to me, but I don't really trust her." Chris held out her glass. "I know she's your friend..." Charlie poured more. "I guess I don't know who to trust."

"You certainly shouldn't trust Patsy. She'd sell you without batting an eye." Chris's voice was even and warm and kind. "Well, in Patsy's case, she'd rent you out." Chris cackled in a delightful, dark way. "It's been my experience, and I'm much older than you, much older than most, that the only person we can ever truly trust is ourselves. Everyone else has their own agenda and it's not your best interest driving that. Don't get me wrong, there are some very nice people in the world.

But you're the only one you can truly count on." She pointed directly at Charlie's chest.

"So, what am I supposed to do?"

"I don't have the answer. You have to decide what you want. What's your agenda? With Patsy? With the maybe boyfriend? With your father? With me? What do you want out of your life?"

Charlie sat back on the plush sofa and studied his glass as if it were a crystal ball. The hint of a song from The Wiz tried to poke through his drunken fog. He coaxed it. It would not come. Finally, he said, "I honestly do not know."

"Well, my dear boy, my advice then is to do nothing. Don't make any choices. Don't force anything."

For the first time, no comedy or songs emitted from the unseen speakers.

The room fell silent.

Charlie cried.

Big, messy, embarrassing crocodile tears that dripped down his cheeks and onto his shirtfront. After a moment of crying, and it hadn't yet abated, Chris handed him a handkerchief. Not a tissue, but a scented piece of cloth embroidered with little flowers, dusty roses, just like on the cookie plate. She draped an arm over his shoulder, pulled him into her, and let him cry. She smelled of a light, sweet, lovely scent with a hint of roses.

She offered no reassurances or platitudes. Simply held him and let him cry.

FORTY-SEVEN

Charlie woke, hungover, in his own bed.

Alone.

The sun out, the light dim. Either cloudy or late in the afternoon or both. With effort, he turned his head toward the nightstand clock. Three in the afternoon if he could believe the device. He had to decide if he would play for Happy Hour or not. Patsy would be there. Quinn would probably be there. Derek would be inviting him to dinner.

The sad part of the story: there wouldn't really be time to take a bath. It would take thirty minutes just to fill the tub. He closed his eyes and stretched and scratched his stomach and scratched his balls.

Once in the bathroom, after he peed, he managed the shower attachment above the tub as best he could and rinsed off. So unsatisfying. He dried himself with one of the big bath sheets Jasper had left. He brushed his teeth. He put on his one remaining pair of clean underwear. When he pulled on his left sock, several toes poked through.

Charlie took a moment to sort out his money. Even after the big deposit, he still had a mountain of cash. Big rolls of bills came together to make big stacks. Almost three thousand dollars. Astonishing. He could go anywhere he wanted with this much cash on hand. He could even fly if he wanted. He'd never been on a plane.

He needed desperately to go to the bank and make a deposit. Too much time had slipped by to do that now.

Unless he didn't play Happy Hour.

That was an option.

Charlie thought of Chris. He couldn't remember how he'd

gotten home the night before. But he and his belongings all seemed perfectly intact. Anyway, he thought of Chris and his question. What do you want?

Charlie still didn't have an answer.

What he knew: he liked to play his guitar. He liked to sing. He liked having an audience. If he walked downstairs, he could do that for a room of gay men who appreciated him. He knew he could drink their appreciation. Deposit their appreciation in the bank. That seemed like the best choice for the moment.

With effort and skill, he broke all that money down into bits and pieces and stashed the rolls and folds throughout the pockets of what he wore, picked up his guitar, and headed out of the room toward the elevator.

FORTY-EIGHT

Charlie entered the lounge. It was empty. He stepped out into the lobby and asked the desk clerk why there wasn't anyone inside.

"It's Saturday, Charlie," he said with a kind smile. "No Happy Hour on Saturday.... Wait, there's a note for you." He retrieved a crisp, white envelope from the row of wood cubbies behind the counter.

"Saturday?" Charlie had lost a day or two or three. He'd never had to keep track of days or time, not since he dropped out of school. Not since he walked away from the last foster family, and from the system.

"Thank you." He took the sealed envelope. Thick paper. His name written neatly on the front. And without a better choice, he went back into the lounge. He sat in a chair at a little table, set his guitar to the side, opened the note.

"Charlie, Sorry to have disturbed your journey. You're immensely talented and I'm proud of you. I would like to talk. The choice is up to you. Quinn." Below his name, a 212 phone number. An old exchange. An exchange that proved he'd been in the city all along.

Derek popped his head in the lounge. "Hi, Charlie."

"Hi."

He stepped inside, came close, "Okay?"

"Don't know."

"Want to talk?"

"Don't know."

Silence enveloped them both.

His mind raced. He heard Milo, "When you're done, be done." Charlie wasn't done. He didn't want to stare at the water.

He thought again about the advice Christopher Marlowe had offered. What did he want? Charlie wanted to play. Not for a big room of people. He wanted a drink. Maybe a pizza. "Can you wrangle up a few beers?"

"Of course." Without ceremony, Derek walked to the bar, around it, and returned with two bottles of beer.

"Oh. Patsy won't mind?"

"No, she'll simply add it to the bill. It's what she does." He smiled as he said it, not at all bothered by the additions to the bill. He cracked open the bottles and sat down with Charlie at a little table.

Charlie pulled out his guitar. "Do you have a favorite song?"

Derek drank some beer. "There're lots I like. Mostly from when I was young. We sort of get stuck in our era. It's interesting that you know so many old songs, being so young."

Charlie hadn't been feeling all that young lately, but compared to Derek, who was twice his age, he realized age, like just about everything else, was a matter of perspective. He tuned his guitar, rolled up his left cuff a few turns, tuned a little more. Took a sip of beer "So, what, a little ABBA? Billy Joel? Diana Ross? Earth, Wind, and Fire?"

"Sure. All of them. God, I loved to go to the discos and dance. Men dressed in open shirts and tight, tight, very tight pants that left little to the imagination. We were fucking in the bath houses and bathrooms and alleys and enjoying a new freedom the generation before us built but never imagined." He drank some beer. "Then many of us died. Most of us. Sorry, I'm in the way-back machine."

"There's a song from then. It's still a hit in New Orleans." He started, "Love Is in the Air." As Charlie played, Derek was out of his chair and dancing, his eyes closed, hands in the air, hips moving in a way that Charlie worried the old man might break a hip.

"It's just like 1980. I came from a small Midwest town," Derek said during the building bridge. He sang along, 'Love is in the air." His hands waving above him.

While he played, Charlie said, "They do this thing with

napkins on the chorus at Café Lafitte's in New Orleans. Toss handful after handful of napkins into the air. The place rains with white bev naps." He went back to singing. A simple, easy, nice song. No genders. "Love is in the air."

He finished and went right into "Sail On."

"Oh, the Commodores. I loved this one, too." Darek sat, drank beer, swiped the beads of sweat from his liver spotted forehead. Listened. Attentively.

When Charlie looked up at the chorus, the older man watched him intensely. He sang the song, looked back down at his hands even though he didn't need to see them to form the correct chords. This song had gender. Another straight love song. Like most of them. Most all of them. By straight, white singers.

"Of course," said Derek while Charlie drank beer. "I also loved Romanovsky and Phillips."

He sang the intro of "Give Me a Homosexual."

Derek laughed. He sang along, "I like my lovers as queer as can be."

They sang the song quietly together and laughed at the end.

"They were what? The nineties?" said Charlie.

"Late eighties. We all had Flock of Seagulls haircuts and wore zippers. And died. So many of us died."

Charlie strummed a chord. He didn't speak. He didn't play a song or sing. He drank more beer. The bottle now empty.

"More?" Derek held up his empty bottle.

"No. I want..." what did he want?

"What can I do for you, Charlie. Gosh, I like you. It's a little creepy, I know. I'm so old and you're so young and so handsome."

Charlie patted Derek's hand. "It's okay. There's something I like about you, too. I just..."

"I know, I'm old and wrinkly. Who wants that?" He smiled as he spoke, but the pain of the statement came through his eyes.

"No, it's not that. Well, if we're being honest, there is some of that. But not really."

Derek went to the bar, came back with two more beers, sat, opened the bottles. "Talk to me if you want. I'd like to be of use to you."

Charlie drank some more beer. "Why is that? Why do you want to be of use to me?" He felt angry, and a little confused. "Sorry. I just..."

"You are so fucking talented. And so fucking handsome. No, beautiful. You're the most beautiful man I think I've ever seen. I'm not alone. The others, we've talked about it. It's like you don't see that about yourself. Your beauty or your incredible talent. I've had my life, my journey. I see you, here in the middle of something. Nearly the start of something compared to me at an end. Your life. Your musical career. Your—"

"That's part of it. It's not a career. I play, make a little money, live."

"Well, when people are talented and handsome and young, the rest of us, and I mean just about everyone, gay, straight, whatever, we want a piece. We get a piece of it by being kind or being helpful or giving you money or buying drinks or dinner. We get to breathe in some of you. Like vampires, you give the rest of us a little more or a little extra life."

Charlie nodded. Like Chris said, everyone has an agenda.

"See, a little creepy."

"Maybe a little, but it's nice, too, I guess." Charlie drank his whole beer, his guitar resting silent in his lap.

"Do you want a career?"

"I don't know. I've gotten a little taste of that the past few weeks. I've been mobbed in places by young kids wanting me to play. They've been posting my songs online and dumping money on me, like it's nothing to them."

"See. They want to be part of you. You give them life, joy."

Charlie looked up.

"You've seen the videos, too? Haven't you?"

"Yes. We all have. We've agreed not to post about you being here," said Derek. "We've talked about it during dinner because we know you won't come in and overhear us. We want you to ourselves."

Everyone had a cell phone, an internet connection, a TikTok account. Everyone except Charlie.

"What do you want out of life?" asked Derek.

There was that fucking question again. "I don't know," said Charlie, his words terse, clipped. "Up until a few weeks ago, I felt like I had everything I wanted. Well, just about. I'd figured out my life. How to live in the world. How to be my own man." All he'd really wanted a few weeks before was to know where he'd come from.

"But now?"

"I don't know." He looked down at the envelope on the table under his beer bottle. "I really don't fucking know."

"What's changed?" Derek finished his beer. He gave Charlie a break by going for two more.

"This." Charlie pointed at the lounge. "Those videos." He thought of Jasper, but didn't say his name. He considered Derek, meeting him had changed things, too. And Milo. "Remembering my parents and then meeting my fucking father."

Derek placed a beer in front of Charlie. That's when he pulled up his guitar. He tuned and fiddled with a picking pattern. He quietly, ever so quietly played the melody for "Cat's in the Cradle." How could he not consider the most famous father-son song of all time. He only played the notes, didn't sing.

Derek drank beer. Tears glistened in his eyes; they didn't fall. "Most of us have crappy relationships with our dads."

"Most of you know your fathers. You know why you have a crappy relationship."

"You know why you feel the way you do about your father."

Charlie stopped playing. "It's changed. It's all different."

"And?"

"The story in my head no longer equals truth or reality. I'm discovering that just about everyone I've ever met lied. All the people who raised me, or whatever they did. They used me. Abused me. Ignored me. None of them were in my corner." He thought once again of Christopher Marlowe, of her saying that no one in his life had his agenda. No one. Only him. He played a different picking pattern: "Dust in the Wind" by Kansas. Again, he didn't sing the lyrics. Finger picked the patterns, a hint of the melody. He loved the song. The melody. The theme. "All we are is dust in the wind." He spoke the words.

None of this mattered.

What did he want?

Charlie didn't fucking know. He stopped playing, drank more beer. In his mind, he heard the violins from the song.

"You amaze me," said Derek.

Charlie finished his beer. "Why?" He wanted another, wanted pizza. Would never ask. He'd certainly never get up and get it himself. Would never take anything from Patsy. Or anyone.... Not without payment of some kind. He considered the songs he'd given Milo for the scarf, for the gloves, for the meals on nights when he hadn't made his nut over the years. Milo never turned him down. Did the old man know?

Derek didn't need a hint. He stood, drank off the rest of his beer as he walked to the bar, a little unsteady. He spoke from there, his head down in the cooler. "You have so much fucking talent. You could be headlining somewhere. Instead, you wander around, doing your own thing. Don't get me wrong." He emerged with two more beers.

How many did that make now?

"Please don't get me wrong. I admire your choices. But with a talent like yours, it seems you should cash in. Ride the...what's the fucking line? Reach for something...the brass ring."

"That's what you would do. That's what you mean?" He twisted off the bottle cap, tossed it on the little table, drank the cold beer, burped loudly.

Through a smile, Derek said, "I think I would. But yet, I admire the choices you've made, too. You've traveled. You've taken risks and chances. You've learned to live lean. You can make money anywhere you are, so long as you have your friend there. It's a beautiful instrument."

"Got it used, in a pawn shop. I don't think it had ever really been played. People buy shit, good shit, and never use it." Once more he wondered if it had been stolen. Charlie set down the beer and played another riff on the Seagull. "I've had this for a few years now." Nearly ten. It was worn smooth in places where his fingers hit, where his wrist often rested. It was scuffed and scratched. He'd never put stickers on it or written on it, like so many street musicians did to their guitars and instruments. Beyond a concern that doing anything would change the tone, he respected the Seagull.

Charlie played the pattern for Dylan's "Don't Think Twice, It's All Right." This time he sang the lyrics. Another of the many anthems of his life, of his journey. His chosen namesake. The road called to him. He'd sat on many, many trains and ridden in many, many buses and played this song.

"You're going to run again?"

"Is that what you think it is?" Charlie asked. Knowing, of course, that was part of it. When you wanted, you moved. Movement always the answer. No need to solve a problem or figure anything out. Move. Play. Drink a beer. He drank his beer. The buzz finally hitting him. Mellowing his brain and slowing the speed of the patterns there.

Dylan was good for picking patterns.

The men drank in silence.

Charlie went back to the pattern of the Dylan song.

"Would you like to join me for dinner?" asked Derek, as he did most nights.

What do I want? He asked himself with internal clarity—was that Christopher Marlowe chuckling in his head?

Charlie said, "I would like dinner, but not here. I'd like a nice slice of pizza." What did he want? "Or perhaps a crusty piece of halibut. Or a huge swordfish steak. Some roasted vegetables. A nice sauce." Charlie's words gained conviction—his mouth watered. "Doesn't need to be five stars. Probably better if it's not. I don't even own a tie. Yes, a nice piece of fish."

"Maybe a crisp glass of wine?" Derek's eyes sparkled in an inviting way.

"Maybe. Although I've had a lot of beer." Charlie finished the latest bottle.

"Another?"

"No," said Charlie. "Fish."

"Hold on." Derek pulled his cellphone out and tapped the screen. "Got a place. In the East Village. We could walk, but it's rather cold. Or take a cab."

"Let me get my coat. We can maybe walk a bit and see how it feels." Charlie hoped the cold air would clear his head. He didn't want to undo the whole buzz, just take the edge off. Not vomit. Not pass out.

"I'll ride up and get mine, too," said Derek. He counted the beer bottles littering the table. "Let me just tell Albert at the desk about the beer."

Charlie reached into his pockets.

"Nope." Derek smiled in a kind, grandfatherly way. The light captured the hairs in his ears. "On me."

FORTY-NINE

Charlie and Derek walked across from the West Village to the East. They found the little bistro, a charming place with old-fashioned windowpanes and soft lighting. Rather a romantic place with violin music in the background. Yet, even on a Saturday evening, which neither of them had considered, they were quickly seated.

It was an expensive place. This check would be many multiples over a plate of cabbage rolls and a beer at Milo's Pub's steam table. Derek had said he would treat. And if he didn't, Charlie still had rolls and wads of cash in his pockets.

"What looks good?" asked Derek after they were seated with menus.

Charlie adjusted his guitar so it rested better in the corner behind his chair. "I haven't looked. I'm still craving halibut."

"Hope you're not pregnant." Derek chuckled.

Charlie chose not to respond. Old men and their dad jokes. He was certain the Aztec and Mayan dads probably told horrible, old, lame jokes, too.

A waiter arrived. "Well, hello." He placed his hand on Derek's shoulder.

Clearly, they'd met before.

"Jorge. Hello. This is the place you work?" said Derek.

Another obvious statement. "Yes. I only pick up those extra…um…shifts at Chanson."

"Well, good to see you again."

Charlie knew Jorge would be getting a very nice tip this evening, and maybe more for dessert.

"Can I bring you gentlemen something from the bar?"

Derek studied the wine selection in a tall, thin, leather-clad folio. "A crisp Chardonnay?"

"I have the perfect thing. A bottle for the table? Or a glass?" asked Jorge.

"I'm not a Chardonnay fan. Do you have a sauvignon blanc?" asked Charlie, thinking of Jasper.

"Of course."

"We could just do a bottle of that. Maybe Cloudy Bay?" said Derek.

"Certainly." The waiter rattled off specials. A beef dish. A red fish dish. A vegan option.

Charlie drank most of his glass of water.

"Actually," said Derek, "My friend would like a nice piece of Halibut." He looked at Charlie. "Right?"

"No rush. But I know I want the halibut." Charlie didn't know why he'd become so single-minded about the damn fish.

"You're Coffee Haus Charlie," the waiter whispered.

Fuck.

"He is," said Derek, a broad smile taking over his face.

Charlie thought about asking for discretion but didn't know if famous people said things like that. He thought about pleading with his eyes but didn't.

What famous people said? Where had that thought come from?

"I've really enjoyed your videos," said Jorge. My dad raised us on that old music.

"Thank you." Charlie drank the rest of his water, hoping the waiter would take the clue and leave to get more. Instead, a young man dressed in black and white livery refilled his glass without comment.

Fuck.

"Halibut. And for you?" The waiter turned to Derek.

"Wait. Do you have swordfish?" asked Charlie.

"Of course." Jorge rattled off the accompaniments as he turned his attention once more toward Derek.

"The beef special." He closed his menu and handed it

to the waiter.

"Many have complimented the strip steak. I think you'll love it," said the waiter.

By the time the bottle of wine arrived and had been poured, a noticeable multitude had gathered on the street outside the little old-fashioned leaded panes of glass. Mostly young girls.

Fuck.

By the time the salad course arrived, people overflowed off the sidewalk onto the street. They'd grown louder in their enthusiasm, at times chanting Charlie's moniker: "Coffee Haus Charlie."

Fuck.

When the fish arrived, there were flashing cop lights, red and white, bouncing off the drippy windowpanes, casting funhouse shadows into the restaurant. A few of the patrons had gone to the windows to take in the commotion.

Fuck.

When Jorge returned to clear their dinner plates, Charlie hissed: "What did you do?" Charlie hissed as the waiter cleared their plates.

"What? Oh, I posted on TikTok with you behind me. Isn't it great?" The waiter picked up Derek's plate and silverware. "Dessert?"

"What do you think, Charlie? Should we at least talk about dessert? Look at the options?"

Charlie didn't want dessert. Didn't want anything else. He had a headache from the wine and beer combination. Although the fish had been delicious, he'd barely tasted it because of the commotion on the street. He said, "Fine."

"Good. And coffee?" The waiter, with one arm full of dirty dishes, poured the remainder of the bottle of wine into their glasses.

"Yes," said Derek.

Fuck. Fuck. Fuck.

FIFTY

There was no choice. They'd lingered over dinner and drank the last of the wine and eaten Crème Brule while sipping coffee as long as they could. The food gone. The check paid. They had to leave.

As the crowd on the street continued to build, Derek paid the check and handsomely tipped the waiter. Finally, unable to avoid the inevitable, Charlie and his dinner companion reached the door.

The crowd had turned into a mob. An actual mob. They were chanting for Charlie. They held their phones up and out, ready to film him when he stepped onto the street.

Charlie thought he saw a local news van.

No one offered a back door to exit through. There was no alley or way around these people. There were several more cop cars now, their gumballs swirling and flashing red and blue lights, creating odd colors and shadows. The cops had closed off the block to traffic. The crowd moved and surged, like a living beast.

The waiter had caused this with his TikTok video. Charlie felt used. Consumed. Afraid. What would these people do to him? They wanted him in a way no one had ever wanted him. Before, just a few days before, no one knew him or even really noticed him as he played on the streets and in the subway and in the park.

The old man stayed back, allowing Charlie to make the choice. It had to be his choice. He reached now for the doorknob. He turned it and pushed into the crowd. The police had cleared a path there, a path that led from the restaurant's door to the street.

The crowd went wild. They chanted: "Coffee Haus Charlie." They held out their phones, photographing, recording. Privacy had died. Anonymity gone. Welcome to the grid. Coffee Haus Charlie.

Charlie had no plan. He saw the sign. A bar nearby, across the street, down one block. Tilde's. Remembered Chris's invitation. He thought they might duck in. Have a drink. This mob undulated now, threatened to consume him. He clutched the strap of his guitar case, afraid someone might try to wrench it from him. He flipped it around to his front.

Around them, these young people, for it was a huge crowd of young people, chanted Charlie's name. They shouted and applauded. They reached for him, toward him, challenging the handful of New York's finest who attempted with outstretched arms to hold the masses back, away from him.

Charlie pointed, just a little indication. He and Derek crossed away from the people, onto the street, to the opposite sidewalk. He led them quickly down the block, and into Tilde's, the bar Chris Marlowe had told him about.

"It's you," said the doorman or bouncer or manager. A man with a black, tight-fitting T-shirt with a punctuation logo over the left pec. "You've chosen to play here tonight? I'll give you half the door. It's twenty bucks a head, so that'll net you ten. Okay?"

"Christopher Marlowe sent me."

"I'll give you the whole door."

Charlie nodded, the man led him inside. Still too early for a Saturday night crowd, the place nearly empty. Once they arrived at the little stage, the mob from the street paid their covers, clamoring into seats as close to Charlie as they could get.

At a spot at the little bar in the darkness off to the side sat Derek.

Charlie tugged his guitar from his back, sluffed off his coat, left the scarf around his neck, it being chilly in the basement bar. Around him red brick walls and a sea of rickety tables. Imagine, commandeering the door without any negotiating.

Half would have been fine, but the whole door? The old drag queen obviously had some pull.

The manager returned, "What will you drink?"

Charlie asked for a beer.

The manager said, "Play as long as you'd like."

Already twenty or thirty young people had elbowed their way into the room, had scraped and adjusted the old wooden chairs, had begun ordering overpriced drinks from the waitstaff, more handsome young men, some of them looking familiar. From Hotel de Chanson?

Charlie took out his guitar. He tuned. There, in the corner, Quinn. How had he found him. He thought of the note in his coat pocket. He would have to deal with this at some point. His father nodded to him. Charlie reached a hand to the pegs and tuned his guitar. Tried to decide on the first song for the evening. An image of the old man playing the bear song traveled through his brain.

This was really happening.

A waiter set a beer on the piano lid. Charlie drank some of it. Centered the glass on one of the ring stains. This wasn't the first time a bottle had been placed on the old upright. He strummed a chord, to test the tuning, the acoustics. The crowd, now at least fifty or sixty people, applauded and cheered. They shouted out song titles, all songs he'd sung at the coffee shop. He'd need to deal with that at some point, deal with Jasper—he knew with certainty that romance had ended. But had now to deal with. He launched into "Ride" by Twenty-One Pilots. "I just wanna stay in the sun where I find/I know it's hard sometimes" and the crowd cheered so loud no one could hear him sing or play for a few beats. Charlie kept going.

FIFTY-ONE

The crowd wouldn't let Charlie leave the stage. They kept clapping and clapping and shouting out requests. The manager gave him a sign to keep going. People were happy and drunk. He held no fear of the crowd. What Charlie knew... he had to pee. If he didn't get off the stage soon, he'd wet his pants. All the beer earlier, the water and bottle of wine at the restaurant, the beer while playing...just too much.

He'd been ending his sets with "Closing Time," so that's what he played next.

There were groans and shouts of "No!" but Charlie played the song. People held their phones up, recorded him. They all applauded like crazy when he finished. He was up, his guitar tucked away, and he headed with instrument and coat in his hands toward the bar.

Derek remained at the same spot at the bar where he'd started.

"Hold this for me," he shouted over the noise.

The old man took his guitar and coat.

The bartender showed up. "Another beer?"

"Restroom?" shouted Charlie.

"Hold on." The bartender came out from behind the bar and like a linebacker moved Charlie through the standing room only crowd to the bathrooms, shoved to the front of the line, and got him inside, in front of the others.

No one complained.

When he came out, people mobbed him for selfies. He put up with that for a bit, taking a step or several toward the bar with each picture. The world closed in on him. He needed to get out, to get some air. Someone tugged on his long scarf. He freaked out.

At the bar, he drank down a beer in a single swallow. He put on his coat. Strapped his guitar to his front to have more control. "I gotta get out of here," he shouted in Derek's ear.

The manager came up to him and handed him a stack of hundreds. A large, thick wad of hundred-dollar bills. "Cash is okay?"

"Yes." Charlie took the money, folded it, and with effort, jammed it into his pants pocket. "I gotta get out of here."

"Sure. You're welcome back anytime. *Anytime.* Even if I've got someone else playing, I'll pull them. Just walk through my door." He patted Charlie on the back and helped him navigate toward the exit, Derek close behind.

Out on the street, the cold air revived him.

"Wow, you were amazing, Charlie," said Derek.

They started walking west. People followed them. People filmed them.

"I need to get out of the spotlight. I need to breathe," said Charlie. His heart pounded, the threat of death circled in his head.

"Sure. Sure. One more block."

They got to the avenue and quickly hailed a cab. The cabbie moaned at the short distance, but then said, "You're Coffee Haus Charlie. Hey man. We gotta get a picture. My daughter loves you. She really loves the duet that went up today. She's played it nonstop for hours."

"Duet?" asked Derek.

"Charlie and Garfunkel. I mean, it's great. 'Scarborough Fair.'"

Derek had his phone out. He did a search. Found it quickly on YouTube. Hit play.

The cabbie rolled his eyes but remained silent as they pulled up in front of the hotel. The three listened to the song. The cabbie positioned himself to get a selfie in his cab with Charlie.

"This is huge," said Derek. "It's got over a million hits. A million. You said this came out today?"

"I don't know when it came out, but my daughter has been

obsessed with it. Been playing it on a loop. Making us all crazy. No offense."

Derek shoved his credit card into the reader and paid for the cab.

The hotel lobby, quiet and empty, pleased Charlie. Instead of heading up to his room, he stopped and sat in one of the big chairs. Derek took the seat next to him.

"Your life is blowing up," said the old man.

"I know." Charlie had already grown to hate it. It had been what, three days a week. He had to adjust the way he sat because of the wads of money in his pockets. He leaned back in the chair and studied the ceiling beams lit by the flickering chandelier. "Thank you for dinner. The fish was great."

"Charlie..."

When Charlie covered his hand, Derek looked hard into Charlie's eyes. "You're welcome. And you were terrific tonight. You're incredibly good at what you do. I don't think I've heard you play anything twice. Well, 'Closing Time.'"

"How have you heard that...you've been watching the videos, too." Charlie, deflated, sunk down deeper in the chair.

"I have." He hit play again on the duet with Garfunkel. Singing filled the lobby.

From behind the desk, Albert asked, "Oh, you've seen that? What are you going to do?"

"What do you mean, do?" asked Charlie. "It's his song. It's a wonder he doesn't sue me."

"Folks do this all the time on TikTok." Albert came out from behind the desk. "Have you watched this to the end?" He pointed at Derek's phone.

"No. Just saw it," said Derek.

"Well, watch it till the end." Albert came closer, adjusted his jacket, released a cloud of pungent cologne covering body odor.

At the video's conclusion, Garfunkel offered to get together with Coffee Haus Charlie. He'd meet him in the coffee shop or anywhere in the city he wanted. He ended his video with, "Just call me," his fingers making a phone up to his ear.

"How do you call a famous person?" asked Charlie. How

would someone call him? Had Art Garfunkel tried?

“Dude,” said Albert. He had his phone up and, after a few taps, held up a contact page from Garfunkel’s website. “There’s an email for him and his manager.”

“Just like that?” said Charlie.

“Just like fucking that,” said Albert.

As Charlie contemplated modern technology, as his head swam with beer and wine and stardom, a shadow came over him. Depression? Fear? No, it was an actual shadow, blocking out the light from the chandeliers. Jasper.

“We need to talk,” said Jasper in a rather harsh, direct, tone. The next words came out softer, kinder: “Sorry. I’m not angry, I’m confused, and I would like to talk to you.”

Charlie studied the looming man’s face. He liked this guy a lot. Just not enough. “Okay. Good.” He turned and touched Derek’s arm. “Thank you for tonight. I’ll see you tomorrow?”

“As you wish.” The old man exuded kindness as he whispered, “Go.”

Charlie stood, picked up his instrument, led Jasper to the elevator. “I think we should go up to my room.” He pointed toward the street door. “It’s not safe for me out there.”

FIFTY-TWO

Inside Charlie's room, he and Jasper remained silent. Charlie waited for Jasper to begin. He'd come here. Initiated this moment.

Charlie rested his guitar in the corner. He shrugged out of his coat, hung it up. Still no words from Jasper. He unwrapped the thick scarf from his neck and hung it on a hook. He immediately wanted it back, the comfort of it soothed him, so he wrapped it once more around his neck.

"Sorry, I don't really have anything to offer you. You know, to drink. There's a little vodka. A warm beer." He indicated the bottles on the dresser.

His pockets bulged uncomfortably with the wads of cash he'd been collecting over the past few days. He vowed to himself to get up early. The bank branch in The Village opened at nine but closed by noon. He could deposit cash in the ATM, but he didn't trust the machine to count it all properly. Not that he had reason or experience that supported his suspicions.

"Charlie, I didn't...." Jasper slumped into the wingback chair. "I'm so confused by you. You played somewhere else tonight. How'd it go?"

"It was impromptu." He'd experienced a twinge of guilt, in that moment, but had easily moved on. "Sort of like being imprisoned. The old man took me out to dinner. I'd been promising him I'd go and he, well, he was nice to me today and I accepted his dinner offer." Charlie sat on the edge of the bed facing Jasper. "The waiter posted something online and within minutes a mob formed outside the restaurant. There were cops and..."

"A crowd showed up for you last night at the coffeeshop. And tonight. Then, everyone rushed out *en masse*. Veronica looked at her phone. She's been following you. Stalking you. I guess you have a hashtag now."

"A what?"

"A hash…it's a keyword system that allows people to track and follow information. You have one. #CoffeeHausCharlie." Jasper held up his phone with the phrase typed into a search bar. A long list of videos and posts showed.

Charlie remembered seeing the symbol with his name on the videos.

He pushed his finger against the screen and scrolled through the list. There, a few entries down, the duet video Art Garfunkel made.

Jasper took a deep breath. He let it out slowly. "Why didn't you come back? What did I do?"

His heart beat rapidly in his chest. Painfully, it pounded against his ribs. "I have a hard time talking about things." He turned his head and found Jasper focused intently on him. He wanted to look away but forced himself to hold the connected gaze. "I didn't think you were really into me."

"How can you say that? I never bathe with anyone. It's so intimate."

Charlie knew that wasn't true. The first night they met they'd talked about it. Ended up in Jasper's big tub. There were multiple towels hung. He didn't contradict him.

"I really do like you, Charlie. A lot." Jasper's eyes became wet, but he didn't cry.

"You…you seemed to…it's not about you. I really wanted to fuck you. I really…you even brought it up, that you wanted it, too. We've slept together several times. We haven't had sex of any kind since that first night. I…"

"You want more?"

"Yes."

Jasper sighed deep and hard.

Charlie waited. He'd said what he'd been thinking what he wanted. He'd rarely been with anyone, maybe twice in his whole life, where he talked about sex in an adult way. Not a growl of desire while naked and everything escalating.

"I...I...don't have an answer to that."

"We went from a hot first encounter to old married couple in like twelve hours," said Charlie. "I don't want to be married." It hurt to say those words out loud. Did he want that type of long-term relationship? For a moment, he thought he did, but now couldn't imagine such a thing in his life.

The word, the idea "Home" flitted through his brain. He did want that.

Jasper didn't say anything.

"It's totally okay if we don't want the same things," said Charlie. When had he become an adult? He embraced it and found it revolting at the same time. He wondered fleetingly once more if he should have gotten on a train while at Grand Central. Charlie wiggled his toes in his new socks. He still could hop a train. Ten minutes. Pack, be out the door, in a cab, at the station.

"Now what?" asked Jasper. He hadn't really responded to Charlie's words.

He heard Chris: "What do you want?"

He heard Milo: "When you're done, be done."

"I guess that's it then," said Charlie.

"What? After...?"

"We want different things, it seems. So..."

"Wham, bam, thank you—"

"Well, that really only works if there's been a wham or a bam." In his head he heard "shama lama ding dong," but didn't say it, or sing it. Charlie worked hard to keep a smile off his face. Yes, he wanted to move on. Wanted to count his money and contemplate this latest iteration of his life. He had to decide if he wanted to be famous. What a choice to have to make.

He heard Christopher Marlowe again, "What do you want?"

"Did you hear me?" asked Jasper.

Charlie shook his head. "Sorry, no. I had a song in my head." He still didn't share the Jay Roman moment. He hadn't done a fifties set in a very long time. He liked that music, the beat, the movement of the hips that happened without effort when he sang that music.

"I was saying...oh, never mind." Jasper, now up, headed toward the door. "I see it. I've lost you. This happens to me all the time."

Charlie did something he'd never done before. He grabbed Jasper's wrist, pulled him into a hug, kissed him hard on the mouth. He wanted one more kiss and decided to take it. He tasted bad coffee breath. When he released Jasper's lips, he saw the hope in the other man's eyes. He again heard Milo, "When you're done, be done." Charlie said to Jasper, "It was wonderful meeting you and I hope you get your beach ending." Charlie opened his door and without much effort, Jasper was in the hallway. He smiled back at Charlie who said, "Goodbye." He said the last word with kindness and closed his door. Tears came. He swiped them away. Clicked the lock. Reached for the warm beer but headed into the bathroom instead. He pushed in the stopper and turned on the hot water tap.

FIFTY-THREE

A moment had barely passed when a knock sounded on Charlie's door. He thought it might be Jasper returning to argue his case. Of course, it might be Derek, checking in. And he might have a lovely bottle of whiskey. He opened the door.

Quinn stood there. A brown paper bag in his hands. "Hi."

"Hi."

"You get my note?"

"Yes," said Charlie.

"Good. You didn't call, so I wondered."

"You came to the gig."

"You're really fucking terrific." Quinn held up a paper bag. "Want to share a beer together?"

"Sure." He didn't, not really. He wasn't ready to drink a beer with his dad, to talk like everything was normal between them. He did what he did: went with the flow. He closed and locked the door. Turned off the water.

They got comfortable. Quinn handed Charlie a beer and took the desk chair.

They drank.

Charlie studied his father. They had similar eyes. Quinn's weren't as uniquely blue as Charlie's but there was a hint of the shade there. They had similar fingers, too. "Did you ever play?"

"An instrument? No. Never had any inclination. Your mother liked to sing. So did her sister. They never did it professionally. Your aunt might have been in a church choir, but I don't remember."

Anger flooded Charlie's brain, flowed down into his stomach, resurfaced in his chest. These people had treated him so terribly.

"Listen. I know you're mad," said Quinn.

As if Quinn read his mind.

"I don't blame you. I'm pissed. At her. Your aunt. At myself, of course. More than I can ever explain. None of us did right by you. I just..." He drank a long swallow of beer.

They even drank the same.

"I can't change any of it. I mean, if I could, I'd go back and change all of it. Most of it. From the moment your mother died, I died. My...I don't know what it was inside me, but I didn't see straight. I lost you. I lost my job. I lost about fifty pounds, which I couldn't really afford to lose."

Charlie flashed back at the visual memory. His father so thin there. So young. So happy. Was that picture real? He searched it for his mother but couldn't see her.

"When I left you with her sister, I thought it would be for a few days. Those days turned into a week. Now, it's been thirty-five years." Quinn burst into tears. Loud, ugly sobs.

Charlie got a roll of toilet paper from the bathroom and handed it to Quinn. He didn't console the man. He owed him nothing. Nothing at all.

"Sorry," said Quinn. He blew his nose and tossed the used TP into the grocery bag. He took out two more beers, handed one to Charlie.

Charlie accepted the beer but wiped the bottle on his shirt before opening it.

Quinn laughed and cracked open his own bottle. "How did you learn to be up there? In front of all those people? Do you get nervous?"

"I don't get nervous," said Charlie. "I don't know why." He thought about the video Art Garfunkel had made. His stomach fluttered. From excitement, not fear or nerves. He realized he wanted to accept the offer to meet him. To figure out how to contact the famous singer.

"I'd shit myself," said Quinn. He laughed through his beer. A silly, snorty sound.

What else was there to say? His whole life Charlie wanted

answers. Now, he had a little piece of the truth, a piece of his childhood reality. All those foster homes. He flashed on the foster with the stack of albums. On the foster who'd forced him to have sex. On the foster brother who'd tormented him. On the teacher who'd threatened him repeatedly. On the foster mom who spanked him and slapped him and beat him for no reason. On the foster mom who fed him amazing foods...foods that reminded him of Milo's steam table. On the foster sister who smashed his first guitar like Ozzy Ozborn on stage and then laughed. On the foster...on the foster ...on the foster ... There had been so many people. Fosters and kids and teachers and social workers. Some had been helpful. Most had been terrible and mean. The men followed. Adult men. Some horrible. Some not so horrible.

He heard her again, "Everyone has their own agenda."

Charlie had more important things to think about and worry about in his life than those old stories. That was the most difficult piece of all. Meeting his father had brought all these memories to the surface. He preferred life in the moment, without those dark experiences. Sure, there were some bright ones, too, but dark always took more power. He didn't want that energy around him. He drank down the majority of the beer in his hand. "Listen, I appreciate you coming forward. You meeting me. You answering my questions. I just don't think I can be around you. Not right now. You understand, right?"

After sucking the remainder of the beer from the bottle, he stood up, set the bottle on the desk. "Sure." The pain in his eyes not directed at Charlie, but instead, more deep set, more self-absorbed.

Charlie followed Quinn to the door, unlocked it, held it open.

"I'll be around," said Quinn. "You have my number."

"Okay," said Charlie, avoiding any type of commitment.

He watched his father walk to the elevator, push the button. Instead of waiting, Quinn pushed open the door to the stairs. He didn't look back.

Just as Charlie was about to close his door, Derek came out

of the elevator. He carried a bottle of whiskey. He held up two crystal glasses in an inviting way toward Charlie. Charlie nodded and the two entered his room.

"My room is bigger. There are two very comfortable chairs, if you'd like." Derek remained near the door.

"That sounds nice," said Charlie. "Let me just wash my face."

Derek didn't move.

Charlie went into the bathroom and closed the door. He pulled the stopper from the tub, peed for a long time. He washed his hands. He washed his face. He dried on one of the big bath sheets. That's what he really wanted, a bath. A tub filled with hot water and oil and the comforting sound of water dripping onto the surface, like raindrops, that moment after he turned off the tap.

They rode the elevator down a few floors.

Inside Derek's room, Charlie took a chair. It was comfortable. More so than the chair in his room. Charlie wondered what their rental charge amounted to. Derek poured them whiskey. He sat in the opposite chair. He sipped.

"I think this is the first time I've ever seen you without your guitar."

Panic rose and tightened Charlie's stomach. He hadn't even thought to pick up his guitar. He couldn't remember if that had ever happened before. Not in at least twenty years. He breathed deep, sipped the whiskey, which bit and nipped at him all the way down.

"Are you okay?"

Charlie didn't have an answer. Instead, he once more heard Chris in his head, "What do you want?"

"It's a lot. Fame. Money. Your dad rising from the dead. What happened with your boyfriend."

"I remain single and independent." Charlie raised his glass. Derek mimicked him.

He still didn't know what he wanted and thought again about the safety of getting on a train headed somewhere. Anywhere. If he left, would this moment of fame quietly fade?

Probably. Possibly. Everyone else had a cell phone. Everyone else knew about these hashtag things.

He thought of the Beatles. Of other bands where the members were mobbed. He'd read about singers who lost their lives to their fame, no longer able to run to the corner bodega or eat in a restaurant or walk down the street or ride a subway. New York or LA seemed like better places to be famous. He'd seen celebrities in restaurants and diners and bars and on the subway. He'd once stood on a street corner waiting for a light with Jake Gyllenhaal standing next to him. People whispered, but generally, the famous were politely ignored.

"Charlie?" Derek held out the bottle. He refilled Charlie's glass.

"I'm drunk."

"Okay. Me, too. It's that time of night, or morning." Derek drank.

Suddenly, Charlie felt like he couldn't keep his eyes open. It all hit him. If he didn't get back to his room right now..." I need to..." He stood up, walked a few steps, made it to the bed, and lay down on top of the coverlet. The bed soft and deep and thick and...

FIFTY-FOUR

Charlie woke with a duvet draped over him, in Derek's bed. Alone. He stretched and scratched and stretched some more. Fully clothed. Even his shoes were still on. Up, after running his fingers through his hair, he slipped out of Derek's and headed up the stairs to his own floor. As he entered his room, Jorge, the waiter from the fish restaurant, exited the room at the end of the hallway, his uniform shirt opened nearly to his navel. He carried his shoes and his coat. He nodded as he passed Charlie, who nodded back.

Sunday morning at Hotel de Chanson.

Once inside, Charlie locked his door, started the water running in his tub, and began stripping off his clothes. He emptied his pockets. They were stuffed with thousands and thousands of dollars, including the folded bills from Tilde's. An actual, what the fuck moment. And the manager said he could return whenever he wanted.

He stacked the bills neatly. He didn't know what to do with all the cash. He didn't like it sitting in his room. He checked the door. Locked. He added the security chain. He had to face the ATM and the cash deposit slot. At some point, you have to trust technology, at least a little.

After pouring oil into the stream of hot water, Charlie brushed his teeth. It would be another ten or fifteen minutes until the tub filled. In the bedroom, he took out his guitar, tuned it. The E-string had started to go again. Strings simply didn't last the way they used to. He finished tuning, close enough for jazz. An average person would never notice that slight weakness brought on by the dying E-string. Maybe he'd go to the music store after he visited the bank. He strummed a chord. Changed it and strummed. Augmented it and strummed.

He played a Django style series through those three chords. Picked out a melody. He knew the melody but couldn't find the lyrics. Something from Broadway. Recent. *Hadestown*. Andre De Shields? Of course, a trumpet played it. "Road to Hell." Great lyrics.

Charlie loved great opening numbers. "Road to Hell" sets up that whole show. The "Prologue" to *Ragtime*, brilliant. He didn't play that one, but loved it, and sometimes, during his library research time, he'd listen to it, just to enjoy the journey. "Good Morning, Baltimore," from *Hairspray*. "Downtown," from *Little Shop of Horrors*. Another song he never played but liked a lot. "Waving Through a Window," from *Dear Evan Hansen*. Oh, not an opening number. Second song. He stopped playing, left his guitar on the bed, slipped into the hot tub. Felt the burn of the water on his feet and ankles and thighs. He turned on the cold water. Waited for the water and his skin to adjust. He hummed "Changing My Major," from *Fun Home*. So much energy. He didn't sing that one in public either. It felt like cultural appropriation for a Black, gay man to sing a white lesbian coming of age song. He returned to "Waving Through a Window." Hummed the line.

Someone had seen him. Acknowledged his talent. People were waving back at Charlie. He could turn this into a huge career.

He heard the company singing, "Sit Down, John," from *1776*. Why? Oh, yes, the closing window, the flies...choosing to vote "Yes." His psyche chimed in through song lyrics. Connections. Of course. Occupational hazard.

It was an occupation. Money in his pockets, in the bank, that was good. He hoped that stack of bills remained safe. That came from occupation, from work, from a vocation. He loved what he did. Loved singing and performing.

He still wanted new shoes.

Who was Charlie trying to convince now? He had no one to convince, no one but himself. They dumped hundred-dollar bills in his case at Coffee Haus and at Milo's Pub. Twenties and hundreds among the fives and singles. Thousands for a few hours at Tilde's before a packed room.

Charlie slipped into the tub, lowered slowly down, suffered the intense, satisfying burn of the water. Experienced being human and alive and longing for something he couldn't name.

Why should he not build a big career? Art Garfunkel wanted to meet him. Liked his singing and playing enough to duet with him on TikTok, for a few bars at least.

Water lapped at the sides of the tub. Charlie went under, felt the heat to his ears, to the crown of his head. The oil doing its job, softening all of him. Soothing all of him.

"What do you want?"

The voice so loud, so real, Charlie surfaced to be sure he remained alone in his bathroom.

Silence. In the room. In his head.

What he wanted, right then? To fuck someone. It had been far too long since he'd fucked anyone, since anyone had.... Yet, he'd had opportunities. Derek. Jasper. He could have pushed that and made it happen. They'd been so close. The Bartender. That asshole.

Something had changed. He didn't just want to fuck. He had a request list. He wanted things to be and go a certain way.

Big thirsty towels. Good bath oil. New shoes.

His dick grew hard in the hot, oily water. He lay back, comfortable. Jacked off in the hot, oily water. A boy is never truly alone...

FIFTY-FIVE

After banking, it appeared the ATM counted the cash as efficiently as Charlie had, and after the thrill of shoving all those bills into the machine and into his bank account, he headed uptown to Brother's for strings. A different clerk greeted him. When Charlie entered, the young guy let out a whoop and rushed toward him.

"Oh my god, it's you! Coffee Haus Charlie. In our store." He had his phone out. "Can I—"

"Down boy," said another guy with a name tag. He held his hand out to Charlie. "Sorry about that. I'm Jason. The manager."

"Hi." Charlie shook his hand. "I just need a new set of strings." He started to walk toward the rack, but Jason hadn't released his hand.

"Congratulations on all your success."

"Thanks. Hand?"

"Oh, sorry." Jason released him and walked him to the rack.

Charlie knew what brand he wanted and grabbed two sets. He had the money, and after that uncomfortable moment, he didn't want to have to come back anytime soon.

"Are those really what you want?" asked Jason. He pointed to a different brand. "I've seen your videos. Heard the stuff you play. I'd recommend these."

Charlie headed to the register. "These are great." He sort of waved them in the air.

Before he'd paid, a small crowd of young people had gathered on the sidewalk outside the store. Charlie found it fascinating that they didn't enter some establishments in pursuit of him but did come into others.

They mobbed him on the street. Tugging at his clothes, his scarf, his guitar. He made the rash decision, got to the street, and hailed a cab. He hadn't decided yet where he wanted to go but didn't want these people following him down the block or into the subway.

While a dreary, chilly day, it wasn't frigid. He thought he might spend some time playing in the park. He wanted to see if he could still just play for passersby without it turning into a concert. And after the brainstorm the night before, he wanted to see if all those theater opening songs, and the few exceptions, would work together as a set. He often worked those things out in the park. Sitting on a bench, playing, with a random spectator stopping and dropping a dollar.

The money wasn't as important. His daily nut was met for the next several months after the past few weeks.

"Where to?" asked the cabbie.

He contemplated. East side or West? He said, "Seventy-second and Fifth."

"You got it." The cabbie started the meter. "You're that guy. The guitar playing guy, right? Charlie, right?"

Had everyone seen those videos?

"There was a story about you on the news this morning. Video of you playing at a coffee shop and then at some club downtown. Art Garfunkel contacted you. I thought he was dead. Nice piece. You must have a great publicist."

Publicist? Charlie hadn't thought of that. He flashed again on the contact page of Art Garfunkel's website. It had management listed.

The cabbie repeated himself. "They showed a video uploaded by Art Garfunkel. Didn't even know the guy was still alive, let alone singing." The light changed to green. "I was at that concert they did back in, what was it? Eighty? Eighty-one? Huge. Massive. Really great. They said on the TV this morning that their old album, from the concert, had jumped onto the Billboard chart for the first time in over forty years. You did that."

Charlie remained silent, not sure what to make of this. Both thankful for the chatty cabbie but also wishing he'd just stop talking. What were the odds now, after being on the news, of going unnoticed in the park? Should he just head home?

Home.

That damn word.

He knew, in that moment, Hotel de Chanson wasn't home. It was just where he currently lived. No different from a nameless SRO.

Why hadn't Paul Simon contacted him?

He heard Diana Ross in his head now, singing "Home" from *The Wiz*. Was it an opening number? No, it came later in the show. He ran through the album. Last. That song came last. A beautiful song. An amazing performance. The song he couldn't find not too long ago.

He considered building a closing number list. Or better, a list of eleven o'clock numbers.

The cabbie kept talking, a nonstop drone. Charlie no longer heard him, instead, he lost himself in Ross's voice in his head, the Broadway soundtrack.

All he ever truly wanted in his life. A home from that song. "Love overflowing." Quinn didn't offer that. Barely offered an apology. His mother danced in his head now, that image of her from the other flashback, the other memory that may or may not be real. He saw her singing the song now, instead of Diana Ross. If she had lived, his whole life would have been so different.

Would he have learned guitar?

Charlie didn't have an answer to that. He would have had a mother who loved him. Probably one home. One arc of growing up.

Yet, he thought of Quinn. He wouldn't have stayed. There would have been hurt and trauma. That was how life worked. No one got out safe from their childhood. Everyone ended up in therapy. Everyone—the song ended in his head. The cab had stopped.

"Buddy? We're here. Is this okay? Do you want to go—"

Charlie shoved some money through the plexiglass. He got out, hugging his guitar to him.

If he had had a different life, a different childhood, he might not be a guitar player.

What would he have been then? What would he be searching for now?

The thought scared the hell out of him. This was what he did, who he was, how he survived. How he survived now, made money, sure, but how he'd survived his childhood. How he'd found his way out of the system. How he'd gained his freedom. How he'd become Charlie Dillian.

It would always be that.

Always.

His Seagull guitar. That was home.

Charlie considered the previous guitar and the one before that. There had been many of them over the years. It wasn't about this one instrument, as much as he loved it. It was about, what?

The cab hadn't pulled away.

Charlie walked into the park. He'd sit in the mall. Find a bench there, even in the chill there would be caricaturists. There'd be vendors selling roasted peanuts and hotdogs and popcorn. Families walking by headed to the Children's Zoo. Into the park, most of the trees bare of their leaves. Tall, empty trees reaching toward a dreary sky.

Into the park. To the Mall. To a bench. He sat, pulled out his guitar, left the case open on the ground in front of him. Charlie tuned. Considered changing a string, but decided to wait until he could change them all. He could afford that today. He strummed a chord, another. Thought of starting his opening number set with "Good Morning, Baltimore," but decided he would do better to warm up a little first. That song so big and commanding—his voice not yet ready.

He strummed another chord, built a scale out of it, bought himself some thinking time.

He quietly played "Corner of the Sky" from *Pippin*. A second number. He considered what a second number list might be.

No one stopped. Everyone passing by ignored him. That's what he wanted. To be an unknown busker.

It came to him. A new era. He played "Aquarius" from *Hair*.

By the time he finished the song, a crowd had circled him. They recorded him. Enthralled by seeing Coffee Haus Charlie playing on a bench in Central Park on a Sunday.

As he finished the song, two cops showed up.

Busted.

There was no way he could pack up and run. No way out of this. There were recordings, videos, probably already posted online. He had no defense. While an acoustic player didn't require a license, creating a big crowd drew attention and harassment.

They weren't there to bust him. One cop dropped a dollar in his case.

"There's a problem because your listeners are blocking the sidewalk," said the other cop. You need to move to a place where that won't happen. Why not walk over to the bandshell by the Bethesda Fountain."

Charlie wondered if the cop saw the irony. He'd been playing from *Hair*, and there were lots of scenes in the park from that movie, including the fountain and the bandshell.

"It's right over there." The cop who'd made the donation pointed into the park.

"And that'll be okay?" Charlie started to gather up the bills in his case.

"So long as you don't play with any amplification. If you stand in the shell, it'll amplify your playing. If you sit on the end of the stage, it won't." The cop smiled. "We'll walk you over."

By the time they arrived at the Naumburg Bandshell, as the cops moved a few young guys who were playing a game of tag up on the stage, a crowd of more than fifty people had gathered.

He opened the set with "Good Morning, Baltimore" to some applause and some shouts that this was New York, that this was afternoon. Charlie hadn't been heckled in a few weeks and smiled at the exchange.

As he worked his way through Broadway opening numbers, and as he played, more came to him, the crowd blossomed. The bandshell did its job, naturally amplifying him. Someone brought a box up to the edge of the stage, on it in marker, “TIPS for Charlie.” He dropped a bill in as he set the box down. People formed a line and deposited money into the box. Filled it up. He worried it would be stolen, but no one took it.

He arrived at the tenth or eleventh song when a tall, older guy came up on stage. Charlie finished “Maybe,” from *Annie.*

“I’ve wanted to meet you,” the man said.

“I’m Charlie.” He didn’t know what this was or… “Fuck, it’s you.”

“Art.” He held out his hand. “Loved what I’ve seen of your work. I’m honored you chose to play our album. Is it true you played the whole thing? In one sitting?”

They shook hands.

“I was trying to impress a guy.”

Art Garfunkel laughed. “Well, you impressed me. Not the same thing, but…”

“Your video was really cool.”

“You inspired me. We’re making money off that album again. You did that.” He pulled a business card from his pocket and handed it to Charlie, then shoved his hands into his armpits. “You should call me tomorrow and we can talk about some things.”

“Are you upset?” Charlie worried again he might be sued.

“No. I really am impressed by you.” He looked out toward the audience. Pointed at them. They applauded. “Do you want to do a number? It’s not from Broadway, but we could do “Homeward Bound.”

“Really? That’d be great.” Could Art Garfunkel read minds? Was he psychic? Whatever the motivation, Charlie launched into the iconic opening. The crowd cheered.

Instead of singing, Art blew into his cupped hands. “It’s cold. You should choose better places to play.”

The story was far too long to go into, so he said, “Good advice.”

Charlie launched into the opening lyrics again, and Art

sang, “I’m sitting in a railway station…”

This was home.

It hit him hard, not a sucker punch, instead, the sensation grounded him to his feet, to the stage, to the shared voices.

Hundreds of phones pointed at them. No need to worry about this historic moment not being captured. It would be online before the applause finished.

Yes, Home.

He’d been here all along.

Standing on a stage before a few hundred people who wanted him to sing another song. Singing with a famous person who found themselves impressed with Charlie. Maybe home turned out to be where you decided it to be. Where you took your Seagull out of the case. Where you had to retune the damn E-string.

Comfortable and safe. At home playing his guitar, singing songs he loved. And there were so many songs he loved to sing.

Charlie didn’t know what might happen next. He hadn’t had a plan his whole life. Not really. He wanted to play. So, he played. He found the harmony with Art Garfunkel. Charlie knew, he could see in his mind, that other performers would love to sing with him, too. To sing their songs with Charlie. It would become the thing. For a while at least. Awhile would be enough for now.

Home, for now, was his Seagull and Art Garfunkel and a random crowd in Central Park.

ABOUT THE AUTHOR

Gregory A. Kompes (MFA, MS Ed.), founder of The Writer Workshop, is an award winning, bestselling author of fiction, poetry, and nonfiction. He's the author of *Shards*, as well as the Broadway series that includes *Flash Mob*, *The Middle Man*, *Tamburlaine*, *Obsequies*, and *Busker*.

Become a VIP Reader at https://Kompes.com.

www.ingramcontent.com/pod-product-compliance
Lightning Source LLC
LaVergne TN
LVHW010606100826
845148LV00014B/2870

* 9 7 9 8 9 5 0 2 4 1 0 1 7 *